THE GO FOR IT NEIGHBOURS

THE GO FOR IT NEIGHBOURS

Melissa L Manning

THE GO FOR IT NEIGHBOURS

iUniverse books may be ordered through booksellers or by contacting:

iUniverse
1663 Liberty Drive
Bloomington, IN 47403
www.iuniverse.com
1-800-Authors (1-800-288-4677)

ISBN: 978-1-4917-6297-4 (sc)
ISBN: 978-1-4917-6298-1 (e)

Library of Congress Control Number: 2015904076

Print information available on the last page.

iUniverse rev. date: 03/27/2015

Acknowledgements

Thank you to my brother Derek Manning for being such a great brother and for helping me to gather more writing skills during the writing of *The Go For It Neighbours*.

Thank you to my parents Jean Manning and Gary Manning for your generous support through the years.

Thank you to Dianne O'Dell. A friend to my mother. You kept on believing in me.

Thank you to anyone else who helped motivate me to finish writing *The Go For It Neighbours*. I found it inspiring to write the more I pictured people reading it.

INTRODUCTION

The day that I wrote my goals on paper and answered a few questions about them was the day that I was able to see very clearly how I had been living my life. Even before then, I already knew what my goals were. After I glanced at my list of goals and the answers I had written about them, I could then figure out something about myself. I was spending time thinking about my goals instead of doing what was necessary to achieve them. I decided two things after noticing this. The first one of these was that I would much rather be doing what it takes to be on the track toward goal achievement. The second of these was the way to go about doing that would be to work on my goals one step at a time.

I knew it would be exciting to complete each step along the way. And it certainly was, as I soon discovered. After some more time and effort, the first of my written goals was completed. Although I had the help of family and friends through a few of the steps before achieving that first goal, my own determination played a large part in getting there. That one goal in particular was especially helpful for me to gain some ground toward where I should be financially. And once I was there, I could look ahead to other goals being possible to reach. Now there were more goals arriving within view to add on to the goal already achieved. There they were. Not too far away at all. With just some more time and effort they would be completed too.

I continued along the track toward goal completion. Soon two more goals were met. After completing these two goals I had already changed my residence and saved a certain amount of money. By this time, I became very interested in goal setting. That is when I wrote a new list of goals. So much had changed in a matter of months (well, it was actually over a year) you can understand why I might feel enthusiastic about a second list of written goals. When these goals were set, it wasn't long before I updated the goal list to include something more. Something I hope many people will enjoy. It is an original idea from me personally. That idea was to write a book about a fun and new way of seeing goal setting. And that is to view it as a sport. Although I didn't end up writing a book about the sport of goal setting at the time, it did lead me to write The Go For It Neighbours. The book you are about to read.

The characters written in this book were invented from my imagination to inspire real people living in the world today to perhaps get together and work on achieving their own highest aspirations and goals. In other words, aspirations and goals can be more simply defined as dreams. Dreams that help to carry you far. Dreams that are with you no matter where you are in life. Today, tomorrow and always. And once these are accomplished, they can make way for even bigger dreams.

Perhaps one day there will be an organization that helps people in many different ways to go after their highest aspirations. The reason is because it is an important matter. It speaks to us. It's easy to go after such dreams if we listen to and follow our hearts.

Regards,
Melissa Lynne Manning

THE NEIGHBOURS OF SUNLIT AVENUE

#1000 Aleisha Forbes' House

#1004 Brooke Akira's House

#1008 Mavis, Damien, Francis and Lulu Hemley's House

#1012 Rita Young's House

#1016 Rain Woodrow and Cullen Dangsi's House

#1001 Zoey and Ralph Holiday's House

#1003 Sid Mathison's House

#1005 Doris, Mark and Edmond Keenan's House

#1007 Hazel and Cora Pepper's House

#1009 Sven and Vic Nicolos' House

And a surprise guest in addition to these nineteen neighbours.

CHAPTER 1

Monday, May 30, 2011

Somewhere on Earth there exists a remarkable place called Sunlit Avenue. It is a new street with a group of ten recently built houses that are quite a sight to behold on a road that still looks freshly paved. It seems so bright and beautiful to live there, the people have noticed, they just knew they had to name it Sunlit Avenue. It is a street that has two lanes going in each direction and is bordered with four blue spruce trees that adorn each side of the Avenue. This is for lasting curb appeal, as blue spruce trees can grow to be very tall trees after a certain number of years. Along with the decorative grasses, blossoming flowers and range of shrubs, the yards along the street are pleasing to the eyes. The houses on the Avenue are simply marvelous to see and are located just a few minutes from two major shopping areas in town. At the time of their purchase, some were a bit more expensive than others to buy. Although that is the case, they still were affordable. The house plans had been designed with a lot of thought put into them. They were well built and had a good quality about them. All of the houses on Sunlit Avenue are identical to each other. They are both charming and elegant. Each one has a two car garage with white garage doors. The asphalt shingles of each roof are a mixture of beige and white and the vinyl siding is terra cotta red. There is a chimney that runs further along the right side of each of the houses and it is made up of beige bricks. There is a nice white trim along the edge of each roof that make the houses really stand out. They are eye-catching to anybody who might pass by the properties. The neighbours could tell that it all works to create a feeling of being noticed. But the neighbours were ready for more than just being noticed by people passing by. They were ready for being noticed by people for what they have been doing as a team from day to day. To someday cause people to say that the neighbours who started focusing on their goals together as a team have definitely succeeded in starting something. And Sunlit Avenue was where it all began.

What happens on the Avenue can be regarded as rather unusual. The people who live there can usually be found spending time talking to each other, neighbours, or other people in town to let people hear how inspired they are for more during the course of any given day. But when it comes down to it, often it is what they keep busy doing and focused on that really matters to them. Such as projects large and small, far and wide that can be definitely interesting. Indeed. "Interesting breeds interesting," or so they say on this particular Avenue. They also say something else. "Watching and waiting to see how the projects will unfold and progress is all part of the fun of it."

The neighbours of the Avenue had talked together and decided that going after one's own highest aspirations or goals is very worthwhile. So they each decided that focusing on following their highest aspirations is what they would do. They talked together to one another about goal setting with a certain serious tone in their voices while standing in the sunlight early one Saturday morning. They then cheered their favourite cheer, "Let's see what is possible to do and be motivated to…go for it!"

They were setting their sights on seeing to what extent they would do so. Goals are what help people to get on track towards moving ahead in life. They are accomplished by taking some positive steps toward a brighter future while enjoying each day in the process. The people on Sunlit Avenue knew exactly those words to be true and felt their future looked bright indeed after communicating about their highest aspirations to one another. Each person who lived on the Avenue would be writing down any goals that were meaningful to them and then once the goals were set the next step would be to get ready for them to be met. Or so they hoped. They wondered if anything stood in their way. The neighbours of Sunlit Avenue would soon be finding out as they continued on to meet their goals.

Each person living on Sunlit Avenue had learned that making a difference, perhaps the smallest difference, for another person's day to day is what makes it more interesting all the while. For it all starts there - making a difference. Making a difference for today and tomorrow. Of course, that is the very special motto that a lady named Rain Woodrow thought of one day. It happened to be a time when she was at home working on her latest ideas for her business, a specialty card business. Being both the store owner and card designer, she started the shop by herself. The cards are homemade by Rain and sold in her store named Cards and More in Store.

It is a store that had been in town for several years and had since become the place to shop for many different occasions.

When Rain isn't sitting at home thinking of ideas or making cards, she can be found at the store talking to the staff and customers or simply arranging the cards on display and making them look neat and tidy. On her days off, she has time to do other things. Such as spending time with her boyfriend. His name is Cullen Dangsi. He lives with Rain Woodrow. Although they are not yet married, they enjoy being together as boyfriend and girlfriend for the time being. And after spending three great years with one another so far, the couple is very familiar with how the other operates on a daily basis. So far so good as they say. Cullen is quite fond of Rain, for he knows how much she cares about him. He comes home from work on sunny days sometimes and says, "Cullen is calling for Rain." That is because he misses her from time to time. She replies, "To the letter, honey, to the letter. Or card, shall I say."

Cullen, a computer salesperson working at a local Yaffs computer supplies store, had become familiarized about all the latest on the many items for sale in Yaffs. Shop at Yaffs the advertisement sign outside of the large store reads. The store had first opened fourteen years ago and can usually be found to have a great selection of computers and other computer related items in stock. Printers, mouse-pads, paper, ink, computer desks and chairs - to name a few of the things found in the store.

Once in a while, Cullen can carry out the computers and other items into the customers' vehicles when someone asks him if he could. Their purchase might be too heavy for them to lift so Cullen is more than happy to help bring it to their car. When he does so, for an added touch of customer service he then says, "Thank you for shopping at Yaffs." Each sale is appreciated and although it is just part of his job, Cullen delights in that little something extra that he gives the customer during their shopping experience.

On this day, he just happened to be at work and was staring out the window to see what the weather was like when he thought to himself, 'I really like this city. Moncton really speaks to me. There is always something new developing in it. Take the Amplitude Theatre for instance.' He began to daydream about how a person in the audience can read about stories that have shaped the present time that are written in words on the screen right there in front of them all created by lasers. The words are displayed one line at a time by the bright beams of red and blue light. Along with amazing music that is played from speakers on each side of the theatre to go with the stories line by line, it is a place that provides many people with entertainment. The Amplitude Theatre was quickly becoming one of the latest ideas for entertainment of its kind around. It had a certain fresh look about it and it attracted crowds of people because the stories carried with them some of the latest technology that went into running each laser line story playing at the theatre.

Cullen thought some more about it and he hoped that he and Rain could go see a laser line story at the theatre soon. He and Rain still hadn't seen one yet. Maybe he would go with her to one to mark some sort of special occasion in the future. Many of the people in the laser line audiences were sure that just going to one of the lighted up shows playing there was certainly a cause for celebration. In the meantime, any way he looked at it, Cullen would be looking forward to the day that he would be attending one.

As he stood there looking out the window, he saw a sunny sky and some clouds here and there. It was mid-afternoon. The day seemed to have gone by so fast that already he would soon be finishing his work shift and heading home. He looked at his watch. It displayed five minutes to three in the afternoon. A seven hour work shift from eight to three was what he had been working. Minutes passed by and after walking along one of the aisles, Cullen saw three o'clock pm reading on his watch. 'Time to go.' Another moment passed. After he got his navy blue fleece sweater, he waved at a few of the gals at work while walking by them. Then he went through the front door and stopped. 'What was it that I was going to do today after work?' He thought for a second or two. "Oh yeah." Cullen suddenly said to himself. "Sven." He started ahead again and approached his car. A black 2004 Toyota Corolla LE.

It was a fairly cool spring day in late May. Some pedestrians were walking by the store. They were wearing T-shirts, shorts and sandals. Already, it seemed, the warm weather was on its way. Although it had been cool during the cloudy days, it was now getting quite warm out on the sunny days. And people of all ages would soon be out enjoying the higher temperatures. The days of sunshine would soon arrive for Canadians both young and old.

Cullen thought about his neighbour the mechanic. He would be giving Sven Nicolos a twenty dollar gift card from a local restaurant as a present for helping to repair his car recently. "It hardly needed any maintenance." Sven had said, "Just a certain part that was worn." Exactly what the mechanic had done to the car he didn't say. Cullen knew the importance of having a valuable repair job done to his car. He would be stopping in at the restaurant on his way home from work to get the gift card. 'Just a little something extra.'

When he went home, his girlfriend Rain was there in the living room looking at some specialty cards that she had made. She was wearing an orange T-shirt, light beige pants, a green rectangular bead necklace and a pair of red and white sneakers. On a nearby table, there were some colourful paper pages, water-colors, a spray bottle and rubber stamps. Where Rain was sitting there were thirty homemade cards that she had just finished one hour earlier.

"Look at what I bought for our neighbour Sven." Cullen said, showing the gift card to Rain. He had on a dark green T-shirt with the name *Cullen* written in yellow on the top left side of it. Along with the work shirt, he also wore black pants and black sneakers. And a silver and blue watch too.

"Oh, that's nice. Italian food."

"That's right." Cullen looked at Rain, studying how she was twirling a piece of her brunette hair in her hand. Her hair was just above the shoulder in length and every once in a while she couldn't help but twirl it.

"It's a great restaurant. Isn't it?"

"Mmm-hmm. I like their decor too."

"You're pretty colourful." Cullen said to her, smiling about his remark.

"Thanks. You're handsomely appealing."

Cullen wrinkled his forehead for a few seconds. Then he watched as she turned to face him. She was eager to hear his reply. She stared at him with her brown eyes and waited.

"Rainy. You're very colourful."

She continued to stare. "Cullen, I know what kind of day you had, a colourful one."

"You might say that."

"Anyway, I made some new cards for the store. Thirty of the same type and I like it. I'll read it to you. Here's how it goes. "A one, a two, a three - four - five… and a six, and a seven, and an eight - nine - ten." Then when you open it, the card reads, "Happy Tenth Birthday. Are you going to do a birthday dance now?" Rain held the card open for Cullen to see.

"Sounds great."

"That is what I was working on today. Kept me busy. I was making the envelopes for them too. Did you know I have a favourite card that I sell? On the front it says, "You look Incredible.""

"Do you sell a lot of those?"

"Yes, especially for anniversary celebrations."

"I know what your most expensive card you sell says on it. "You're sweeping beautiful." God, where did you come up with that?"

"That's easy. A person can be swept off their feet sometimes by their boyfriend or girlfriend, right? By a hug or something they actually did."

"Yeah. But how many of those cards do you sell?" Cullen asked.

"Ah, let's see…five maybe, on a busy day." She said to him.

"And how much do those ones cost? I forget. But I know that card, "You're sweeping beautiful" does seem to attract the attention of the shoppers, doesn't it?"

"Yeah."

"So how much does it cost?"

"That one is twenty-five dollars."

"Twenty-five dollars!"

"That one is specially made." Rain said.

"By the hands of my darling." Cullen said. "Rain, you're sweeping beautiful."

"So are you. My sweet blonde haired, blue eyed guy."

Cullen laughed. Then he went to the kitchen to get a drink of cola. Rain stood up from her desk and followed after him.

"Do you want some cola?"

"Okay. I'll have a few sips. You know how I like my beverages." Rain opened a can of cola and took a sip. "Guess what. I'm going to write a book about the rainforest."

"What? You are?"

"Yeah, I have been making a few notes about it lately and I decided that it will be called, "A mini-book about the great and tall rainforest." I already planned out what the first words are going to be. Let the Sun shine forth and the rain tickle." Rain said, sounding a bit overdramatic.

"Neat. What will it be about?"

"All about the rainforest. How we can help the trees there to grow and continue to grow because you know how important it is to keep the rainforest growing."

"That is for sure." Cullen paused, opening his can of cola.

It came as a surprise to Cullen when she said it. Here he was thinking away for days about how the weather was going to get warmer after seeing the four seasons of grow, mow, blow and snow that went by last year; even so, Cullen did get a feeling of exhilaration from the excitement of the year so far. It would soon be June again and he was more than ready for its arrival. He already bought some sunblock for the warmer days ahead. But now, it seemed, this summer was going to be different. With Rain writing a book and everything, it all was bound to be exciting. He certainly wondered what projects all the neighbours on Sunlit Avenue could possibly be working on in addition to Rain's mini-book. Cullen realized it was time for him to finally figure out what he would like to work on.

After a minute he said, "Please save the trees. Please save the rainforest trees."

"Hey, that rhymes." She took a few more sips from her cola, and placed it on the kitchen counter. "I like it."

"Can you put it in your book?" Cullen asked.

"Okay. I'll just write down what you said." She went into the living room where there was a pen and a notepad by the telephone.

Just then, Cullen turned to look out the kitchen window and he saw a man casually walking through the backyard. He was wearing a brown leather vest, a mustard yellow long sleeved shirt, blue jeans and red sneakers. Cullen watched as the fellow retraced his steps while looking around the yard and then went to the front of the house again. Cullen stepped into the living room and looked through the living room window to see where the guy was going next. There was no sight of him. Then finally the man jogged up the street at a fast pace to the left side of the house and it left Cullen wondering what the man was doing walking around the yard. Soon after that when there was no sight of the man, Mr. Cullen Dangsi looked to see if Sven's car was in the driveway. There was no car in sight. He looked at his watch. It read three fifty-five pm. Sven always worked from nine o'clock am to five o'clock pm. Even though a stranger had been roaming around the property for a minute, Cullen still looked forward to talking to Sven with anticipation to see what, if anything, was new with him. Sven was a good neighbour. He was also a guy that a person could really talk to about things. Both Cullen and Rain knew him to be friendly. He sometimes made a joke or two to be funny, especially when his brother Vic was spending some time with him.

Sven and Vic, close brothers, had been living together since they purchased their house on Sunlit Avenue a year ago. All ten recently built houses on Sunlit Avenue were first purchased either one or two years ago. The houses that are located on Sven and Vic's side of the Avenue were built one year ago, while the houses that are located on Rain and Cullen's side of the Avenue were built two years ago. And ever since then, the residents of this street have been pretty happy to say that they enjoy life on Sunlit Avenue.

Cullen stepped into the kitchen again to finish his can of cola. He heard Rain walking toward him from the living room. He hid her cola behind his back. Cullen tried not to laugh. She saw him holding his cola as he stood leaning against the counter and looked for her drink. It wasn't where she placed it.

"Where's the pop I had?" Rain asked, staring at Cullen for a few seconds.

Cullen couldn't help smiling. "Voila!" He held it out for her.

"Very funny." Rain held her drink. She smiled at Cullen, taking a couple of sips.

"Cola, cola. All right." She sang to him. *"Cola, cola. Tonight."*

"That's a fun song isn't it?" He said, drinking the rest of his can of pop. Cullen enjoyed listening to the sound of Rain's singing voice as she sang.

"Yup. Sing it." She said.

"Cola, cola. All right. Cola, cola. Tonight. Oh yeah." He sang back to her.

"I like singing it. It's my song." She watched him put his can on the counter, and then sang, *"Cola, cola. Hurray. Cola, cola. Today. Sing the song with a beat and have a sweet treat."*

"You really are something else."

"I know. It's really different."

"I'd say. Hey Rain, when you write the book about the rainforest are you going to make it fun too?"

"Yes. It will be fun to read about the rainforest. And fun to learn about it too. So that people can see that the rainforest is…something to take care of and enjoy." Rain drank the rest of her pop and put her can on the counter beside his. She placed it down with a thud that echoed throughout the room. "The living rainforest, I like the sound of that for the book."

A minute went by and she said, "In fact, I could write a little bit about that. The living rainforest sounds nice."

"Go get your notebook. I think you should write down those words."

"Good idea."

Before long, there was a car parked in Sven's driveway. Sven's car. It was just about five-thirty pm. He was home from work and Cullen noticed it after looking through the living room window for the tenth time. He had been talking to Rain about his plans for the summer. All she really said, short and sweet, was the following, "Whether cloudy or sun, have fun." The rest was about what he said he felt inspired to do. "This summer, I'll paint acrylic paintings full of contrast. It's my new hobby. You're inspiring me Rain."

He loved this idea of his. For sure. Just what he would be painting was half of the enjoyment of it. He had some ideas. A little bit of blue. A little bit of green. Some white. Some black. His girlfriend Rain had nodded quite a few times while he was talking about painting with acrylics on canvas as she sat looking over some of the things she wrote for her mini book.

"See you later. I'm going to give the gift card to Sven now."

"Okay."

Cullen walked over to Sven and Vic's house and soon knocked at the front door. The two houses were just across the street from each other. As it was, Sven and Vic were considered close neighbours.

Sven came to the door. "Hi, how are you?" Cullen asked.

"Oh, what can I say? I'm keeping it real. How have you been?"

"Good. I've got something for you. A gift card. I got it for you from an Italian restaurant for a present. Thank you again for the repair job on my car."

He took the gift card from Cullen and held it in his hand. "Thanks. Anytime."

"You're welcome. Oh, could you say your favourite saying again to me? The one you wrote about progress?"

"Sure." Sven smiled. Then the mechanic said, "Progress is made like a car. It carries you forward. When a lot of progress is made, what you have is a good car. A car you can count on. Count on counting the many kilometers of such a car. When enough progress has been made, what you have is a lot of places in life that you have traveled to."

"Beautifully said."

"Ah, yes."

"Of course."

"Rett's Italian Restaurant. I think I'll try their spaghetti again. I ate there once and I ordered spaghetti then."

"Spaghetti? Spaghetti and meatballs?"

"Yes. Spaghetti and meatballs."

"I like their salad."

"Salad? What do they put on the salad?" Sven asked with a look of curiosity on his face.

"Oh, tomatoes, cheddar cheese, lettuce, spinach, peppers, and pieces of almonds with ranch dressing."

"Is that your favourite?"

"Yes, it is." Cullen thought about it for a few seconds. He liked how they put almonds on the salad. 'Ranch dressing is tasty but to top it off with pieces of almonds, now that's quite a salad.' No wonder he liked eating there at the restaurant every so often. A pinch of this and a dab of that made for some mighty fine menu items at Rett's.

"Glad you like their salad. So, what's new? How is your day going?"

"Great. I told Rain that I'm interested in doing canvas paintings now."

"Really? Paintings?"

"Yeah, I would like to add some contrast colors to each of the canvas paintings to make things colourful indeed."

"That's great. Contrast colors, eh?" Sven looked around the yard for any dandelions. He couldn't see any as he held the door open. "If you could see some yellow dandelions against a background of say…blue forget me nots, you would have a contrast."

"Oh? Blue and yellow?" Cullen was intrigued.

"Sure. That's curious." Sven said. "Speaking of contrast colors, Rain told me the other day that she has a type of blue and yellow card that she makes to sell at her store. It's a joke card. It goes like this. A heart surgeon went to go see his girlfriend after operating on a patient. She asked him, "Would you be so kind as to write me a love letter?" What was his response? "Yes. In a heartbeat."

Cullen burst out laughing. Then the laughing got louder. Then it stopped and he said, "That's funny!"

"That's a hilarious joke isn't it?" Sven said with a curious tone in his voice that beamed with excitement.

"Yeah. I do laugh at the drop of a hat though. But it sure is nice to hear a new joke. Do you have any more jokes that you can tell?"

"That's all I can think of." Sven let go of the front screen door and it latched shut. He looked at a few of the shrubs around his yard with his neighbour since they were already talking about plants and such. He stepped off the front deck and stood on the walkway. Cullen was beside him.

Rita Young, a lady that lived next door just on the left to Rain and Cullen, facing the avenue, happened to be outside and soon noticed that the two neighbours were talking to each other across the street. She went over to see them and they saw her as she approached.

"Hi, I was getting ready to wash my Dodge minivan and I heard you guys and thought I would come and see you."

Sven greeted her. "Hey Rita. Yeah. What's new with you?"

Then Cullen greeted her. "Hi Rita."

"Oh, I've been enjoying my day off today. I have been doing some cleaning and went out for a drive. My sister is coming to visit in two weeks."

"That's nice. How's Sonja doing anyway?" Sven suddenly frowned because he saw that his screen door was barely on its hinges.

"Alright. I'm looking forward to seeing her."

"She's a personal trainer isn't she?" He tested the screen door some more by opening and shutting it a few times while Rita was talking away to him.

"Yes. And she's pretty muscular too."

"Is she going to be staying at your place?"

"Yes, she is."

"Cool. How long is she staying at your place?" Sven kept playing with the screen door until it fell off one of its hinges. It swung to one side and rested on a slant against the black metal railing by the front steps.

"Fifteen days." She appeared to be puzzled by what she was seeing. "Is everything alright? You seem to be having some trouble there with that door." Rita paused.

"Nothing like a wobbly screen door, eh folks? I think my brother Vic must have done this when he brought that new coffee table into the house the other day. He's gotta learn to be more careful."

"Maybe you can fix it." Cullen shook his head. He folded his arms in front of him and said, "You're used to fixing stuff anyway neighbour. That's what mechanics do after all."

"Yes, but this screen door is brand new. Vic must have been kind of rough with it. No worries though. I will fix it."

Rita looked like she was ready to change the subject. She folded her arms and stared at her watch for a few seconds and let out an impatient sigh. But after doing so, she soon started laughing for no apparent reason and pressed her hands together in anticipation of what she was about to say. "Been at the zoo lately? Come and see our new look." She quietly giggled to herself. "Actually, that is part of the ad for the new grand garden zoo that is due to open on June the fourth. I talked to my sister on the phone about the zoo the other day. So I thought that I would spread the word and tell you two about it.

"Did you say...grand garden zoo?" Sven looked at her with a serious face as he waited for a reply.

"Yeah, it's a garden and zoo. Its name says to me "grand scale" with many plants around the place to see. This is a different type of zoo. This zoo has all kinds of shrubs and flowers and of course new animals to look at all around it."

"Marvelous. June the fourth you said?"

"Sure did. And I'm going to take lots of pictures. Being a professional photographer I can get some nice pictures."

"Thanks for telling me about it. I'm sure Rain and I will go too." Cullen stared at Rita.

She giggled in response. "Cullen, I always get a kick out of talking with you. I admit that I'm usually bashful around you. That's because I'm still getting used to the thought of having a neighbour like you who always seems to be so funny whenever I'm around and I can tell you enjoy it too. I'm glad you live nearby."

"Well said Rita."

"Vic and I will have to go too."

"Good. Be sure to bring your camera. Oh, you know what? The rest of the ad said, "We hope your zoo going experience will be the highlight of your day.""

"Rita, I just thought of a joke about a physical trainer. You mentioned your sister is a physical trainer a minute ago. Here goes. A physical trainer was helping one of his clients with a workout. He just so happened to ask him, "What is your favourite muscle group to work on?" "My eye muscles because I'm a magazine article writer.""

Then at that moment a car was heard peeling around the corner quickly as it sped by and came to a sudden halt at the opposite end of the street from where they were standing. It came to rest near the curb on the side of the street to drop a man off and he went into a neighbouring house that was located on Sunlit Avenue. After a short pause the car did a full circle in the middle of the street and sped away into the distance.

"Funny stuff Cullen. Hey, there's Cally Ryerson." Sven said with a dry sound to his voice.

"Cal. But don't call him that. He might get angry." Cullen felt that although Cally was nearby, there was only the slightest chance of him heading straight toward them. "He probably didn't see us."

"Who is Cally Ryerson?" Rita asked.

"Who is he? He's Mr. and Mrs. Holiday's bad boy son and he's a drummer in a rock band in town. It looks like he's visiting his parents."

"How come I haven't heard of him before? Does he go over to see them every so often?" Rita asked.

"I don't know but he did come over to me when I was busy in my yard raking some leaves last week to tell me what he thought of the idea of the entire street working on their goals together." Sven saw the look on Rita's face. Her jaw was wide open as she listened.

"What did he say?" She questioned, appearing eager to hear every word of what he was about to say to her.

"He wanted to find out how many people I thought would be attracted to the idea of our whole street of neighbours going after their goals together." Sven said plainly.

"What did you say?"

"I said that I only would be guessing. After that he tightened his fist and shook it in the air close to me. I also said don't worry. The guy walked away after a while. So I continued raking the leaves."

"What?" Cullen said through his teeth in disbelief.

"He hasn't come around here since." Sven swept his brow.

"I've been busy at the photography studio taking pictures of people. This is the first I've heard of him."

"You'll probably be hearing more about him soon. By the way, Cullen, did you know his rock band's name is Wind Spontaneous?"

"No, I didn't. Imaginative name, isn't it?"

"Yep, it is. He's a talented professional drummer. His parents told me so. No one understood his attitude when he was a child. He's been drumming ever since." Sven looked very mellow for a moment. "Don't let him bother you, Cullen." He stared at the gift card again.

"Do you think that guy Cally is going to come over and talk to us one of these days? You said he already talked to you Sven."

"We'll have to see if he does. And if and when he does I will be prepared for it."

"I hear you. We have to find out what he is going to say about everything we are going to be working on. But even when we do find out, we still have to be willing to listen to him."

"That's right. Hey Cullen, I appreciate your thoughtful present. Thanks Dangsi."

"Treat yourself to a night out at Rett's."

"I'll do that."

"Nice talking to you guys. I'm going to go wash my minivan now. Remember, June the fourth."

"Okay Rita." Sven watched her as she walked across the road to her house. "Going to the zoo should be fun."

Cullen commented to Sven. "Hey, what better way for a mechanic to wind down from his busy day at the shop than to watch his good neighbour Rita wash her minivan?"

"You said it. Silver paint too."

"Deservedly so."

"What the heck does that mean?" Sven thought Cullen went a bit overboard by what he was saying.

Cullen then said, "Wheel clever, isn't it?" And soon Sven realized Cullen was just being his jokester self and thought nothing more of it.

The man that had walked through Cullen's yard appeared from out of nowhere and walked along the side of the street by where Cullen and Sven were standing. Cullen soon headed home after that. He had his suspicions about the guy and he wasn't much in the mood for talking to Sven about what he had seen. Not even to his girlfriend Rain.

CHAPTER 2

When Rita Young was only eight years old she had seen pictures of butterflies in magazines that her mother had at the time and thought they were quite something. It was then that she knew she was going to be a photographer. And it was then that her fondness for butterflies started growing. She wanted to capture nature on film. It was her fascination with butterflies that started it all. It all grew from finding out all she could know about them by reading information from grade school and on, to practising taking pictures with her camera, to studying photography courses and finally her career as a professional photographer. Everything led to where she was now going with photography. Seeing that first picture of a monarch butterfly resting on white yarrow with green stems was a picture that said it all to Rita. The monarch butterfly has a beautiful wingspan of orange, black and white. And it is just one example of a variety of different organisms that nature provides us with.

Monarch butterflies reminded Rita of the colors of sunrise ever since she moved to Sunlit Avenue. Rita really liked that too. She has often enjoyed watching the variety of colors in the early morning sky of a sunrise. Yellow, orange, and red. Usually she can be found waiting each morning for the perfect sunrise just to say she took a snapshot of one. Still, at the age of twenty eight, the young woman can be intrigued by photography during the course of any given day. People can definitely tell too. It all can be due to any aspect of her work and how she can get people to not only pose for the camera but to get the right angle. The right lighting. The right look. With nice results. With great effect too. Rita Young does seem to understand that each photograph can involve some amount of preparation. Miss Young's work has been admired by both the people that have their photo taken at the studio where she works and by magazine readers who get to see some of the work she does when she has been spending time out in nature. Rita has hope that the magazine readers will look at the beautiful photographs the same way she did when she looked at that first photograph of a monarch butterfly so many years ago. That way, at least to Miss Young, they too just might find mystery and intrigue in photography as an art form.

CHAPTER 3

Tuesday, May 31, 2011

"I checked the weather report. It's going to be another sunny day again today." Cora Pepper said to her mother Hazel Pepper. "And that means it's time to wear sunglasses."

"That's nice." Hazel said, while washing the upstairs bathroom mirror after spraying some cleaning solution on it. "Are you working today?"

"Yup. From ten o'clock to six o'clock."

"I'm going to keep this mirror spotless."

"Glad to hear it mom. So what are you going to do today? It's your day off." Cora noticed her mother was wearing a navy blue T-shirt and beige pants. She had a turquoise bracelet on and that was new.

"I think I might rest for a while today. I've been having fairly busy days at work lately. My co-worker Hugh and I are going to set some tiles at a few places tomorrow."

"Rest up then. Be back later. See ya mom." Cora was wearing a light brown T-shirt and striped black and white knee-length shorts. Her matching shoes were of course white sneakers. The kind of outfit that had a certain appearance about it that looked neat and fashionable. As far as style went with Miss Pepper, neat and fashionable said it all.

"Bye."

Cora went downstairs to the hall table beside the front door where she left her sunglasses. She put them on and headed out the door. As she walked to her car that was parked in the driveway outside, she thought, 'Today is going to be one cool day.'

Already, she had received by mail some information that her new company called Neat Street Robots had been doing great. "It is in the making." The letter had clearly stated. It went on to say, "Neat Street Robots is now co-owned by Cora Pepper and her business partners making up a team of five known as Team ON-ST, a shorter version of the word Honesty, and we are sure to begin production of the first of the robots of "Take it to the Max, Robot" in our factory by the end of the month." To Cora that meant they are giving it the go ahead.

Cora was waiting for the letter to arrive for days and it finally arrived. It meant so much to her to find out how her company had been doing lately. Now that she received the notice she could look forward to hearing from them again as soon as the first few robots were finished being manufactured. Soon, she hoped, there would be six-foot tall life-size robots saying different messages including, "Life. Live it. Take it to the Max. When you are making good traction you are taking good action. My name is Catchy Petunia." It seemed like the robots would be sold to people so they can keep them in their homes as decorations to make it all the more futuristic. But only recently Cora felt that they may even be sold to businesses with their simple messages being something to hear by many people. Added by her own personal touch. Cora's touch. With the push of a button the robots would say the messages. Each one of the Take it to the Max robots would be saying messages about life that people haven't really heard of before. At least not from a robot.

With the turn of a key, Cora started the car engine and sped off down the street. She drove to the hair salon where she worked as a hairdresser and parked in the parking lot. There she sat in front of Refresh Haircutters thinking about how her day had been so far and how it would be for the rest of the day. It had already been quite exciting. She thought about it and thought about it some more and then took her sunglasses off as she got ready to start her shift. People would be getting haircuts from her and her co-workers for most of the day if it so happened to be a busy day. She hoped it would be busy at work because that way there would be lots to do. As soon as she focused on what the haircuts would look like she stepped out of her car.

A minute later she was at her own salon area dreaming to herself for several minutes about her new type of robot called Take it to the Max, Robot. A robot nicknamed Catchy Petunia looked more male than it did female. It had, in fact, a regular sounding male voice. There was a nifty sounding recording of a guy saying each of the inspirational messages that Cora came up with and had later written down on paper around the time when she had first invented the Catchy Petunia robot. She had actually heard how they sounded when the people at her company contacted her over the phone earlier on. "It does sound like the kind of robot voice I was hoping for Catchy." She told them when they played it for her. Although that was so, Cora secretly did find that both working at a salon styling the latest hairdos almost every day stood in stark contrast to being an entrepreneur of a company dealing with the technology of having realistic life-sized speaking robots. That is because they seemed to be like something out of the future. Even though the robots had an appeal of all their own, Cora knew only too well the many emotions she regularly experienced that made her feel funny about being a haircutter and a new robot line inventor. After finishing her hairstyling duties at the end of her work shift every day she had only to imagine what having two incomes would be like.

She stood looking at the items around her salon chair. There was a mirror and all the hair styling accessories like scissors, combs, brushes, a hairdryer and even a small rectangular shaped card on a table with her name on it. Cora. After looking at the mirror in front of her to see herself, she fixed up her sandy blonde short style hairdo and looked at the nice blonde highlights that ran through it. Cora had blue eyes and was five-foot-nine in height. She was quite thin looking but still very shapely. She had light toned skin with freckles in some places, especially her arms. Miss Pepper felt like washing hair for people at the salon today more than usual for some odd reason. To see the shampoo foam up as she scrubbed away at any particular customer's hair during washing was interesting. Also, to rinse the conditioner off after finishing the hair wash and dry it with a towel and walk the customers to their seat where she would soon begin the hair styling was all part of the enjoyment of it for her. At only twenty-one years of age, there was much to celebrate about for her on this day. Cora decided to wait until her shift was done before telling anybody about the robots that would soon be made. People like Sven, her neighbour, for starters. And Laurence, another hairstylist in town that she knew as a close friend, who she met one day while getting her hair done at a local salon where he found employment. She discovered him there about six months ago. He liked to talk about the latest hairstyles. Cora imagined his reaction upon telling him about Neat Street Robots. 'What is he going to say? Probably "Neat Street Robots…that's exciting!" And I will answer, "I'll say." My oh my.' Cora thought. She wondered what her mother would tell her about it, for she knew the time would soon arrive for her to discuss Neat Street Robots with Hazel. She was looking forward to it.

"Are you ready to start styling?" A co-worker asked Cora after walking to where she stood.

"Sure."

"I thought so." Cora's co-worker said with a smile. She appeared to be cheerful. "You know what I thought of saying after I finish doing each haircut? Get this. "What do you make of it?"

"Oh, that's a good one."

"Isn't it though?"

"Yes it is. Plus they can tell you what they think of their haircuts and such."

"Yeah, that's right." Flo said with a mixture of excitement and gratitude. "Now I'm all prepared for the day ahead.

"So am I." Cora crossed her fingers hoping for the best for her new line of inspirational type of robots. As imaginative as she had been when he had created them, there was one thing about Cora that caused her to feel tense.

She didn't know what reaction people would have toward finally seeing those life-size robots she had talked to the robot developers about with on the phone all those times. Although she had some investors backing her up financially for the business, she felt as though she was on a rollercoaster with all the emotions she was experiencing about it. She had so much riding on this new robot business. She had nothing to do but wait for it all to play out so that she could see where her company was going with it. She was relying on a team of people to ensure the robots would be made correctly. On top of that, she wondered what the public reaction would be to having the futuristic Catchy Petunia robots brought out and available to the public.

* * *

"That one will do just nicely." A customer said about a tabletop water fountain that he was purchasing for his home. After a few minutes of looking around, he was very pleased about the one he decided to buy. One of the staff could tell right away by the expression on his face. There it was in plain sight. There were quite a few of a dove with wings outstretched. Even though he considered purchasing one of the ones with a dove and looked at them for a while he nodded contently at the one that was of two cats rubbing themselves against each other in a sort of embrace.

"Yes, that one. What is it made of?"

"The cats are copper and the rest of the fountain is brown and grey slate."

"And it's four-hundred and twelve dollars? I would like to purchase it."

"That one is called Meow Fantastic." The store employee said to the customer.

The tabletop water fountain measured twelve inches in width, twenty-four inches in length, and eighteen inches in height. It had a copper water pipe two inches wide with water flowing out of it onto some river stones and a bamboo plant that were just underneath. Little flat red stones placed about the fountain could be found within it. They were almost hidden with the word "Meow" painted on each one in black lettering. There were exactly twelve of those. They were glued there so they would stay in place and looked nice just the way they had been arranged. The copper cats were at the front and nearby the water pipe. It was as though they appeared to be frolicking in the streaming water.

"A charming water fountain like this can add character to a room. It also has a quiet motor and the water will keep flowing. Just clean it with some water cleaning solution to clean the algae and white scale deposits off of it every month. We have some cleaning solution just over there." The store clerk pointed to the section at the other end of the store where the cleaning products were located.

"Really?" The customer said, scratching his chin as he was thinking about it. "Okay, what kind of cleaning solution do you recommend?" He had on a yellow silk tie, a green dress shirt, black suit pants and black shoes.

"Follow me, I'll show you." The young gentleman said as he looked at the customer who appeared to be in his fifties. He had some noticeable grey hair throughout his black hair.

"Well, alright." The customer beamed a bright smile as he looked at the orange and pink designs on the employee's short sleeve shirt. There were zigzags all over it. Grey pants went along with the shirt and a white belt and black shoes that made for a one of a kind sort of overall appearance. The employee had brown hair and was about five-feet-eight inches tall.

"What is your name, young chap?"

"Damien."

"Impressive store you have here. I've been meaning to shop here for a while now, so I thought I should stop by."

"Glad you did."

"Me too. Damien, where did they come up with the name for this place? Hemley's Great Fountains Alive.

"Oh, ah…actually my wife and I run the store. We're the Hemleys."

"You're kidding? How long has this store been here? I moved to this city recently."

"Six years."

"Gee. It's a fine business. Been nice seeing some of the creative creations you sell. The name really says it for me."

"Thank you." The customer walked to the cleaning solution section where there were bottles of solution displayed on shelves.

After the man made his purchases and left the store, Damien Hemley was feeling glad to have made a sale. Then he thought about his wife, Mavis Hemley, who he shared a house with on Sunlit Avenue. They enjoyed playing soccer together on weekends on family outings along with their two kids Francis and Lulu. At six years of age, Francis was starting to score some goals by running faster than usual the closer she got to the net, while Lulu, at five years of age, usually shouted "Watch this!" and made a goal every now and then. They often rewarded the two girls by taking them out to get ice creams or smoothies afterwards as a way to relax after the big game and to celebrate any points that they scored that they made each time they played. It always brought smiles to their faces when they received the treats. Francis was going to begin grade one in September and already she knew how to write a lot of words. Her mom taught her in her spare time how to spell the words and how to do some simple math too.

Damien had a certain fondness for bringing in new fountains from the backroom each time there was room for new ones to be displayed. Often the other employees would help carry them because some of the heavier garden fountains required some heavy lifting and some muscle power to move them. This kept the twenty-nine year old Damien in shape during his work duties. The store staff had mentioned to Damien recently that they thought he could sell pretty much anything in the store to pretty much anyone because he was such a successful salesman. They were well aware of how much money that Damien must be making. They considered that he should be pretty wealthy by now after being in business for a while. Customers often came into to the store feeling like they would like to buy a fountain already and Damien was always right there with a big smile on his face ready to help them with their next selection and make the next sale. There was something about Damien that made people want to buy from him. He didn't miss out on every opportunity to listen carefully to what the customer was looking for and each customer could tell that he was a natural at his job. He had the spark for being an entrepreneur.

His wife Mavis, at thirty years of age, paid close attention to her husband and sometimes wondered if she should help to sell more fountains by talking to the customers the same way that her husband always did. However, she was definitely improving at making the sales on the job a lot lately by watching Damien at work because she focused on one noticeable detail that he didn't. Her fine edge for sharing vivid information on the fountains that Damien missed seemed to draw even more people into the store by word of mouth. Mavis could hear them talk behind her back about how she had said to put on their fountains when they are sitting and relaxing at the end of the day and picture that there is a peaceful and serene sounding stream of water flowing nearby their feet that was their own little piece of paradise there to enjoy. She said there was a quiet and alluring way of having a water effect in front of you that helped you to imagine yourself being on top of a mountain where there was scenic views all around. Mavis had a vivid imagination and her customers were fully aware of that being so. Between sales she spend most of her time cleaning fountains around the store so they would be in good working order for the customers. There were plenty of them. And the cleaning supplies section of the store had to be restocked every so often, as many people who bought fountains at Hemley's Great Fountains Alive also stopped in to get some cleaning supplies to wash their fountains. This made for a fairly large sales volume from the cleaning supplies section of the store.

Two hours later, Mavis walked into the store to start her work shift. She would be cleaning some of the fountains and she had already tagged the ones due to be cleaned with a white sticker on the front of each one the day before. She saw Damien talking to a customer who was looking around at the fountains they had on display. After the woman spoke to him for a few minutes she continued to look around the place watching the water as it circulated through the fountains. She always found it peaceful to hear the sound of water coming from some of them.

Mavis greeted Damien, "Hello, how are you doing?"

Damien replied, "Great. We sold the Meow Fantastic tabletop fountain earlier today."

"That's good. Would you believe Rain Woodrow said that there is going to be the opening of the grand garden zoo in a few days?"

"In a few days? When? What time?"

"June the fourth she said. We could find out what time they open and go see it. She said Rita is going on the day it opens."

"Maybe. We could check it out sometime soon anyway." Damien pushed his glasses closer to his face. Mavis studied her husband's relaxed tone of voice as he talked to her. It seemed as though the subject of a grand garden zoo calmed him. She looked at his facial expression and then at his fair skin and brown hair. He appeared to be daydreaming a little. Then he looked at her face and her short, light blonde hair and her shirt that was just as colorful as his. It had vertical stripes of red and blue. Some thick and some thin. She had the same color of pants on as he did. Grey pants. Her dark orange and navy blue sneakers were a little bit worn at the toes but still comfortable to wear. It was all part of her work uniform. Just as what Damien was wearing was his work uniform too.

Mavis sighed. "I went to Rain's store today. She wasn't at home so I went there to see her. She was talking away to her staff about a card that says on it…"Really? I mean really? Really. You're thirty-five? Have a Happy Birthday and a really splendid year."

"Nice card."

"It cost eight dollars."

"Nice price."

"I'd say."

"Well, I'm going to head over to the bank and get some more money. We need some more twenties and more rolls of coins." Damien said.

"Okay. I saw two men fighting in the parking lot a few minutes ago. You might want to be careful. See you after."

"Oh gee. They were rough were they?"

"You might say that."

When Damien left the building and went out into the parking lot, he just so happened to notice two men standing beside his white Dodge Charger. They appeared to be checking the tires of an orange Chevrolet Corvette parked right beside it. Damien took a final glance at the tires on the other car to see what shape they were in before getting out his keys. He was dangling the keys in front of him while searching for the right one. It was at that moment when it happened. All at once they grabbed him. The two men handcuffed him and threw him in the back seat of the car. Then they put grey duct tape over his mouth and threw a black cloth sack over his head and fastened his seat belt for him. After that was done they got into the car. Between the muffled cries coming from Damien and the shushing sounds coming from the two men to quiet him down, there was a pause for only half a minute as the men scanned the parking lot to see if anyone had spotted them. When it appeared no one had seen them, the men turned to face Damien who was sitting behind them. His heart was racing and he was scrambling to try and get away.

"We are kidnapping you."

"We might want to hold onto these." The guy in the driver seat said while holding Damien's keys in his hand.

Damien shook his head in an exaggerated way. He didn't know why this was happening to him. He took some big breaths and watched as they drove off with him out of the parking lot to some unknown destination.

A short while later the kidnappers stopped the car in a paved driveway. They brought Damien into a two storey house with beige siding and a black roof. Damien was carried down a flight of stairs by the men. They removed the black sack that covered his head and the duct tape that covered his mouth.

"Who are you?" Damien asked right away. He remembered overhearing one of the two men saying to the other earlier in the car, "This is no ordinary kidnapping." It made him wonder who these guys were and what they planned on doing with him.

"The name is Griffin." The first man said.

"I'm Lenny." The second man was reluctant to say. He pointed to Griffin. "Don't try anything, Damien. This guy is huge."

"I'm tough too." Griffin sneered.

"Bye, I have to go take care of other matters." Lenny waved.

Damien could only listen. He watched as Lenny went up the flight of stairs and closed the upstairs door behind him. Holding back the tears he asked, "Griffin, why did you and Lenny kidnap me?"

"We don't plan on revealing that just yet. What we do plan on is keeping you here until we figure things out."

"Where is the other guy going?"

"Don't concern yourself with that."

"I'm thirsty. I have a dry throat."

"Oh, you would like some water?"

"Yes." Damien cleared his throat. He still had the handcuffs on and hoped so much to have them taken off soon. He didn't like the idea of drinking water with handcuffs on.

"Can you please remove these handcuffs?" Damien said with a shaky voice.

"I will get you the water and remove the handcuffs if you work on something for me. Make a drawing. One drawing of anything you want. You can color it in too."

"Ah, yeah. Sounds alright." He gulped. "What are you going to do with it?"

"Mail it to your wife."

"My wife?"

"That way your wife and kids will take the hint that you are, in fact, okay."

Damien cringed at the thought of anything happening to his wife and children. He cried out, "Don't you hurt them. I love them."

"Sure, Damien. I will get you that water now."

Griffin, a man who was six-feet in height with short, red hair and a grown out beard, left the room laughing with uproarious laughter. "I've got you now Damien." He shouted quite loudly.

When he came back a minute later with a plastic jug of water and a metal cup filled with water, he walked by Damien and set the jug on a square wooden table. Damien was in a renovated basement apartment of some sort. He could only tell so far that it had dark blue walls and different types of fake plants. Some tall and some short. But Damien was in no way taking it all in. He missed his own home. He missed his family. There was even a growing suspicion for him that he may be living in the basement apartment for some time. Damien hoped that he would get out of it alive. It had happened so fast. He was situated there in the living room of the place slouching in a soft armchair of a light mauve color trying to catch his breath.

Damien lost his puzzled expression once Griffin brought the water over to him. Soon after, he sat up straight and watched as the handcuffs were taken off. His hands were sore from struggling to get away from the two kidnappers for the fifteen minutes it took to get to the house. Now that he could finally see where he was thanks to the black sack being removed from off his head, he had decided to stop struggling so much and remain focused instead on keeping his wits about him.

"Relax Damien, you look worried."

Damien wrinkled his forehead. He had a sense of overall concern for his safety. "Tell me you're not going to hurt me, please."

"I won't hurt you." Griffin held the metal cup up to Damien's face for him to drink from it. Damien held it in his hands and took a sip. He then drank down the rest of the cup of water. Damien frowned. The kidnapper's words weren't so comforting. "Stop worrying because…"

Griffin scratched his head as he started to say something. He stared into Damien's eyes. He knew the young man was being very patient with him and he liked to see that from him.

Damien sat waiting for Griffin to continue and then flew out with it. "Because why?"

"Because I said so. It's a bit chilly in the basement apartment here but luckily you have a jacket on. Damien's jacket was peach and aqua colored. Griffin looked at Damien, I better turn off the heat in the place. That way you won't be hot because it is getting warm out." So he turned down the thermostat on the wall nearby. "Is that enough water for now?"

"Yes."

"Good. Now I want you to draw that picture of whatever you want to draw and I will mail it to your wife like I mentioned." Griffin passed him a pencil, some pencil crayons and a large notepad of paper.

"Wait a second. Aren't you going to tell me why you kidnapped me?" Damien was nearly gasping for air. His nerves were shot and he couldn't take it anymore. He counted the seconds it took for Griffin to reply to his question that he felt compelled to ask.

"Yeah, I guess Lenny wouldn't mind." He stretched his arms while glaring toward Damien.

"I had to after I learned how wealthy you must be. C'mon, I mean, you sell anywhere from five, six or seven four-hundred dollar fountains a day. You're right up there with someone like Brooke. Do you know what this means? You're one of the richest people on your street."

"You're joking. How did you find that out about me and my neighbour?"

"I'm not joking. I'm going to leave you alone for a while now Damien."

Damien looked at the brown laminate flooring and then turned his gaze up at the ceiling made up of grey metal tiles. "I'll make that picture for you then."

"Next time I return to see you, I hope you will have drawn just the picture I've been waiting to see. Until then, cheers, my boy." Griffin brought the handcuffs with him while going up the stairway to the rest of the house. Finally, after a few seconds of silence, Damien heard the sound of Griffin locking the door behind him. There was no other ways of escape. At least, none that Damien was aware of at the moment. Even if he did escape he knew they might be after him. So he began tapping his notepad page with the tip of his pencil and stared so long at the pencil crayons in front of him he began to daydream. He figured the drawing may take some amount of planning if it was to meet Griffin's expectations. Every line had to be carefully drawn until the picture was complete. 'Just what kind of drawing should I make?' He thought to himself. 'It has to be something that is beautiful and cheerful to me anyway. After all is said and done, it would still be something that I may be proud of making.' He realized that after working on such a drawing, he could only sit and wait for one or both of the kidnappers to return to him. He dreaded the thought. It would only be a matter of hours before he would be seeing where it would all lead. One way or the other.

* * *

At six-forty pm Cora was home from work. She went over to see Sven Nicolos to tell him of the news about her new business she was keeping secret. There were two cars in the driveway. One was Sven's and one was Vic's. She knocked on the door and rang the doorbell and soon Sven came to the front door.

"Hi Cora. What's new?"

"I have something cool to tell you. Me and four other people are the business owners of a new company called Neat Street Robots and I received a letter saying that they will soon begin production of the robots. Isn't that just wonderful?"

"What are the robots like?"

"They are six-feet high and they are each green, black and grey in color. And they say messages that inspire people. With the push of a button you can play the messages. I'm so happy they are finally going to be made. They are called Take it to the Max, Robot. What do you make of it?"

"Where are they being made? C'mon, let's sit outside. Vic, come over here and listen to what Cora is saying." Vic was in the living room listening to his two lovebirds singing. The green, orange, and red birds had white eye-rings. They were cute and were a vision to see. But their names were equally as cute as the birds themselves. Vic had named them Fizz and Bizz.

"I heard her. Fizz and Bizz actually stopped singing long enough for me to hear Cora talking to you. That is great about your business." Vic walked over to Cora and nodded at her. The three of them went outside and sat on the wooden front steps.

"Cora, how many robots are they going to make?" Sven asked.

"A lot of them hopefully. There is a factory where they will be built and factory workers that are getting ready to make them right now." She smiled, "Fun eh?"

"I guess so. Just wait until they make some of them and see what they are like first."

"Yeah, they have the know-how though when it comes to creating robots. I'm waiting for them to send the next letter about the company. I'm part of a team known as team ON-ST. Get it? Neat street robots. We made the word Honesty into ON…dash…ST? It's so wonderful."

"Hmm. Cora, what a surprise." Vic said.

"The letter stated that when the first few robots are done being manufactured they will send me another letter. It's to keep me informed about how the company is doing."

"Thanks for telling us about it." Sven said.

"I thought you guys would like to hear about it."

"That's for sure." Vic said.

"Hey Cora, good job." Sven said. "In case you're wondering, we took the screen door off because it came off its hinges. Vic was a little rough with it but he said he will remember to be careful with stuff around the house more often. That's Vic for ya."

"We aren't exactly two peas in a pod." Vic blurted out loud. "He fixes stuff and I'm a little rough with stuff."

"Curious. Well, I should get going guys. Talk to you again soon."

"Yep. See you." Vic sounded like he could hardly wait to hear what his brother was going to say next about him. But Cora left before he could say anymore. Vic liked being talked about by people. Especially when he was there to listen to it all.

Before long, she went back home and phoned her friend Laurence. He wasn't home but the answering service machine came on and she left a message. It was a short message and she thought he might be home as it was his day off and just after suppertime. "Laurence, call me. Wait until you hear about the letter I received in the mail yesterday."

Cora's mom was home. She decided not to tell Hazel about the business just yet. She cooked some Thai stir-fry for herself and sat down to rest for a while. After standing on her feet all day, she liked to sit on her favourite living room chair. A black leather recliner. And to Cora, after such an exciting day and fairly busy work shift, that made all the difference.

CHAPTER 4

Wednesday, June 1, 2011

The next day at around one thirty pm, Francis was playing out in the front yard with her sister Lulu and they were both looking at the dark clouds covering the sky above and watching to see if it would start raining while they were outside. They heard it might rain. It looked as though it may start drizzling any second and they wanted to be outdoors for a few minutes to see if it would be any warmer than usual. It was starting to get windy outside and the trees were rustling nearby. The two girls listened to the gusts of wind come and go. One after another the gusts blew the spring air around them. Francis and Lulu then looked up the Avenue to the house just two houses away from where they both were standing. Aleisha Forbes, the woodcarver of fine lamps, lived there and could usually be found working away on her latest woodcarvings whenever anyone she knew stopped in to see her. Francis missed her and wondered how she had been doing lately.

"I haven't seen Aleisha for a while." Francis said.

"Me neither." Lulu answered.

Ever since Francis and Lulu had last visited Aleisha Forbes a few weeks earlier, she had been working away busily at her most recent woodcarving of two female dolphins named Tickle and Tackle pulling a lady named Lily Sumner on a water ski cart across the open water as Lily held the reins of the dolphins' harnesses in front of her. In the woodcarvings Lily Sumner always had a big smile on her face. It was all part of the detailed work of each homemade lamp that Aleisha spent time completing before selling the lamps to people interested in purchasing them. She sold them online mostly and she had her own website that described the lamps and the original one of a kind idea of dolphins being trained to pull a water ski cart through the water as though they were horses pulling a cart along a road.

"I liked seeing Aleisha's lamp she has of Lily Sumner and the dolphins a few weeks ago. She said she saved it for us to see. Maybe she will sell it soon."

"I learned a lot about dolphins. She said you can train dolphins how to do things." Lulu said.

"Yeah, like flips in the water. Do you think they really could train them to pull a water ski cart?"

"Yes. Horses know how, why not dolphins?"

"Good thinking Lulu. I think so too."

"Kids, come on in the house. I have to tell you something about your dad." Mavis called out to Francis and Lulu. She wasn't prepared to tell them their dad had gone missing. But she still had to tell them before they wondered about him. She had a look of concern on her face. The kids noticed it right away as she stood at the front door.

"Let's go in the house now and see Mom. It's starting to sprinkle." Francis held her sister's hand and swung it back and forth.

"Yeah, I don't want to get wet." Francis stepped into the house.

"Me neither." Lulu said softly as she followed behind Francis.

"What I have to tell you about your dad is important." Mavis held the door open for her children as they walked inside the house. She looked at them and thought to herself, 'God, how am I going to do this? How am I supposed to tell my kids that their dad has been kidnapped? I just received a call from a strange man telling me he has Damien. And from the sound of things he just may be holding him captive for a while.'

* * *

Vic Nicolos and two other professional siding installers had just finished putting new siding on an older two storey house when it started to rain. The construction crew had perfectly timed completing the installation of some medium brown siding with the rain that was forecast to arrive in the afternoon. And as they collected their tools and things and sat in the truck, the rain really started to come down. Before long, they had the wipers on and they were about to pull out of the driveway while taking a final glance at their work to see how different the house now looked than when they first arrived a few days ago. There it was in front of them. They thought the homeowner was wise about the color he picked for the siding. It matched the tan color of the roof. The seconds went by until it was a minute later. They had admired their work on the house and now it was time to drive off. And away they went. Down the road they drove with the rain streaming across their vehicle's windshield and windows.

It suddenly occurred to Vic Nicolos, 'Why don't I give myself a nickname too? My brother Sven is nicknamed Flare because he finds hot cars to be appealing and he is a mechanic. Mid-Town will be my nickname because I like it and I'm into putting siding up all over town. Mid-Town.'

He sat in a white truck in the passenger seat with one of the guys to his left in the driver's seat and one behind the driver's seat in the back seat. They were done for the day. It was time to go home.

The name of the business they worked for was Howda's Siding. Vic had been in business with Howda's Siding for nine years in total. And he found it rewarding career. Sometimes they played the radio and their favorite song C'mon-C'mon would play. On the way home one of the guys would usually sing it or talk about what they liked about it. Vic sat in his seat thinking about it and then sang the song. "*C'mon-C'mon now everyone. To say-you say-we say the bell rings, ding-ding-ding-dong. To say-you say-aww-you've got to reach those heights, say yes you can and be part of the crowd. And not just stand out in the crowd but be part of the crowd that stands out. You said you can, you surely can and it's all up to you. But no matter what and no matter when you know what you've got to do. Just say you will be the best you can and the day will carry you through. I heard you, I heard you. I saw you, I saw you in the crowd standing there. Remaining true to the same old you but now you're being the best way you can be you. That is what a person can do. When they go about their* day, go about their way, they are already in shape or shaping up. To show you what they can do. Oh, what they can do. And doing all they can to see-see-see you. And to see all they can do-do-do. So what can they do? They can do. Yes they can too. Don't you know it, oh yeah. We can too."

Vic sang it softly and slowly. The song had a soothing and relaxing beat to it and a great guitar sound for it too that stirred the emotions of its listeners. That is part of the reason why Vic, Rex, and Sampson liked to sing it so much. Plus, they also enjoyed hearing the words to the song. The three of them heard on the radio station that the music and lyrics are by a band called Peace-eba.

The professional siding installer, otherwise known as Vic Nicolos, kept himself fit by weightlifting in his spare time at home. He even had his own home gym in one of the extra bedrooms of his house. This made him all the more effective in his job duties when he had the task of putting up new siding at any house he was working on, as he always had the muscle power and strength to lift his arms for extended periods of time. He usually teased his brother for not weightlifting when there was a weightlifting bench and a set of metal weights laying around for him to exercise with if he ever felt like pumping some iron. Vic usually cried out a loud yell that echoed from room to room whenever he was doing some leg squats due to the huge amount of weight that he put on his barbell. It seemed to Vic that Sven was turned off by this certain behaviour he showed in his exercise routines. Because of that, Vic had developed the habit of rolling his shirt sleeves up high on his arms do show his well-developed muscles and he had a tendency to do it while on the job with the other guys. Vic usually had a blast working away with the siding thanks to all the remarks the other workers made in front of him. Their upbeat attitude they showed as a team when the owners of the houses heard them talking away made it easier for them to get more customers from word of mouth recommendations to other people they knew. As it was, they were putting new siding up all over town now that the warmer weather had arrived. And Vic was ready as ever to tackle the work load.

"Hey guys, I just thought of a nickname for myself. Mid-Town. What do you think of it?"

"Wonderful." Sampson said. Pretending to play the drums on his lap the same way a teenager would do. He was dressed in a pink T-shirt and tan colored pants. He had just enough room in the back seat as he leaned over to tie the shoelaces of his steel-toed shoes. All three men wore the same style of black shoe.

"Mid-Town it is." Rex said.

"My brother Sven has a nickname too. Flare. He's a mechanic, remember?"

"A mechanic. Oh, we remember. Right, Sampson?"

"Yes." Sampson said, taking a quick glance at the bright hot orange and yellow plaid short sleeved shirt and white jean shorts that he was sporting. "You didn't tell me he also went by the name Flare though."

"Yeah, but now you know." Vic said while looking at Rex driving the truck beside him. Rex wore a checkered black and white T-shirt and navy blue shorts that had one big white stripe that ran up each side.

"Ok, Vic."

"You won't believe this but I have been seeing the same red SUV all day. The one that is two cars behind us. I wonder if someone is following us." Rex stated with a concerned tone of voice.

"No way. I didn't even notice. I was working hard to put the siding up before the rainstorm came." Vic said.

"Yeah guys, I really do think someone has been following us. They were parked on the road for an hour near the customer's house and after that they circled around to the street where we were working at least a dozen times."

"Maybe they were waiting to use the driveway." Sampson suggested.

"But that doesn't explain why they are two cars behind us now." Rex replied shaking his head.

"Just keep driving man. That's all I can tell you. Maybe it's a lady looking to date one of us." Vic commented.

"No, it looks like it's a guy. Yeah, definitely a guy."

"Oh jeez. Just who could it be?" Vic said. He was distracted by what his co-workers were saying so he listened to the sound of the rain being wiped away by the windshield wipers to calm himself down. Half a minute later the red SUV had pulled away and he felt a sense of relief.

* * *

The rain let up after six o'clock pm that day and Hazel Pepper thought she just might go outside for some fresh air after having supper with her daughter Cora. They had eaten several plums and brown rice, boiled eggs, spinach and sliced apples with cinnamon. Hazel came home with groceries after work and supper had already been made by the time Cora was done talking to Laurence on the telephone upstairs in her bedroom.

Hazel stepped out the front door and looked at the cloud covered sky above. She had asked Cora what she and her friend were talking about on the telephone and Cora told her during the meal, "A line of robots named Catchy Petunia. A type of grey, green and black robots they are making in a factory and hopefully people can start listening to their messages soon."

Hazel talked to Cora during their meal. "Messages from robots? The part about the robots being six-feet tall is what I'm mostly thinking about. It seems like you know a lot about them. I have to go get some fresh air." The fifty one year old lady went and checked to see if the birdseed feeder beside the front walkway was still full. It was half full. It was quite dark outside so she came back in the house after taking in a few breaths of spring air. All was quiet on Sunlit Avenue. She stepped back in the house.

That is when Cora approached her and said, "Mom, I have to tell you. Me and four other people are the ones that are the company owners of Neat Street Robots and I think the robots are really going to sell. I mean isn't it unusual to have robots say inspirational messages?"

"What? You and four others are the owners of the company? You're kidding. Since when?"

"They are beginning production pretty soon."

"The secret is out. My daughter the company owner."

"Co-owner."

"Well, don't just stand there. For starters tell me what they say."

"I'll tell you some of the things they say. "The fun has begun." "I can tell by the way that you look at yourself that you are a stargazer. Stargazer." "Take it to the Max, Robot.

Neat Street Robots." "Life. Live it. When you are making good traction you are taking good action."

"Oh my goodness. How much are these robots going to cost?"

"Twelve thousand dollars each. We have to pay for the factory rent and all the parts and labor too. But I was told that I would make five-hundred dollars profit on each one since I thought of the idea for the robots.

"The rest of the investor team are helping to fund it."

"Gee. You are only twenty-one and you thought of that?"

"Wait and see Mom. The robots have to be made first. Then we can see what they will look like and sound like."

"I'm glad you told me about it."

"Me too. We'll talk about it some more later."

"Sure."

Cora had already talked about it to Sven, Vic, Laurence and now Hazel. The next letter was soon to arrive in the mail. The people at the Neat Street Robots company had said it might.

Hazel Pepper had a busy day of putting tiles of slate down on the entryway floor and marble on the kitchen floor of a house. And hours later, ceramic on the bathroom walls of another house. Hazel and her co-worker Hugh usually worked together on a daily basis on all sorts of projects. Professional tiling was their career. Both Hazel and Hugh felt it was a good career to have actually. That is because setting down tiles for a living kept them moving and on the go. Most days, for them it had usually been either challenging or easy. And after being in professional tiling for seven years, Hazel had been finding out for herself that the job can be rather easy to do overall. Hazel started out working at the tiling store as a sales clerk and then she thought of taking up tiling when she heard they were hiring another full time tiling professional. She said she would give it a try and ever since that day she had been employed as a tiling professional.

Hazel had been seeing all the new styles in her work lately and it really made her feel eager to do her work. She was ready to call it a day and go to bed early. She wanted some more time to think of exactly what her daughter told her about the robots they were making. Robots with inspirational messages. Hazel soon walked to her bedroom and she then lay down on her bed with her head resting against a pillow. She heard Cora go into the next bedroom and said aloud, "Cora, you're very inventive. I hope you are successful at whatever you do for a living. Robots, what a concept."

"Thanks Mom." Cora peered into her mother's bedroom and saw her laying down on the bed. "I have to say that living on Sunlit Avenue sure has helped me to be more productive."

"Hasn't it though? When a group of people like us decide to work together and are as determined as we are, you really get to thinking how you can accomplish things. Isn't that so?"

"Yes mom. I'm just glad that we moved here and met all the neighbours here. We're lucky, aren't we?"

"We sure are dear. Yes, we sure are."

CHAPTER 5

Thursday, June 2, 2011

Sven "Flare" Nicolos the auto mechanic went to work the next day at nine o'clock am rotating some tires on a car in the garage. It was due for a tire rotation because the owner of the car had said that he put another six thousand miles on it. The car was a 2010 Toyota Camry LE with a white exterior and a grey interior. As he saw how new and shiny it still looked, Sven noticed it had a tiny dent on the front bumper. "A zing." Sven said to himself. "Ah! I mean of course a ding."

To Sven, rotating tires was simply a part of the work routine, just as changing oil was routine too. He knew the importance of doing a professional job. To him, being a mechanic was all about keeping automobiles running smoothly. Auto maintenance involved doing some tune ups every now and then. With the right tools and enough concentration he could usually figure out why a car was making a particular sound or what really should be repaired.

'Mid-Town is it, Vic?' Sven thought to himself while getting out the tools to start work on the car. 'I'm Flare. Been Flare since I was twenty-two. Now I'm forty-six and my brother is forty-five. Time flies.' Sven noticed the tires were in pretty good condition. He soon saw that they were a little bit deflated though after a closer look. He would be filling them with air so that they would be properly inflated and that way they should last longer.

Sven Nicolos was quite a tall man at six-foot-one. He had light blonde hair and he was bald at the back of his head. Sometimes the wisps of hair in front of his forehead had to be brushed back a bit. He still liked to let his bangs grow to his eyebrows in the front. Whenever he was puzzled while working on a car, he moved his hair away from his eyes with the back of his hand a few times while checking to see how to make the car run properly. It helped him concentrate. The value of great service was the key to Sven's quality of work and after twenty years of being a mechanic, he really knew a lot about automobiles. The garage where he worked was owned by a company known as Desmarol Auto Shop. Working alongside three other mechanics at a time with a total of four work stations meant that a lot of customers could be served on any given day. The team at Desmarol Auto Shop really knew how to get things done. The customers could rest assured knowing that the mechanics were taking care of their cars while they waited in the seating area reading newspapers and talking to each other before paying the mechanic fees when the cashiers brought in the bill statements. The people at Desmarol Auto Shop, during their years of running the business, have always been about providing precision and accuracy to each of their customers. And the customers that have regularly brought in their cars for tune-ups often leave feeling satisfied to be able to drive away with their vehicles after a short period of waiting because of how the mechanics can get advice and learn from each other which often leads to speeding up the work they do so that they can serve the next customer sooner.

Sven was not aware that the car belonged to the bad boy son of two of his neighbours, Ralph and Zoey Holiday. Cally Ryerson was a man in his forties who had developed a career in a popular rock and roll band as a drummer. The four person musical band was made up of a bass guitarist, singer, keyboard player and drummer that played during the weekends at a local night club. Every night that they did so, the audiences screamed and cheered for more not only because of the spectacular ability of the band itself to play but especially the skilled beats and rhythms that Cally Ryerson performed on drums. The audiences grew wild whenever the rock and roll band went on stage for a live performance with Cally often saying on microphone to everyone, "Are you ready to jive it up?" Then they would play their songs along with Cally who would keep in rhythm to his band members with his own completely mesmerizing drum music. Although he was known to be an expert drummer, people that knew him more on a personal level were surprised to discover that he had a hard up-bringing as a child. So tough, in fact, that he completely transformed himself stage after stage of growing up through the years just to escape the life he knew way back when no one seemed to understand him and his tough guy attitude. He began on drums at a young age and moved past where he was each time he saw he was improving at playing the instrument. He also became a little more well-rounded as a person as he went along. He even got better grades at school and spent an extra amount of time talking with his family. Through it all he still seemed to have parents that cared for him. Little did he know it was all meant to carry him forward in life into becoming the drummer he has always dreamed of being. If someone were to tell Cally he was meant to shine from the get go, he would act out by gripping them by the shirt and shaking them until they were freaked out enough to back away from him. This still made for somewhat of a rocky ground for Cally in his personal relationships which was one part about him that he still needed to refine. His memories of a childhood left untamed were a part of his past that he would rather not be reminded of to any extent.

Sven had heard about Cally and was aware of his upbringing from the talks he had with Cally's parents. He had seen and even heard the man from afar during one of Cally's visits to Ralph and Zoey Holiday's house when he had shouted loud enough for everyone on the street to hear him. It happened at a time when he was talking to his ex-wife about visiting his kids for an extra hour when they were there at his parents' place with him and it was time for them to go home again to see their mom. He had wanted that extra hour with them. After hearing such a loud shout that evening only four months earlier, Sven hadn't felt like meeting him in person in too much of a hurry. He later found out that Cally only got to see the kids, Dance and Xavier, once a week.

After talking to his neighbours about going after one's highest aspirations or goals, as each person on Sunlit Avenue had readily been focused on accomplishing, Sven often wondered what he could do for his highest aspirations to be fulfilled. It amused him when he sat down each day to think of his goals. He recently had decided that his wisdom sayings he wrote from time to time and then said to people in town would be a good one. He usually had a few but now he would be writing them more often with the goal he had set. Wisdom sayings are nice to hear and he hoped to tell them to people more often, with new sayings coming up whenever possible.

While he was there in the auto shop, he started thinking a bit about his wisdom sayings goal. Then it happened. One of the cashiers went up to Sven while he was working away on the car and said, "Right now you're working on the car of some tough guy named Cally Ryerson. I don't know why he wanted me to tell you but he insisted."

Sven was caught off guard when he told her. "Gee, what's the difference? Anyway, you can tell him I'm almost done the work on it."

"Will do."

"Now that I like the sound of. Will do."

"Got it. Oh, and one of your neighbours, Damien I believe, has been missing for over a day."

"He has? I wonder where he could be. Thanks for telling me about it."

"I received a call from your brother fifteen minutes ago."

"I'll find out more about it after work today."

Mr. Nicolos began whistling to himself as he checked the car over for another minute.

Shortly afterward the bill statement was given to Mr. Ryerson at the front desk and by then the mechanic had parked the car in the parking lot outside the auto garage where Cally would find it in good condition and ready to drive away.

"Here's to a job well done dude." A fellow mechanic mentioned to Sven as they both sipped from some cooled bottles of spring water that were set down on a wooden table between their workstations.

"That's right. Hey, I'll see you in a jiffy. I've got to go get the next car."

"Sure. A jiffy. Dude, you rock."

"What did you just say?" Sven looked at his co-worker. He had gelled-back hair of a medium blonde color. He was five-foot-five in height and had a big tattoo on his left forearm of a heart. Sven admired Joe's skill and determination that he often displayed while working beside him at the garage.

"I said you rock."

"Ah, you haven't heard of the band called Wind Spontaneous have you, Joe?"

"In fact I have."

"Oh. Have you heard their music?" Sven looked puzzled.

"Sure I have. I just gotta say though. Man, that Cally is one great drummer. Wait until I tell my friends he brought his car in for a checkup. Anyhew Flare, I'll let you go get the next customer's car."

"Certainly."

"Rock on."

* * *

It had been two days since Griffin and Lenny had taken Damien to the basement of the two- storey house. During the hours that had slowly ticked by on his watch ever since he had first arrived to the basement apartment, Damien had discovered that the colored in drawing of a monarch butterfly he made did not meet Griffin's expectations.

Neither did the second drawing which was grey all over. All he did with them was put them on a nearby table and tell Damien that at the rate he is going there will probably be a pile of his drawings on the table a week from now. This shocked Damien. He had been asked to make one drawing during each day that he was being held captive. This time, Damien figured, Griffin might think differently about the latest one he had been working on. The third one. It had a different quality about it. This time the tough guy was present there in the same room with Damien as he worked on it. For the most part, he kept to himself. It made the minutes he spent on the drawing go by easier. Damien watched as the colors he added to the butterfly brought out the added detail he was hoping for. He made the colors of the butterfly seem to float across the page. Although he only had a yellow, a red, a green and a blue pencil crayon to work with, and some pencils, he was pleased with what he saw. And after a quick glance at his kidnapper, Damien passed the drawing over to him.

"Look out your window and imagine yourself breathing the air. You are getting somewhere with it after all, Damien. Keep at it and by tomorrow maybe your talent will have improved to the extent that you will be giving a whole new meaning to the drawings. You're getting more artistic as you go along."

"Oh my God."

"What? Tell me."

Damien didn't want to say that he thought what Griffin said sounded crazy. So he said instead, "I'm wearing the same clothes I had on days ago."

"I've been thinking ahead. In your bedroom closet you will find a change of clothes that I have set aside for you."

"Are they your clothes?" Damien asked Griffin.

"Yes, they are my clothes but I'm giving them to you for you to wear."

"Well, can I use the washer and dryer you have in a corner cabinet in the kitchen?"

"Uh, yes, but just don't spill the soap all over the place." Griffin hollered.

"I'll be careful."

"See? You have talent you didn't know you had."

"I'm not laughing."

"I'm not being funny."

Damien shook his head and leaned forward a bit in the mauve chair. He felt a little uncomfortable and he didn't want to give his kidnapper Griffin the slightest impression that he would have liked to just lay down and cry to release some pent up emotions. Griffin was putting him through a lot and he didn't like it. Not one bit. For the more time he spent talking to his kidnapper the more he felt uneasy. And the more he felt uneasy the more he felt impatient.

"When am I going home?"

"You have some raw talent coming through my boy..."

"My boy?"

"...and I'm going to keep you here until we learn more about it and let it develop."

"God."

"In the meantime, I will be mailing the first three drawings to your wife and kids."

"I miss them so much."

"I bet."

"Let me go."

"No, Damien. You just keep on doing those drawings for me. We'll talk again later."

"Will Lenny be coming back?"

"What I'm not hearing from you is thank you for helping me develop my talent, Damien."

It was then that Damien thought of Rain, Cullen, Cora and all the other neighbours that he missed so very much. Including his family. It was apparent that Griffin was only interested in the drawings. Damien was interested in his own well-being. That was what mattered to the young man. Damien smoothed out his hair with his hand, feeling that he had already come a long way with his business at Hemley's Great Fountains Alive. It was a relief that the business was a success. It was fast becoming a popular place to shop. He liked coming in to work and spending time selling fountains and fountain supplies to people. As he sat thinking about his experiences at the fountain store, it suddenly dawned on him. His kidnapper Griffin mentioned before that he regarded him as a wealthy person. He did have experience talking to all different kinds of people and somehow he could use that to his advantage. He no longer felt that something was pushing him over the edge. All he had to do was work with Griffin and maybe Lenny. He sat staring up at the metal tiled ceiling and remembered that sometimes artwork can have a certain raw look to it. He decided that he would keep it in mind for the next drawing.

"I'll keep making those drawings for you Griffin."

"Oh, that's what I like to hear."

"Until the time comes for you to bring me back home and I'm no longer held captive anymore. I'm an entrepreneur and I have to get back to my work there at my business and be with my family."

"I'm into art."

There was a pause for a minute before Damien went on to say, "You could just as easily make the drawings instead of me."

"You're not listening. You have to get the ball rolling."

"I'm listening alright." Damien ran his fingers across his freshly shaven face. Griffin went so far as to supply him with all the essentials that came with apartment living. Although that was true, Damien in no way wanted to keep spending time as a captive. He went on, "But you can do it on your own. Do the drawings yourself, Griffin, and let me get back to my family and business."

"Get the ball rolling and I might."

"Sure." Damien felt enthusiastic. He was getting somewhere. And where he felt that he was getting was away from his kidnappers, or at least he hoped. It meant so much for him to be getting through to Griffin. He knew he had to make sure the next drawing was something else entirely to look at. He already had in mind what the next drawing would be like and he wasn't going to tell Griffin until the time came for him to show him the drawing the next day.

"I heard about one of your neighbours making a career out of selling drawings of cars of the future. I like that style of his and you're the person that is showing me how to develop that kind of talent he lives by each day."

Finally, the kidnapper had revealed why he was doing it. Griffin was after Damien to get him to do artworks with the same raw edge that Brooke was working while doing his. Damien felt curious to know how Griffin found out about him and his neighbours. Someone must have announced that the neighbours are perfectly intent on going for their own goals and aspirations. They had recently talked to one another about how one at a time they are going to live their dreams until they are each living the dream together and to keep on going further and further along. There had not yet been a media story about it that Damien was aware of but the news of it did seem to be attracting people like Griffin. Maybe Griffin heard it from Brooke, the Sunlit Avenue neighbour who skillfully designed the colored futuristic car drawings. Griffin hinted of it. Damien shut his eyes as his kidnapper stood by.

"There is no better time than now to accomplish your dreams and desires." Damien quipped.

"You're pretty clever."

"Yes I am, in fact."

A few seconds later Griffin left Damien and headed upstairs again. It gave Damien a chance to get some shut eye. He felt sleepy even though it was only four o'clock pm.

CHAPTER 6

Friday, June 3, 2011

"Hi, is it your day off today?" Edmond Keenan asked.

"Yes it is." Cullen said. "What's new? How is it going?"

"Wonderful."

"Wonderful? That's good."

"Yes, I've got some paintings to sell that I have been working on and I think I'm going to be working at Fiona's Fine Restaurant sometime next week. The interviewer said after they call a few references they may soon be calling me for the job."

"Way to go Edmond." Cullen felt happy to hear what Edmond was saying. "When did you have the interview?"

"Yesterday afternoon. I hope they are going to call."

"I hope so too. Is that a western style restaurant?"

"Yes, sirloin steaks, beef ribs, and baked potatoes with dipping sauce is their specialty. I applied for the waiter position. I've been keeping busy with school and those paintings."

"That's a coincidence because I'm interested in doing paintings too. Contrast colors on canvas. What kind of art do you do? What stuff do you paint?"

"I paint a chef bringing a large round tray of cupcakes out to serve the customers that are waiting at their tables. On the tray are chocolate cupcakes with vanilla frosting and vanilla cupcakes with chocolate frosting and there are candy rainbow sprinkles on the cupcakes."

"A chef carrying some cupcakes. That I've got to see. You should bring a painting over so I can see your artwork."

"Yeah, I could do that."

"What else do you paint?"

"The people actually eating the cupcakes for the second painting. And for the third painting, the chef takes a bow to the people to thank them for sampling his tray of cupcakes."

"You mean there are three paintings of the same scene?"

"Yeah. I call it "Compliments of the chef." Good idea, isn't it? People can put all three of them up on their walls."

"Yes, how many paintings did you paint so far since you started?"

"About twenty-one."

"That's a lot. When did you start painting as a hobby?"

"Since last winter. My paintings will be about cupcakes."

"Oh, I know what I could paint. How about this? Different shaped glasses of colorful beverages."

"Yeah, that's something. Good idea Cullen."

"Thanks Edmond."

"You just may have something there." Edmond put a hand on Cullen's shoulder. He gave Cullen a few friendly pats as he watched Cullen's interest beginning to grow. "Remember, interesting breeds interesting."

"Oh, I know. It's going to be great having a hobby. Wait until Rain hears about this."

"That's for sure."

"She has really been inspiring me because she comes up with the most bizarre ideas."

"Bizarre?"

"Yeah, unusual yet fantastic ideas for her business."

"Unusual is good. Maybe she's just getting creative."

"Oh, she's getting creative alright." Cullen folded his arms across his chest. "That's why I tell her that she's inspiring me." He looked toward the beginning of the street on the opposite end from where his house was located and thought for a minute. "You know, there are a lot of creative women on this street. Such as Aleisha for instance. And Rita."

"That's true. Hey, you have to admit it's interesting though."

"Definitely."

Edmond Keenan was a black adopted child as a baby by two very supportive white adoptive parents named Doris and Mark Keenan. They were glad to have a son of their own the first day they brought him home. Both of his adoptive parents grew close to him over the years as they watched him from day to day. Sixteen years later, Edmond had grown to become a handsome teenager and he measured just over five-foot-seven. He was still their son and very much a part of their family. Edmond had been an exceptional student in his tenth and eleventh year of high school and enjoyed learning all he could about the many subjects he studied in school. In just a matter of days, Edmond Keenan would be finishing grade eleven. During the school year, he usually had lots to say about his neighbours to his friends and other high school students. Sometimes he brought his friends to Hemley's Great Fountains Alive to see Mavis and

Damien and to browse around the store looking at the water fountains. They liked talking about the latest new fountains to the entrepreneurs and often told them which ones they would buy. Their feedback was appreciated. And as a result of it, the couple had some ideas about what young people enjoyed seeing in their store. Of course, the discussions they had each time actually led to some of the items going on sale and that led to more people shopping at Hemley's Great Fountains Alive. Mavis had called it "a fresh perspective" for the fountain store. She and her husband Damien felt that it was sure to attract some shoppers.

Edmond lived right across the street from the Hemleys. The high school student was about to write his final exams of the year. He and his friends had only one more year of high school to finish after their exams and were well on their way to graduating.

For a moment, as Cullen stood in his driveway with Edmond standing beside him, the two guys exchanged glances with each other before Cullen made a rather smooth move and gave Edmond a high five. And as they continued to talk to one another, Cullen soon learned that Edmond had a day off from school. He was enjoying his break from studies for the day.

"Oh, what to do, what to do." Edmond said, looking at his watch. He paused after seeing it was eleven forty-five am on his watch.

"If you want, you can visit Rain and me. She hasn't seen you in a while."

"She's home? Alright then, I'll just go get one of my paintings that you mentioned about and be right over to see you guys."

"Okay."

It was just another day on Sunlit Avenue. Cullen felt a nice breeze in the air while he waited for his neighbour to return. The sky was clear of any clouds and displayed a bright blue hue. As he thought about the weather some more, he started thinking about his idea of different shaped glasses filled with colorful beverages as he waited for Edmond. A few minutes went by and then Cullen saw his neighbour walking toward him again. He was carrying a painting. By the time Edmond approached him, Cullen saw that it was a canvas about twelve inches by twelve inches in size.

"Woah! Look at that. Good detail work."

"I'd say so too. It took a while to paint though."

"Yeah? I like how the chef appears to be grinning as he prepares to hand out the cupcakes to the customers."

"It's a special treat."

"Let's go show my girlfriend, Rain."

"Sure."

Just then, the same man that Cullen had seen walking through his yard days earlier was strolling by. He saw Cullen and Edmond standing nearby as he walked up the road and waved. "How are you guys today?" He shouted in a reckoning voice.

"Good day to you." Edmond answered.

The man continued walking along Sunlit Avenue. He was wearing the same brown leather vest but this time he had a neon green T-shirt and khaki green shorts on.

"C'mon Edmond. Let's go inside." Cullen didn't mention anything about the guy to Edmond. Instead, he motioned for Edmond to go through the front door.

As they walked into the house they soon saw Rain Woodrow working on some cards at her desk in the living room. She was surprised to see Edmond. "Hi, how are you?" She asked.

He replied, "A friendly hello to you Rain."

"Thanks."

"Wait until you see the painting that Edmond made." Cullen said.

"A painting? Yeah, what is it of?"

Edmond stepped closer to Rain and showed her what he had painted. "It's a chef carrying a large round tray of cupcakes for people to try as they sit at their tables in a restaurant."

"Yes, it is. That's great. And it shows talent. Have you painted for a while Edmond?"

"Since last winter." He replied, holding the artwork carefully in his hands. "I'm going to see if I can sell paintings like this one."

"Yeah, and did you hear Edmond is expecting to hear from the people at Fiona's Fine Restaurant? He may just have a job there soon."

"Glad to hear it." She was intrigued. "Sit down and stay a while. You know what? Cullen talks about painting as a hobby."

"Yeah, and I came up with an idea. Different types of beverages in a variety of glasses. I could paint that."

"That's true." Rain said, looking at her neighbour. "Anyway, keep up the painting and you'll see your work improve enough to sell paintings Edmond. All it takes is a little time."

"That's right." Cullen added.

"I really like to do the paintings so I'll be painting plenty more of them."

"Do you want a drink of juice or some spring water?" Cullen asked Edmond.

"Juice? Okay. What kind is there?"

"Apple juice, orange juice or vegetable juice." Cullen replied.

"Orange juice, please."

"Be right back." He swiftly moved out of plain sight in a funny way to draw attention on himself while getting the beverages in the kitchen. Edmond laughed as he looked at Rain shrugging her shoulders.

"That Cullen Dangsi."

She watched Edmond carefully place his painting on a small square shaped wooden table beside the beige curtains that were opened to let some sunshine into the room. After he did so, he sat down on a dark brown leather sofa that faced the living room windows. The living room walls were painted a copper orange color. Also, there was a hardwood floor made of birch that matched the rest of the colors throughout the room. Rain still sat at her desk and faced the entrance to the living room. Edmond noticed some cards piled at her work desk and was curious about what she had written on them.

"What are you working on?"

"Oh, just some cards. It's a funny type of joke card. I will read it."

"Okay."

"Why was the dragonfly all over the news? Because he was walking on a newspaper."

"Geez. Funny card though." Edmond chuckled.

Rain laughed but only for a few seconds. "I'm making a dozen of them to see if they sell."

"They probably will sell."

"I hope so."

"What? The cards? Of course they will." Cullen said, stepping back into the room with a can of orange juice for Edmond and a bottle of water for himself and one for Rain. He passed them their drinks and soon sat on the sofa beside his neighbour.

"Edmond...did you know Rain is writing a mini-book about the rainforest?"

"No, I haven't heard anyone mention anything about it. What a good idea."

"Isn't it though?" Cullen said, opening his bottle of water and taking a few sips.

Edmond opened his can of orange juice and drank until it was half full.

"What is it going to be about? Protecting the rainforest?"

Rain sat back and held her bottle of water in her hands at her desk. "Yes, so that the cutting down of the rainforest stops. There is some stuff that is possible to do instead of farming where some of the rainforest trees used to be, such as selling arts, crafts and clothing. There are a number of things that can be done to make sure we keep the rainforest safe for now and the future."

"Glad to hear you are interested in keeping the rainforest the rainforest. I like how you said other things are possible to do instead of farming." Edmond drank the rest of his orange juice and walked to the kitchen to set down his empty can on the countertop. When he went back into the living room, Rain had already put the cards she had been designing into a purple square shaped box to finish later. For now, Rain thought she would enjoy the rest of her day off. On the days that her boyfriend Cullen was having a day off, she often took a day off too. But even on a day off work, she usually started working on the cards again in the evening to prepare for the next work day.

The seconds went by and they continued on with their discussion. The rainforest seemed like something great to talk about together. And the direction their talk was going was making for an excellent way to get the message across to each other that they and others too cared for the rainforest.

"I have an idea about what we could do for starters. After the mini-book about the rainforest is published, we could see about selling a type of writing pen called Fine Point Rainforest Pens. People could buy them left and right for rainforest conservation so that a company called Fine Point Rainforest Inc. could contribute fifty percent of its earnings to the communities of people that live and farm nearby there so that they would no longer have to cut down the trees there to farm. Who knows, once Fine Point Rainforest Inc. is established one day soon, I could hire some people to set up a workshop near the rainforest where the people there live and they could make a good income selling clothing and such for Fine Point Rainforest Inc. What do you think?"

"You've made a fine point. When did you think of all this?" Cullen asked.

"After thinking some more about the book this morning."

"Rain, you are very creative." Edmond simply said. "Fine Point Rainforest Incorporated. Sounds great to me."

"And me." Cullen looked out the window at the sunny day and took a few more sips from his bottle of water.

"I'm glad you guys think so."

"In fact, I would like to help if you set up the company." Edmond stated with a serious tone of voice. "I have a feeling that your idea is something people will like. It's well thought out. In fact, maybe in the future I can work for you too."

"Alright. It may take a little bit of time but I think that it is going to be possible."

"Very possible." Cullen said.

"Oh my goodness, I should start writing the mini-book today. I've already got a few words and notes but it's time to start writing more about the rainforest."

"I can just see it now." Cullen said with a dramatic tone to his voice, "Rain Woodrow brings smiles to many people's faces with Fine Point Rainforest Inc."

"What? Oh, Cullen. Let me write that one down."

Edmond laughed for a few seconds. "This is one great idea you have. Let me know when you get your book published."

"Sure."

"Yeah, definitely." Cullen was glad to hear it. His girlfriend Rain was just getting things started with the discussion they were having and he felt proud to have asked Edmond to come over to see both of them. Cullen hoped he would see it all happen. One day at a time.

Edmond Keenan visited for a short while longer and then went home again. It had been quite a talk they had together. To the three, it had been a special time that they shared. Mr. Dangsi and Miss Woodrow both stayed home for the rest of the day after the discussion was over and talked about things some more. The hours went by and before long it was eight in the evening.

"All it takes is a little time." Cullen repeated to himself what Rain had said earlier. "That's for sure. Hmm, Time, Experience, Development. Yeah, that's it. T.E.D. = Time, Experience and Development. What if I could invent a new super hero? One that has the ability to change his hair colors by just imagining his hair to be certain colors and then his hair is those fantastic colors. That sure would be awesome. Every day his hair could be different colors. And people would notice, oh wouldn't they? For eight days in a row each month he says before bed every night, "T.E.D. = Time, Experience and Development." Then he can change his hair different colors. Eight nights in a row each month he says it, but if he forgets then he has normal looking hair for a whole month afterwards. That's it! I'll call him Straight Eights the superhero. It's an excellent idea. I still have to give him a regular name though. But what name should I give him? I'll figure one out for him."

Cullen was doing a lot of thinking. He had decided to invent a superhero instead of painting some paintings just yet. And he also decided that he would write a book about him. 'Straight Eights will be a young adult twenty-five years of age.' He thought.

Cullen Dangsi went to go lie down on his bed. Just to hear himself say it, he said, "T.E.D. = Time, Experience and Development." The excitement of coming up with such an exceptional idea made him feel like relaxing for a while. As he did so, more thoughts about the superhero gradually got him thinking again about what he could write about for a superhero story. Then he remembered a red glass pendant necklace that he sometimes saw his sister Kina wear. His sister lived in Halifax, Nova Scotia.

Just then Mr. Dangsi got out of bed, went to the computer in the spare bedroom and sat down to look for glass pendants and wood carvings online. After seeing a few websites and some pictures of them, Dangsi thought that he should have the superhero working at a shop that he owned called The Glass, Metal, and Wood Shop. Glass pendants, various iron metal works of art and wood decorations would be found throughout the store.

He thought of the name Isaac and then Isaiah. And then he thought it over some more. It was when he found himself beginning to daydream about the two names he already came up with that he finally came up with the unusual name Isaiek. That was what his name would be. Isaiek Sheer. That was it alright. And it would be a good name for him. Cullen was sitting there staring at the names Straight Eights and Isaiek Sheer that he wrote down with a pen on a page in his address book while feeling sheer enjoyment out of coming up with the idea for a superhero.

Cullen thought to himself, 'He would be a superhero with certain qualities about him that many people could find themselves relating to in a surprising way. Someone that had very colorful hair and a just as colorful personality. The fact that Straight Eights could color his hair whatever colors fascinated him most each day purely by thinking of it would still be kept pretty much a secret. People he would be meeting and talking to would certainly be able to tell the difference if they saw him. Even so, every now and then people would surely notice just what Isaiek Sheer had been doing to his hair as they saw him on a regular basis.'

Cullen stopped daydreaming about it and wrote down the main points of the superhero idea of his. The information about Isaiek Sheer would be there for him to refer to time and time again. Before calling it a night, Cullen decided to name the mini-book. It would be called The Twenty-Fifth Year of Isaiek Sheer.

Cullen looked forward to writing the story of the superhero as a mini-book, just as Rain herself was writing a mini-book. Rain was writing about an important topic. The rainforest. And making plans about taking care of it already. Cullen decided that his mini-book would be something special to read in addition to her mini-book. He decided to keep it all a secret. A very beautiful one.

* * *

"Would you look at that? This brings new meaning to the word butterfly. This is gorgeous. You've colored the butterfly from head to foot with blue and green and you've still managed to keep the right orange color on its wings to make it appear to be a monarch butterfly."

"Remember I had both a yellow and a red pencil crayon to color it in orange. Along with a blue one and a green one."

"That's right. This says so much. This was just what I was looking for. Instead of being black and white from head to foot you colored it blue and green."

"That's true. Am I free to go?"

"Uh, wait just a second. Now I want you to work on something else for me. Get the ball rolling further for me by thinking up some really great wood carving ideas for me."

"Oh no, I have to think of more ideas before you let me go?"

"Yes, you do. But this time you don't have to draw anything on paper. You can just tell me what the ideas are."

"I don't have any ideas for wood carvings right now but I'm sure I can think of some."

"That's what I like to hear."

Damien got the chills just thinking about how Griffin managed to get him going on another task in addition to the one he already completed. He reasoned it was probably an excuse to get him to stay with him for another twenty-four hour period. Damien hoped to go home before the day was through.

"Out with it. You must have some ideas."

"Not yet. It might take a few hours."

"A few hours? Alright, if that's what it takes then I'll be waiting."

Then all of a sudden he thought of it. "Hey, how about this? Tribal wood carvings the kind you would see when you travel to tropical destinations."

"Yes, I see. Except a person wouldn't have to travel to those destinations to get them if I were to make them. Yes, my boy, thank you for your idea. Just like the artist Brooke Akira puts the final line of color on one of his one-thousand dollar drawings, you're free to go."

"I am?"

"That's the finishing touch for me."

Damien sighed a huge sigh of relief. He watched Griffin reach for his cell phone with one hand and say to him, "One moment please." The young man felt glad to be going home again and working at his job some more.

Griffin made a quick call to Lenny on his cell phone. "Len, could you come by the house? Damien is free to go."

Lenny replied on the receiving end, "Already? That boy sure must be kicking it. I'll stop by in a few."

"Oh, he is. He can figure out what to do on a dime. I've got this plan thanks to him. Wait until you hear. Let's bring him back now."

"Got it. See you soon."

Thirty minutes later, Damien went racing through the front door of the Hemley's Great Fountains Alive store vibrantly cheering. "I'm free! I'm free! Yes, I'm free!"

"Darling! It's you. It's really you. Are you okay?" Mavis asked, as she threw down a big box full of plastic bottles of fountain cleaner from off a flat cart and wrapped her arms around him.

"Yes…after everything that happened…I'm still okay."

"I'm so relieved."

"I just hope this guy Griffin can carry on with his own business enough so that he won't have to kidnap me again."

"His own business?"

"Yeah. He wanted some ideas for making artworks and woodcarvings."

"Is that all he was after?"

"Yup. Thankfully."

"God. Damien, I'm glad you're back."

"So am I."

"I felt worried about you when you were gone."

"Let me tell you, Mavis. I was worried too. But I kept telling myself that everything is alright. And it is."

Chapter 7

Saturday, June 4, 2011

Rita was sent a note in the mail two weeks before the day at the zoo and after much consideration she phoned Sven an hour before going to the zoo. She said, "I found this note that reads, "Good day, Rita. You are welcome to go on a treasure hunt to the likes of which you've never seen before. I have heard of you going after your aspirations along with your group of people and I hope that the treasure hunt will help you each on your way. I like to call it eye-opening format. You can call it what you will. During the treasure hunt your eyes will surely be open wide to the possibilities. What this means is simply that you and your friends amaze me with what you have set out to do because more and more people are going to be observing your efforts. And since the time to alert the public to your efforts is approaching as I've heard, then by whatever means or however you end up doing that I congratulate you.

Here are some instructions. In the fantastic garden at the end of the zoo trail you will find something under one of the stepping stones that is surrounded by a patch of red mulch. Just look under the fourth stepping stone and you will find what you are looking for. This letter marks the start of the treasure hunt. From: Anonymous one."

When Sven heard her read the note in its entirety he made a remark about it. "Sounds decent enough. Let's go see what is under that stepping stone in the footpath then. I'll see you when the zoo opens at noon."

"Okay, sure. See you then."

"Bye Rita."

"Bye." She nodded to herself as she was hanging up the phone.

* * *

Aleisha Forbes, Rain Woodrow, Mavis Hemley, Damien Hemley and Francis and Lulu, along with Sven Nicolos and Rita Young met at the grand garden zoo at twelve o'clock pm. They were to meet at the front entrance to the zoo. They had spent time talking on the phone to each other the night before to see exactly who was coming at twelve o'clock pm and who might be making plans to go to the zoo at a later time. It was going to be an exciting event. Each of the neighbours of Sunlit Avenue felt curious to find out just what was so different about the zoo now that it had been given a new look. If there were many new wondrous sights that had been added to it they were sure to please. And by the looks of things already, the opening day of the new zoo season was one that actually held much public acclaim. Crowds of enthusiastic people were showing up at the front entrance to see what was new about the zoo. People that lived in town already heard the news that all kinds of new plants and even some new animals had been placed around the zoo in addition to the already existing ones. As it was, it looked like scores of people would be showing up. People were driving cars to the empty parking spaces in the parking lot one after another. And it was happening a few minutes even before noon. The old Bixxi Zoo, now named the Grand Garden Zoo was one happening place.

After each of the eight neighbours found one another as they waited beside the big line up of people they could now get in line too and they did so with looks of amusement on their faces. Everyone wanted to burst through the door with certain anticipation in celebration of the momentous day. Then the minutes went by and it was noon. The staff began stamping the hands of the customers after they paid a fee with cash, credit or debit. Each customer received the word 'Zoo' stamped in ink on their hand to mark that they had paid and should they leave the zoo temporarily for a while or for the rest of the day, the ink mark would prove they paid the small zoo fee.

The eight neighbours finally stood at the cashier booth and soon they each had their own ink mark. By that time, they had already seen Damien in the crowd. He waved at his neighbours who had taken notice of him standing nearby his family.

"Look everyone, Damien is back!" Rain shouted cheerfully.

"Yes he is. How are you?" Within seconds Sven was standing right beside him carefully watching Damien's every move to see how he was coping after the ordeal of being kidnapped.

"As good as could be expected." Damien put his hands on his hips. He was taken aback with the joy of co-mingling with the mix of neighbours. And from his standpoint, he was certainly ready for some fun times with them once more. "I'm just looking to get in the swing of things again."

"Welcome back." Aleisha patted him on the shoulder to reassure him that she cared. It was a friendly gesture.

"Thanks. Pleased to finally be back."

"Mavis told me she called the cops the other day. Man. It's good you're here." Rain wiped her brow.

"That's right, she did. I just hope the kidnappers have had enough."

"You mean there is a chance they might be back?" Rain gasped.

"Yes, a small one."

"What did they want from you?" Sven questioned reluctantly.

"The guy Griffin wanted me to sort something out for him by using my creative abilities and doing some drawings of butterflies and telling him that tribal art, the kind that you find at tropical destinations, could be a good idea for making woodcarvings."

"Butterflies?"

Damien nodded. "Monarch butterflies actually."

"That's strange. And you say they want ideas for some woodcarvings? What's that about?"

Rita asked with an unexpected dryness to her voice.

"That is a tough cookie to bite into." Aleisha said.

"The guy Griffin said I'm his role model. He's been observing us somehow."

"Say it ain't so. Observing us?" Sven had heard enough.

"I know eh?"

"Well, at least they brought you back after only a few days." Sven shrugged his shoulders.

"Only a few days? I had all I could take."

"Damien, Damien." Mavis reached out her arms. "Come and get a big hug."

Mavis embraced her husband lovingly. "I missed you."

"I missed you too. It's great to be back."

They started on their way, walking past the entrance and saw a sign that read, "Now that is Zen, citizens." Then they were filled with excitement at what they were seeing. Rocks from one- foot in length to two-feet in length were arranged among shrubs with a soft, round foliage to them. All around the rocks and shrubs was fine combed grey sand with lines going in one direction. It was a circle. They were seeing it right before them. Of course, there was some green grass too, but then they noticed some water along with the grass beside a few of the rocks in the shade. It appeared to be stream about a few inches deep.

"It's a Zen garden." Aleisha said.

"Oh it is?" Sven said. "Yes it is."

"I like how they shaped that grey sand in lines going around the garden." Mavis said.

"I have seen small Zen gardens with sand for something special for home décor but this is the first real Zen garden I've seen." Aleisha said.

Rita took a photograph of it with her digital camera and smiled. One person standing beside her laughed as she did so. Rita turned to see who was laughing and saw that a woman was staring at the garden.

"Look at that!" A little boy said to the young lady standing beside Rita.

"Yes, son. I see it." She replied to him.

The neighbours began walking from the Zen garden on their left toward the next area of the zoo just to the right. Already they had seen it. They caught a glimpse of an animal. An ocelot. Then there was a second one. Two ocelots. One sat on the grass beside a tree. The other was there laying down and was rolling from side to side, enjoying the warm weather. As they were doing so, the sunlight beamed brightly for a few seconds and then some clouds covered it. Lulu looked up at the sky and saw that the clouds soon went by and the sun beamed brightly on them once again. There was a bunch of clouds in the distance. Lulu knew there would be a break in the sunshine for a few minutes as soon as the clouds came nearer. For now, the ocelots were warming in the sunshine. Lulu watched the ocelot rolling some more in the grass. She gazed at the other ocelot still sitting on the grass. Everywhere around her there were people that had gathered to look at the two cats.

"These are new. Last year I visited the zoo and didn't see any ocelots." Aleisha said.

"Oh, really?" Rain said.

Rita took a photograph of them. She would be taking lots of pictures during her visit. After all, it was the new and improved zoo that she was viewing.

"Maybe in the future there will be a lot, yep, a lot of ocelots." Sven said.

"You're funny." Rain said.

"Very funny." Damien joked.

Just then, some of the neighbours walked further toward the next zoo area to the right, down the path and the others soon followed after them. There was a long stretch of grass and soil with some trees at the next spot. It appeared that whatever animal stayed there would have lots of room to move around in, if it was occupied by one or more. They were there at the far end of the area. Two cheetahs were sitting and watching what appeared to be the animals in the next fenced in area just across from them on the left. The cheetahs themselves were quite a sight. They were noticing the three snowy owls resting within plain view on a wooden branch set across a little owl house the zoo keepers had built for them to shelter them from the elements. And it had a roof and some branches for the owls to sit on.

The snowy owls had just closed their eyes to rest when Lulu shouted. "Look mom, owls!"

"I see that." Mavis said. "They are snowy owls."

The owls had opened their eyes again. One of the owls was suddenly surprised at the loud shout and made a high pitched sound followed by five deeper pitched sounds.

"Snowy owls?" Francis asked, staring at their large yellow eyes.

"That's right." Aleisha said. "And those are cheetahs."

"Cheetahs. They run really fast. But then they have to rest or they will get too overheated."

Sven said, nodding at Francis as she eyed him for a few seconds.

"You mean they get too hot from running? Yeah, they must run pretty fast."

"They're built to run." Sven emphasized his point by slowly moving his hand from the right to the left all the while making a definite whistling sound to hint about how fast they can go.

"C'mon, let's go see more animals." Rain said, looking ahead at some people reading a sign further along the path.

"Okay." Mavis said. "Ready kids?"

"Yup. Lulu…I'll race you to the next one."

"Sure, Francis."

"Meet us at the sign then kids. So that we know where you are." Mavis called out before they started running ahead. Then with a mark, get set, go they were off, dashing toward the sign in the distance.

They walked on after Francis and Lulu sped ahead and a couple of minutes later everyone was gathered together looking at the designs on the sign. There was a map of the zoo pictured on it with a 'You are here' marked by a red dot showing people where they are located and where the path would take them if they went to the left side or the right side, as the path was now in the shape of a letter T. That meant they had to decide where to go. To the orange section on the left side where the bigger animals were located or to the blue section on the right side where the smaller animals were located. They had seen the green section. The map showed that the path coming up was a rectangle shape and how they, at the present time, were at the bottom of the rectangle shaped pathway that later continued on at the top of it with a winding letter S to mark the end of the trail. The purple section, or S part of the trail, clearly indicated on the map that S is for surprise.

"Let's go see the big animals first." Rain said.

"The big animals. Yes, let's go to the orange section to the left." Sven replied.

Everyone walked together enjoying themselves with mixed emotions between what recently happened to Damien and the fun day at the zoo they were having. Some of the neighbours that had not been to the zoo for a long time were thinking about what kinds of animals there might be to see in this section, and yet, others that had been to the zoo recently were thinking about the new gardens they have not seen before that may be coming up. Onward they went until they saw a giraffe. The animal had a long neck and long legs as giraffes are known to have. That along with brown spots on light tan colored hair. The giraffe saw the group coming and peered at them as they approached.

"Mom, look at that giraffe. She or he is so tall." Francis said.

"That's why they are good at spotting who is nearby. Get it, spots?" Rita joked.

"Good one." Sven said.

"Yeah, I guess."

"I like giraffes." Mavis said. "I should order a fountain that has giraffes for the store."

"Good suggestion." Damien said.

"I think so."

They soon walked by and noticed three zebras standing beside each other while nibbling on some grass on the right just across from the fenced in area with the giraffe on the left. The area set aside for the zebras was large and there was plenty of room for them to roam about eating and running and resting, or just for hanging out together. The giraffe had plenty of room too. Although there was only one giraffe it appeared that the animal could always see what the zebras were up to. Being a tall animal it could also see what the people would soon be up to while they visited.

After a few minutes they walked further along until they noticed some stone steps going up a hillside within the next area to the right of the path. There were some rocks spread around the place and it appeared to be a rocky terrain of some sort with new sod and wet soil. There among the rocky terrain were four llamas. Right away, Rain noticed that a sign giving a general description of llamas stated that llamas are of the camel family. She told the group what she read and they stopped long enough to see two youngsters playing and running to and fro around the other two llamas that were the adults. The mother llama was chestnut color, while the father llama was a dark brown color. The two youngsters were both black.

Sven took a big breath that very minute to prepare for what he was going to tell the group. While leaning against the fence surrounding the llamas he mentioned, "Have you heard that Cora Pepper has a company called Neat Street Robots and that they are making robots six-feet high that say inspirational messages and are known as Take it to the Max, Robot?" He then asked, "What other projects are the people on Sunlit Avenue working on lately?"

Rain said, "I'm writing a mini book about the rainforest. That's a coincidence that Cora has a company because I hope to start up a company to help care for the rainforest."

"Huh. Jeez." Sven combed his hand through his hair.

Mavis said, "Me and Damien have been listening to more music lately when we are away from the store."

"Oh my goodness." Rain said, "Edmond told me he would like to work for the company I was talking about that I named Fine Point Rainforest Inc. So named because of the point I'm working on getting across to help keep the rainforest rustling away."

"Rain, you surprise me." Sven said.

"Me too, Rain, or should I call you Sunshine?" Aleisha said.

"Funny."

"I'm thinking of carving two horses named Chocolate and Bubble gum for the next lamp that I make. If I decide to make them, Chocolate will be a brown horse and Bubble gum will be a white horse. If so, there will be more variety to my website."

"What? Aleisha is going to make a new type of lamp different than the Lily Sumner lamps? You guys amaze me." Rita said.

"Well, the people of Sunlit Avenue are going to be known for the projects that they do sooner or later. And not just between us but many people hopefully." Sven said. "Who knows what will be happening even a few months from now?"

"Yup." Rita looked at Sven.

Rain commented to the group, "Amazing stuff… amazing stuff."

"This is me being plain." Sven said as he turned from side to side. "This is me looking casual." He said with his hands in his pockets. "And this is me looking at you." Sven grinned at everyone around him. He observed the looks on their faces as he joked around. "Funny enough, isn't it Rain?"

"Yeah. Funny stuff."

"Thems the stuff dreams are made of." Sven clearly stated with a mellow tone to his voice so that everyone would hear.

"Fantastic saying." Rain said outright. "I like that saying."

"Of course. I've been waiting to tell you guys that saying. I thought of it myself only today while I was getting ready to go see you guys here at the zoo. That along with another saying, "I'm honkers for you…kidding.""

Mavis clued, "It sounds like a bumper sticker."

"Do you think so?" Sven replied.

"Gee, it does." Rita said. "Sounds like you have been having some fun to me."

They continued on looking at the animals in the zoo. As they walked onward they saw two camels, three hyenas, three wolves, a tiger, five antelopes, two black bears, two lions, a white and brown horse, six buffalos, a white rhinoceros and later a group of swans and ducks near a lake. Then they came up to a sign that marked where the small animal section would begin. They had a choice of seeing what small animals there were or seeing what new surprises the trail had before them where the trail led to the final part of the zoo. They told each other that going to the final part of the trail where the new gardens might be found sounded alright to them. And they could always see the small animals after seeing the rest of the zoo.

"Daddy, here's some rose bushes. They smell nice don't they?" Francis asked, while taking some sniffs.

"Yes, they smell just like perfume."

"Now that you're back we should stop and smell the roses more often." Francis crossed her arms and threw them up in the air feeling filled with the wonder of a new day. "Yay, daddy is free again."

"Yeah, daddy." Lulu exclaimed.

"Would you guys like to come over to my house later? I have a new chinchilla. He's my pet and his name is Orom. He is a grey chinchilla and is one year old." Aleisha asked.

"Mommy, let's go see him. Please?" Lulu asked, still wondering what a chinchilla looked like.

"Yup. After."

"What is a chinchilla?" Francis asked.

"A type of rodent. Like a mouse but he's like the size of a bunny." Aleisha said, looking at Lulu and then Francis.

"I bet he's nice." Mavis said. "Do chinchillas bite?"

"They nibble. They are known to be very affectionate actually. Some of them live fifteen to twenty years."

"I didn't know that." Rita said. "I'll go see him. We all will, I guess, right guys?"

"Yeah. Totally." Sven said, putting his hand on Lulu's shoulder.

"He's ever so cute. Hey, I like the sound of that. My chinchilla is ever so cute."

Sven looked at her and nodded his head with approval. Aleisha put her arm around Rain with the excitement of the moment. Just then, Damien put Lulu up on his shoulders while making sure he held her carefully. Onward they went, walking past the sign that marked the purple section of the trail that was in the shape of a capital S. Lulu herself remembered how the letter S on the map stood for surprise. Whatever it was that was going to be the surprise, Lulu knew it may probably be something special to see. She could hardly wait to find out. Her dad carried her up on his shoulders while continuing on with the rest of the group of neighbours toward it. Within seconds they were looking at the first part of the surprise. It was something that could be enjoyed all season at the zoo. A gorgeous garden that could be admired for hours had been perfectly created by what seemed to be some folks that were very talented at landscaping. It was there right before them. All in its fine detailed splendour.

"Mommy – mommy look at the garden!" Lulu shouted upon seeing it for the first time. There she was still sitting on Damien's shoulders. Damien looked around at it as they approached the entrance where there were two large column shaped shrubs that were a magnificent and welcoming addition to the garden. Standing dozens of feet high, they made it all the more beautiful.

"I see it Lulu. It's so spectacular." Mavis answered. Damien lifted his daughter Lulu off from his shoulders and placed her on her feet again.

"What a sight." Rita said, taking a picture with her camera.

"Oh my God, that's pretty." Rain said, noticing what kinds of trees and other plants were in it.

"This sure is a grand garden, just like they said that it would be."

"As a matter of fact it is." Sven said.

"Pretty special." Mavis said.

"Special alright." Francis added.

Aleisha said, "I wonder what the next woodcarving will be. Maybe one covered in brown and silver paint. Triangles and other shapes too."

"What?" Sven said, "You're talking about lamps at a time like this?"

"Yes. The garden, I'm checking it out now. Yeeha!" Aleisha paused and then she grinned at what she saw. Not only was she seeing the garden but she was also picturing the possibility of her new lamp idea. Such as tiny checkered squares of brown and silver paint covering some shapes like triangles and rectangles, all carved on a lovely new style lamp.

"Guys, wait until you hear this. I received a note in the mail saying there is a treasure hunt that begins here in the grand garden. I will just look under the fourth stepping stone in the pathway here to see what is there."

As she did so, Rita found a key set with a black leather key tag and printed on the key tag was a license plate number. Everyone took a look at it as Rita passed it around to them. The neighbours made their comments about it.

Rain gasped. "Whoa, that's neat."

"Looks like we're supposed to go find a car with that license number." Mavis clued.

"Yeah, it does, doesn't it?" Sven glared.

"We'll go to the parking lot later. For now, let's just enjoy this beautiful grand garden." Rain let out a gasp.

"Alright, Rain. Yes, it is beautiful indeed." Rita said, looking through her camera as though she was going to take a snapshot of it.

ˋ They were in the midst of the garden now. All around them there could be found islands of round shrubs, pointy shrubs, some wild grasses, rose bushes, ornamental trees of miniature sizes, dwarf trees, and hedges in the shape of animals and such. One was of a gecko, another was of a bird, still another was of a horse, and yet another one was of a flower. Some even were spiral shaped.

The garden was accented with a flat stone pathway running through it. Some people began arriving into the garden and could be seen gathered at the flat stones located nearby where they stood. The grand garden was grand indeed. Such a place was not only grand to see but was also grand in size. That made the first part of the S shape. The second part of the S shape was now in front of them. A large greenhouse containing seedlings of different sorts of flowers was open to zoo visitors. Once the neighbours walked into the greenhouse they also discovered all kinds of bonsai trees set on display tables arranged in a variety of plant holders, some with pieces of river stones on top of potting soil and some with just potting soil. The neighbours were delighted with how many bonsai trees they saw inside the greenhouse. After they walked outside of the greenhouse at the opposite end of the building, there was a large sign with big lettering for everyone to notice. It read, "Thank you for looking at our fantastic zoo. We think our fans are fantastic too. We hope you have had a wonderful time and that you like our sign that makes a rhyme. Please visit our gift shop by the main entrance. As sure as the sun will shine, we hope your day will be fine. From the staff of the Grand Garden Zoo."

"No, no. I've got it. The checkered brown and silver squares are on the base of the lamp itself and the triangle and rectangle shapes are painted either silver or brown." Aleisha stretched out her arms and let out a loud yawn.

"Hmm. Aleisha likes being a woodcarver I guess." Sven said.

"I guess." She answered Sven.

"Wanna buy some happy faces from Sid, Aleisha?" Sven questioned.

"I'll paint some on my lamp." She replied.

"Don't do that."

"Why not?" Aleisha asked. She felt curious to know the reason behind his comment.

"Because Sid's creations are exactly that. Sid's creations."

"Oh brother. Sounds like you need another one of those good laughs. Anyway, let's go to my house now."

"What about the small animals?" Francis asked.

"Don't worry. We'll see them on our way back to the car." Mavis stated.

"Lulu exclaimed, "Pew! Francis did you fart?"

"Yes." Francis blushed. "Lulu, shush okay?"

Lulu only laughed.

Soon they headed off toward the small animal section that they had yet to see and a few minutes later they were looking at a couple dozen guinea pigs of an assortment of colors, two swift foxes with light brown and grey and white fur and two red macaw parrots with green and blue wing feathers. After that they saw ten black-footed ferrets of a white, black, brown and yellowish color; two black and white porcupines, five pygmy marmosets with brownish-gold fur, two golden lion tamarins of a reddish-gold color, eleven ring-tailed lemurs of a grey, black and white color and five red pandas of a rust-red and white color.

The group of neighbours walked to the parking lot. After checking almost the entire parking lot of cars they came across the right license plate number. They took a good look at the vehicle. Rita opened the car door on the driver's side and sat down on the driver's seat. On the left side sun visor there was another note with two rubber elastics holding it there. Rita took them off and held the note in her hands.

"Hi Rita, you have just been given a free car. It's a black 2011 Ford Fusion SE. I'm a multi-millionaire and this is a present for you. What better way to spend about half an hour to an hour than going on a treasure hunt? Go to Tran's Flower Shop on Mountain Road and ask for the gift basket from Anonymous one. They will have it waiting there for you. Your neighbours will be pleased to find out what it contains. They each can come along too."

After she read the note, Rita said to her neighbours standing nearby the car. "A multi-millionaire gave me this car."

"How exciting. Let me read the note, Rita." Rain said.

"Okay." She gave her the typed note.

"There's more."

"Of course there is. This is quite a treasure hunt. I think we should go to Tran's Flower Shop now. It's on Mountain Road."

Everyone was huddled close to see Rita sitting in the driver's seat of her new car. After another moment went by Rain said, "Let's go to the flower shop then."

Soon afterward they were there. Rita left her new car in the parking lot and drove there in her old 2005 Dodge minivan because she still had to bring the new car to the automotive place to get it put in her name. Once they were at Tran's Flower Shop, everyone piled in to the place to see what the gift basket contained. In it were gold award ribbons with the words 'Goal Achievers' written on them. There was also a note.

"Remember to work on your goals a little at a time. Over the long run you will have definitely moved along with your goals. Go on from there. A little word of advice: You can totally have what you want in life, you just have to make the commitment to keep going after what it is you would like to go after. And if it is to be then it is to be. That's where goals come in handy. They help you to get to it.

You have been awarded a special prize. On the back of the gold ribbons you will find a sticker stating your name. Show your Goal Achievers ribbon to the limousine drivers at Watoosis Limousine Service and they will give each of you (that's EACH of you) two free hours in a limousine. Tell them what some of your favourite foods and drinks are (non-alcoholic) and they will put them in the limousine for you to enjoy. Go ahead. Have a fun time in a limo.

Oh yes, one more detail. In the trunk of the new Ford Fusion, Rita, you will find one wallet for you and each of your neighbours. Each of them contains a one hundred dollar bill. It's a little incentive from me for you to keep continuing on with your goals. Don't forget to get the wallets. They are inside a green cloth shopping bag. Thank you for going on the treasure hunt today. I hope that it will inspire you. And that, ladies and gentlemen, is the finish of the treasure hunt."

When they got back to the zoo parking lot to pick up their new wallets from the trunk of Rita's new car left by Anonymous one, they soon were driving away in their cars while feeling glad about spending the afternoon at the zoo. They thought the opening day at the zoo would be a good day to spend time with one another in the out of doors and it had been. They really liked seeing what animals were there.

There was much to talk about after arriving at Aleisha's house on Sunlit Avenue. From the moment Rain stepped inside to see Aleisha's pet chinchilla along with the rest of the group of neighbours, Aleisha felt it was a welcoming party for her pet. She only had him for a week and already she wanted to show everyone what it was like to have a chinchilla for a pet.

Sven began by saying, "Hey, this Orom of yours is a gentle little fella, isn't he?"

"Yes, he is. He keeps me company when I'm at home."

"What does he eat?" Francis asked, looking at him sitting up on two legs while watching him through the large, dark grey cage. It was five feet high. Francis noticed that Orom had a cozy habitat of all his own, including soft blue paper bedding, and places where he could run, jump, climb and play. That along with a soft, thin but cushioned purple material for a bed when he decided to rest.

"He eats timothy hay, chinchilla food pellets, dried fruit, pecans, and sunflower seeds. And he drinks fresh spring water."

"I'm glad you got him." Francis said.

"Yeah, but you have to be careful when you hold him because they have delicate ribs. I hold him gently." Aleisha picked up a piece of soft hay from the side of his cage and passed it to him. Orom then nibbled it and ate the hay in front of everyone.

"He has little hands that hold things." Sven commented. "I can tell. He held that hay in his hands."

"Isn't that neat?" Rain said.

"I bought a straw mat for him too. He moves the straw mat around his cage though, from one platform to another."

"Sounds like chinchillas are pretty intelligent." Francis said. "I remember you telling my sister and me about how

99

smart dolphins can be. Can I come and see Orom again soon?"

"Yeah, sure you can. Want to feed him a piece of dried apple?"

"Okay." Francis followed Aleisha to the kitchen to get the dried apple and then they came back to the group standing around his cage in the living room. Everyone watched as the grey chinchilla, at one year of age, ate the dried fruit as he munched away at it. Sure enough, he was there holding onto it in his hands just as everyone thought.

Aleisha asked, "So dear, what are you going to buy with the money you got from anonymous one?"

"I'm going to buy lots of chocolate roses with that one-hundred dollars I got."

"Sounds yummy." Aleisha replied.

"I have to try one." Francis said.

"Aw, what a cutie." Mavis sighed. "So guys, what did you think of the zoo animals today?" Mavis asked her two children, changing the subject.

"I liked seeing the cheetahs." Francis said.

"Me too." Lulu smiled.

"I liked seeing the lemurs." Rain went on.

"How about those red pandas?" Sven beamed a smile, laughing a little as he did so.

"Oh, there goes Sven having a good laugh like I mentioned he should earlier."

"That goes without saying Aleisha. So, have you decided what kind of woodcarving you will have for your next lamp?"

"Bubbles the fin whale and Swirl the bottlenose dolphin actually. They're friends."

"Aha. So then pretty soon you'll have a picture of that type of lamp on your website?"

"Yes, I will."

"Can I see one of Lily Sumner and the two dolphins if you happen to have one?" Sven asked, he appeared curious. "I haven't seen one of the popular lamps."

"Yeah, but the one I've been working on is a little rough around the edges."

"I don't mind. Whatever you have handy." Sven poked his finger through the side of the cage to touch Orom's grey fur. The chinchilla made a little chirping sound after he did so.

Aleisha was already opening a cabinet in the corner of the living room that contained her latest woodcarving of Tickle, Tackle and Lily Sumner. Soon it was in Sven's hands and he looked at it, noticing the details of Miss Forbes' work. "Do you have a photo of one that is finished being carved?" Sven gave it back to his woodcarver neighbour.

"Yes, right here. I have one framed here on the wall. Right over here." She motioned for Sven to come over to her. There it was sitting on the wall nearby the hallway, opposite from the chinchilla's cage.

"Gee. How many years have you been making the Lily Sumner lamps? Five to ten years?"

"You guessed it. Ten years."

"Is that so?" Sven rubbed his chin. His fingers grated over some stubble starting to grow on it. He played with the stubble for a few seconds and then turned toward Aleisha. "This is the first time I came over to your place. I'm glad I visited you. Go for it. Have you thought what your highest aspirations are?"

"I thought about it and just have to do more thinking."

"Think. Do. Think. Do. But do think."

"Oh, Sven." She patted him on the back.

"I determined that I'll have wisdom sayings to say for people. Then maybe I can get them printed."

"That sounds cool." Aleisha nodded. Just after she did so, Rain and the other neighbours that had been listening to the mechanic and the woodcarver talking soon stepped toward the framed photograph on the wall and listened to see if either of the two would be saying anything more about the subject they were discussing.

"What is it guys?" Aleisha asked, breaking the silence.

Rain started by saying, "You know…ever since we all decided to follow our highest goals or aspirations as the people here of Sunlit Avenue, I thought it would be easy to work on but now I know there are some challenges to it. We just have to figure out what they are and keep moving forward. Like for me, I have to start writing my mini-book about the rainforest by sitting down and doing it. I've talked about it enough."

"And Cora has to see what the robots will be like when they do complete the first few." Sven said.

"Yes, and I'm starting school in September." Francis reminded the group.

Lulu exclaimed, "Mom, what is school going to be like? One more year and I will be in first grade."

"By that time, I'll be in grade two." Francis teased.

"Yes, and I'll be a whole year older."

"So will I."

"Ha, I got you there." Lulu hollered.

"Very intriguing. Grade one. I remember way back when. There's spelling and math and reading." Rita suggested.

"That's right." Mavis answered.

"Projects and more projects. Sounds like we are doing good. After all, I've been getting my pictures in magazines lately." Rita continued.

"I can hardly wait to hear what our other neighbours are up to. People such as Brooke Akira. Even Doris and Mark Keenan." Rain said.

"Isn't it getting exciting though? If you really think about it? Sure, we have some stuff to do to get there but all the while here we are going after our goals and aspirations. We should just figure out what it is we are going to do and go for it." Mavis pointed out to them to help cheer them on.

"That's right and it's definitely days like today that can help us do that." Aleisha said eloquently.

"Stuff. That's it. The stuff that life's made of can help us all to get up to speed." Sven said with excitement ringing in his voice. "How's that for a wisdom saying?"

"Good. We're all getting there. Let's make it possible by being smart and taking one day at a time like we have been doing. Only now, we'll keep it moving on." Rain said.

"Moving on, I like how you say that. Alright Rain or I mean Sunshine. Let's do that."

Aleisha felt relieved with her reply. "Everybody, let's keep moving on towards those goals."

"Remember that writing down your goals to goal set is the first step to have your goals met, so that you will meet your goals." Rain reminded them.

"Gee, this has been great today. It really has." Sven mentioned.

"Whenever you're met by a challenge just figure out what the next step would be in finishing that particular goal." Mavis shrugged her shoulders. Then she held her hand up to her forehead and broke down. She couldn't hold back the emotions that she felt toward Damien. She started crying a little bit and said, "My husband is back. I missed you so much darling."

"I missed you too." He said back to her.

"Mom, smile okay?"

"Wisest thing I heard all day. And it's coming from a smart six-year-old." Sven wanted to cheer Francis on but he didn't know what to say.

"My sis is smart and so am I." Lulu replied.

"How true." Mavis didn't feel quite as concerned as before. "Thanks. I had a grand old time with you guys at the grand garden zoo."

"That's for sure." Rain had an uncontrollable urge to grin. So she gave everyone a humungous grin.

"Okay guys, let's go now and we'll see what steps we can take so that our goals and highest aspirations can be met." Mavis felt motivated and ready for some achieving, not only for herself and her family but for all the people who lived on her street. It was happening. The results of their progress would soon be seen.

A short while later everyone left and went home. The moments they had spent together during the afternoon had made them realize on this day that it was all turning out to be the makings of one special year. One in which all the efforts of each of their projects worked on during it would begin to take shape.

At the end of the day, Edmond Keenan called Cullen and Rain on the telephone and announced that he got the job at Fiona's Restaurant. They were pleased to hear it. So was Edmond. Miss Woodrow and Mr. Dangsi could tell by the sound of their neighbour's voice during their telephone conversation that he was very happy. He told them that he would start the job on June 23. One day after the last school day of the year.

CHAPTER 8

Sunday, June 5, 2011

At about two o'clock am, when everybody living on Sunlit was sleeping, there just so happened to be a sudden loud screeching of tires followed by noisy horn blasts a second later. An automobile roaring at full speed came to a sudden halt before continuing onward along the Avenue. The horn honking that was occurring soon caught them each entirely by surprise and stirred them from their sleep. Then the honking stopped for a minute and everything was quiet again. After a rather gripping moment passed by, the automobile circled around and sped quickly along to repeat the tire screeching and horn honking a second time. And as soon as that happened the automobile was last heard speeding away into the night. It left the neighbours concerned as to whether there would be more horn blasts going on again in the quiet of the night. It was very possible that whoever had done it appeared to be trying to tell the neighbours something. They wondered what it was and who it could have been.

The next morning Cora Pepper wrote a note for all of her neighbours to read. She made copies of it and put a note in each mailbox for them. She had written it out really quite quickly. It read, "Dear neighbours, the automobile noises you heard last night were probably due to the fact that an article was published in a nearby city's newspaper emphasizing the fact that I mentioned all the people living on Sunlit are working on their highest aspirations and goals together. I told the people working at the Catchy Petunia robots factory in Fredericton that simple fact about us when I was asked how I thought of such a lovely idea for a business. The business of life size robots that talk. The Catchy Petunia robot was of course my goal. Let's hope they will be advertising the robots soon. Regards, Cora Pepper."

While Cora was out delivering the notes to each of the neighbours' mailboxes, she noticed big skid marks that ran several feet in length on the pavement of the street. Cora felt concerned as she wondered some more about whether something else might happen. After all, Sunlit Avenue was a rather quiet street because it was part of a new neighbourhood. She hoped it would stay that way, at least until everyone finished their projects. For now, she would be getting used to the fact that people were going to notice their efforts sooner or later, however small or large the neighbours' goals were turning out to be.

* * *

Early in the afternoon, Ralph Holiday and his wife Zoey decided to give a copy of a children's story book to Francis and Lulu for a present. When they went over to see the two children at their home they were happy to unwrap a book called Key Notes. When they did so, their mother Mavis was astounded to discover it was only about a dozen sentences but the words along with the illustrations within it stretched beyond imagination.

"Thanks for the book Mr. and Mrs. Holiday. I like it." Lulu said.

"So do I." Francis said, noticing that the name of the author was Ralph Holiday. She gasped, for it suddenly dawned on her that the same person who wrote the book might be the same man standing in front of her. Their neighbour Ralph. "Did you write this book?"

"Yes, I did. Four years ago. Isn't it great?" Ralph chuckled to himself and his wife Zoey. "Let me read it to you." He said.

"Alright." Lulu said, inviting him to sit with her on the purple sofa. Surrounded by some grey walls in the bright living room, they sat and read Ralph's book.

"Key Notes
By Ralph Holiday.

"Yessiree I really love you, love you.
Yessiree I really love you, love you."
"I'm growing up."
"Where's my little guy gone to? Gone to?"
"I'm hiding from you. I'm playing hide and seek."
"Where's my little guy going to, now that you're getting older?"
"I'm facing the music along with you and I really love you.

And since I've been doing so, I really hear it and it's a nice tune.

It's the song of life."

"Your mom loves you too. As I hear you say those words about the

song of life, I listen carefully and I can hear it clearly just as you do."

"It's really something. Feel the rhythm. Every day is a different note."

"That boy of mine is a nice guy. He's touched by the music of life."

"My Mother is a kind lady. She listens to the music in everyday living.

What's great about that is she's learning to soar just as I am."

The storybook had black and white stick figures of the two characters, a mother and a son, with pink and green colors for illustration. The son had short spiky hair and the mother had long straight hair with curls. There was very talented stick figure artwork of the two in the story and as the years went on line by line in the children's story book it showed how the mother and son looked different as they got older. Ralph had written a simple story but one of very enduring love. After he read the story to them, Lulu rubbed her eyes and Francis sniffed. They had tears in their eyes.

"Did you know that I and my wife and two grandchildren Dance and Xavier have been working on a comic book about two animals named Awesome Opposum and Witty Kitty? The kids are both nine years old and are fraternal twins. Dance is a girl and Xavier is a boy."

"No, I didn't know that." Francis replied.

"You are?" Lulu asked with her hands on the story book while still looking at the pictures.

"It's something Zoey and I have been doing to keep busy since we are both retired."

"Yes, and it gives us time to spend with the grandkids when we share our ideas for the comic book and design the pictures and do the writing. Who knows? Someday maybe the grandkids will have it published."

"When I get older, dad said I can carve wood like Aleisha. The lady that you live across the street from Mr. and Mrs. Holiday."

"You can? Keep working at it and you'll get to liking your artwork. Aleisha sure does. In the meantime, keep to carving bars of soap instead of wood. You want to stay away from sharp knives like what Aleisha uses."

"Thanks for the pointer." Mavis winked.

Ralph paused and then continued to speak more on the subject of comics. "The only trouble is when we get together to write on the comic pages we don't know who should work on what. So I finally mentioned we will each do an entire page at a time and then there will be four pages done. After a few touch-ups it should be good. Anyway, I think they liked my idea."

"It really works." Zoey said.

Ralph hesitated and then went on to say, "It might take many months to do up a comic book."

"That's for sure." Zoey grinned. "But you can be sure it will be one that is great to read. At least I hope."

"Gee." Ralph looked puzzled. "I mean, who does the front cover?"

"We all do." Zoey seemed to answer her husband's comments all in stride. Sure he had concerns but she was ready to go with it.

"How many pages is a comic book?" Mavis questioned. "You could make one that has more pages than usual."

"That's what we are doing. I have one with a few dozen pages." Ralph slapped his knee.

"Well, we just thought we would stop by for a few minutes. We should be off. We're going for a walk."

"Thanks for the present. I'm sure the girls will find it inspiring." Mavis said. "After all, it's about how two people that love each other share what they have learned. To me that's what the story is about."

"As inspiring as Brooke Akira is, right? Anyway, I'm glad you said that. Thank you too." Ralph nodded, heading for the door with Zoey. "Ta ta, Mrs. Hemley."

* * *

Brooke Akira, sporting beige khaki pants with a brown leather belt, a white short-sleeved shirt and brown leather shoes, relaxed at home listening to some electronic music on his computer. It was his day off work. He was thinking to himself how great it would be to complete his latest sketch of a futuristic car he had been working on. A car that looked very different than cars of today. At times he found that he had a vision of what to sketch in the line of cars of the future by looking at some toy cars found in the toy stores. They had edges, curves and shaded windows and other features of the kind of car he otherwise saw as a car of the future. He wondered how long it would take to sell the sketch once it was all filled in with color he had yet to choose, with wheels that looked slick and a style that was sure to be seen as sleek for a future car. He had been working on the drawing of a car of a type that existed far in the future. Such as fifty to one-hundred years from the present day.

Doing up sketches of the sort was his second job and he usually sold four sketches a month with each sketch going for one-thousand dollars or more. He made them in a room reserved for artists who sat together talking about certain topics up for conversation while they worked on their works of art. Their out of the ordinary sketches of cars of the future were done with an artistic skill that had a certain magnitude all its own, for it supplied the artists with income and even the owner of the building where they worked with rental income. Given that three-hundred and fifty people altogether had jobs in the various rooms within the building making different assortments of artworks, people far and wide knew that the area of the city of Moncton they were in seemed to be fast becoming an artist's haven. Many people living in the city had second incomes selling products to the rest of the world. It was catching on all over town. The people that lived there were seeing it. Brooke Akira, a Japanese neighbour living on Sunlit Avenue was seeing it. As were the other people living on Sunlit Avenue. And the sales from the artworks produced at the O'Byron Mihi Loft that were sold online were enough to tell anyone that the business had a website that was a sure success. It was becoming quite the place to shop for just about any type of artwork.

It had been Brooke's third year at the shoe company. And his eighth year at O'Byron's. Between selling shoes while working at Calizro's shoe store, his first income, and selling framed sketches he named The Kalmetta Series at the O'Byron Mihi Loft, his second income, he had been finding out lately that learning to take a day off on Sundays was important to keep him in shape for business. It was the one day each week when he could get the rest and relaxation to keep him rejuvenated for the next work week. Although he had some vacation time coming up in two days with his job at Calizro's shoe store, five days of it, he was still determined to make the most of his day. The day was another one of those days that kept him wondering about his life and where it was headed. With no girlfriend he was still a bachelor. But he liked being a bachelor. It gave him room to roam about on his search for all the best home décor, the best music, and the best foods that money could buy.

"To what capacity?" Brooke said aloud to himself. "To what capacity do I go after my highest aspirations and goals when I believe I'm doing so now? I mean, of course I'll always have goals, it's just that I'm so busy with work already at two great jobs. What would my neighbours say is the best approach to achieving goals when you already are?"

Brooke sat for a while and then started daydreaming about cars of the future flying high in the sky. 'Cars that fly. It could happen sometime. Maybe sooner than we think.'

He visualized them going up, up, higher up and then got wind of something. 'What if instead of seeing goals as something that brings you to the road ahead as represented by the cars of today, goals could be something that lifts you up to the sky with positive upliftment as represented by the cars of tomorrow? And what if each day a person can work to achieve positive upliftment by accomplishing their goals one by one?' He thought for a moment. 'Now we're getting somewhere.' Brooke Akira said aloud to himself, "I can just see it now. Goals in regards to flying cars of the future.

That's definitely something I can work on. A little bit of positive upliftment goes a long way."

Brooke Akira, a charming man of Japanese ancestry, suddenly stood up tall and proud at a height of five-eleven and became fully convinced of the importance of his words when he came out with it and said, "This isn't an over exaggeration but I think it's really time for those flying cars I've been dreaming about to move people in life and precisely that. Oh the possibilities."

To say the least, it was a marked improvement for Brooke already with his new way of thinking about the cars he had spent so much time sketching. Until now, he found designing them to be moving. But now he was seeing how their very design could move him even further. Beaming with joy, he let his imagination soar for a while and felt glad that he did. It took him farther toward setting his sights skyward as far as goals were concerned. And really that was what it was all about for him. So he sat down and wrote down his own goal. 'My goal is to help other people achieve their goals with my cars of the future designs. I will start a website that provides the information necessary to get people to be positively uplifted with their goals and aspirations.' That was where it was at for Brooke.

'Over-zealous of me…maybe…but how enthusiastic can a guy like me get when it comes down to it? I mean, ideally I could call this new addition to my designs "The Goal Getters" or maybe "Goal, get it?" or possibly "Play the Sport of Goal Getting." Yeah, that's it! I'll call it "The Sport of Goal Setting." People will be playing the goal setting sport when they are going after a positive upliftment of sorts.' He thought.

Brooke continued to think the whole sport of goal setting through some more and he liked what he was seeing. To him, the point of the sport was feeling eager to live each day in a way that brought out excitement in a person with renewed vigor toward the accomplishment of each new goal. "The Sport of Goal Setting. Are you up for it? Let the task begin." He said to himself.

Mr. Akira went outside for a breath of fresh spring air and saw that there was something in his mailbox. He noticed a corner of a page. At first sight it appeared as though it was a flyer or an advertisement hanging out from under the top of the mailbox. Upon opening the mailbox, he soon was surprised when he found out what it was as he held it in his hand. A note from Cora Pepper regarding the loud tire screeching and horn blasting that occurred last night. 'Curious.' He thought.

After a minute, he was baffled by it. Cora somehow seemed to draw the attention of some readers of a local newspaper by describing Sunlit Avenue as the place where there are neighbours working together on their goals. People already knew of them. Brooke himself had been answering so many questions at the O'Byron Mihi Loft by one of the other artists working along with him that it was causing him to think that someone was spying on him and his neighbours. The fellow artist always wanted to hear just what had been happening on the Avenue and exactly what each of them had been up to every time there was free time to talk at the Loft. It was enough to make Brooke bite his lip. 'What about the newspaper article readers?' He thought. It seemed the neighbours were facing their first real challenge since making their goals together. Brooke wondered if there would be more soon on the way.

Chapter 9

Monday, June 6, 2011

As soon as the noises of construction work began on the next street in the morning, Cora noticed it and checked out the work they were doing for the new houses that would be built there. She told the construction workers the story about her company Neat Street Robots. At first they found it hard to believe that twelve thousand dollar talking robots would soon be available for the public to buy.

When they found out from talking to her that the factory workers still had to build them, the construction workers found what she was saying might possibly be true after all. In fact, the way that Cora described it made them imagine it to be very true and they wanted to know more details. The details she too was still waiting to hear about. She assured them it would be worth the wait.

Having heard that one of the things the robot Catchy Petunia will be saying is about the stars in space, the construction workers had some ideas of their own. She said to them, "I can tell by the way that you look at yourself that you are a Stargazer. Stargazer." One of them paused and said back to her, "Hey, that really does sound great." Within a minute they decided on a name for the new street. Starlight Street. Cora was delighted and hoped it would soon only be a matter of weeks before they named it Starlight Street.

On the way back to her house, she saw Sid in his front yard swaying back and forth on an orange mesh hammock that rested on a white metal frame. As she stepped closer she heard him talking away on his cell phone. "Doris. That is sure a surprise. T-shirts that say, "This is turning out to be one sweet awesome turn of events. Kokomoz." And you're starting a new line of T-shirts? Huh. When?" He was talking to his neighbour Doris Keenan on his cell phone.

Cora was curious so she thought she should go see Sid Mathison. Sid emphasized each word of "This is turning out to be one sweet awesome turn of events. Kokomoz." When he said it he really drew Cora's interest in the telephone conversation he was having with Doris.

Miss Pepper went over to see him. By the time she got near to him, he was still talking away on the phone. "I haven't been selling too many Happy Face Heaven artworks this month so far. I wonder if there is anything I could do to sell more of them. Hmm, I don't know. You've got your T-shirts to sell. I've got my happy faces." Sid waved to Cora with a frown on his face.

"Oh my God, I know what. Happy faces with T-shirts on. That's what I'll paint on metal. Yes, I'm serious. I'm very serious. It's a good idea, isn't it?"

"Hi Sid, you're looking bright today." Cora said.

"That's for darling sure." He answered. "Do you think that they will sell?" Sid listened for a few seconds. "You think I should do a website write-up on them? Maybe I could add something dramatic to one my online business webpages to catch people's interest in the artworks. And advertise."

Several more seconds passed and then Sid said, "Cora is here. I read your note Cora. Just keep it a secret. The fact that we are all working together on our goals while living on the same street. Okay?" He coughed. Sid was still a little concerned about the loud automobile honking that he had recently heard.

"But Sid…" Cora started to say.

"Doris says getting Cora to keep a secret is like getting me to stop drinking a fruit smoothie every day. That's what she just said. Anyway, I like my smoothies. Speaking of which, I have the day off today. So I can spend some time sipping a smoothie or two." He laughed hysterically, as though he found it to be extremely funny. "I've got to go. Cora is waiting patiently for me to finish talking on the phone. I'll talk to you later Doris. Okay. Bye."

After Sid was done with the phone conversation, he turned to face Miss Pepper. "I think I just might have something here. Happy faces with T-shirts. Seems like it."

"I'd say." She quietly answered.

"What's new?"

"Got the day off, huh?"

"You know what? This really is something. Doris is starting her own company too.

Kokomoz is the name of it. She has a T-shirt that says, "On a breezy day may you have smooth sailing. Kokomoz." She also says that "Kokomoz is like a strawberry sherbet."

"That's one for the books." Miss Pepper said.

"What?" Sid gasped eagerly.

"Another lady on Sunlit starting a company. Go figure."

"And then there's Rain who might also have a company to help the rainforest." Sid paused.

"But it looks like Doris is going to be the second one on the street starting a company."

"I would think so after hearing you talking about it to her on the phone. What does Mark think?"

"Her husband is looking forward to it. Mark actually thought of this. "One fun sun. That's the beauty of Kokomoz."

"What does Edmond think?"

"He likes it. Doris told him that it would be a month before the business opens here in town. She's going to start off small with it. Then go from there."

"Good idea. Neat Street Robots is starting off big."

"Speaking of Neat Street Robots. What will the robots sound like?"

"Like a normal human voice. No added effects." She smiled.

"Oh yeah. I hear you. I hope they start selling them soon." He beamed a smile back to her.

Just as they were thinking some more about their goals a car peeled up the street and passed by them. When it stopped at the other end of the street someone was heard screaming really loud, "Woo! It's Sunlit Avenue!"

"Looks like there's another one of the newspaper article readers." Sid gasped, still feeling all wound up and over excited after talking to Doris.

"Apparently." Cora remained calm, cool and collected.

"It's getting to the point that so much is riding on our decision of working together on our goals."

"Yes, there is. And it's up to us to get it done."

"We're going to get her done. You can be sure of that. I'm just worried about what people like the one who just screamed out a minute ago will be doing once we are going places. After the fact, I mean."

"They'll be shaking your hand, Sid. Won't they?"

"Ha. That I'd like to believe. As long as they don't take it any further than that."

"You mean, if they start going overboard at having met us in person?"

"Yup. That's what I mean."

"Get used to it. That's all I'll say about that. Things are about to change and change for the better too."

"It's still a cause for concern to me at least." Sid cleared his throat. "Maybe tourists from all over will be coming to Sunlit Avenue to see us."

"Hey, you could be right. That could happen."

"For now, I've got to get working on some more ideas for my business."

"Good luck with that."

"Thanks. Good luck with your robots."

"Okay."

* * *

After Doris was done talking to Sid on the phone she went to talk to her husband Mark. Along with Edmond, the family was certainly pepped up about what would be coming up in a mere four weeks. The opening day of the new company. Until then, Doris would be enjoying four weeks of vacation time and doing all she could in the process of getting everything ready in time. She had a lot of stuff to take care of and she would be busy for a while enjoying her vacation days she had accumulated from her full time job at the clothing manufacturer Reyonders. After being a worker at her job for twelve years so far, she had developed a liking for the making of classy T-shirts and pants. Reyonders was a fairly popular name brand in Canada.

Her husband Mark worked at a furniture store as a salesperson at a place otherwise known as Sopuzela Furniture. Mark had eight years of experience working there since the day he was first hired. Although he had gathered knowledge about furniture at his job, there was always something new for him to learn from his interactions with the people who were making furniture purchases. But he found that nothing attracted their interest like finding the perfect furniture for the perfect price.

Lately he was discovering a change in the air. He knew it and so did the others on Sunlit Avenue. Soon his attention would remain focused in a whole new way. Within a few days there would be something new for him to learn. It would be from the result of meeting the people who were wondering what he and his neighbours had been up to lately. It would be one more week, to be exact, before he saw what was really going on in regards to Cora letting a few people in on some details. Although he was beginning to wonder what else could possibly occur, he didn't realize just how a few remarks to the public could cause everybody on Sunlit Avenue to get noticed.

News had been reported already that the people of Sunlit Avenue were known to be following their highest aspirations. And the news report was now starting to draw the attention of many. The neighbours were going to be confronted.

Chapter 10

Tuesday, June 14, 2011

At around six-thirty am, at a time when the birds were heard singing away in the nearby trees and the clouds were covering the sky above, two people got out of a yellow car that was parked on the side of the Avenue. By mere coincidence, the car was parked just in front of the house where Doris, Mark and Edmond lived. And Mark had been wondering for days if anything unusual would be happening during the week.

One person was a young woman with short, red hair who appeared to be around thirty years of age while the other person was a man with some noticeable grey to his short, black hair who looked to be fifty years of age. The lady was dressed in a green business suit and white high heel shoes while the gentleman was wearing a purple T-shirt, black shorts and black and grey dress shoes.

Within seconds they were waiting for someone to answer the doorbell at the Keenan family's house. Mark rolled out of bed still in his pyjamas and was greeted by a lady newspaper reporter and a cameraman at the front door. They appeared to be friendly and for someone that just woke up and gotten out of bed, that certainly helped keep him alert and on his toes.

"We're here to conduct an interview with you to gather some information for a newspaper article that I'm writing to discover what you and the rest of the people that live on Sunlit Avenue have been doing together to achieve your highest aspirations like we heard from Cora Pepper."

"We would like to tell the public more of the story." The cameraman added.

"Sure, my name is Mark Keenan."

After they shook hands, Mark welcomed them into his home and the cameraman soon found a place to set up his camera for the interview. It was in the kitchen where there was a table to sit down beside. There were four pinewood chairs set around a pinewood table. The walls were painted a medium red color. The floor was made of square slate tiles of a variety of grey, red, black, and tan tones. The countertop had a tan hue. And the rectangle backsplash tiles were dark red.

By this time, Doris and Edmond soon made their way downstairs to see who had come to their house. They entered the kitchen. Doris had a pair of black and navy blue tartan pyjamas on and Edmond was wearing a pair of blue shorts and a red T-shirt.

"Hi, what is your name?" The cameraman asked Mrs. Keenan while noting the young Edmond. It was apparent that both of the guests were feeling somewhat enthusiastic about having the chance to meet three of the people they had heard so much about recently.

"Doris Keenan. And this is my son Edmond."

"We're very pleased to meet you. Aren't we Barbara?

"Yes we are." Barbara answered.

"My name is Jacques. Thanks for inviting us into your home for an interview. Barbara is writing a newspaper article on the latest that has been happening on your street to find out what your highest aspirations are and how close of each of you are to achieving them. The public is interested to hear all about it. So am I." The cameraman said.

"Okay, we will get dressed and be back in a few minutes." Mark said, feeling a bit more alert and awake now that he had a few minutes to get over his sleepiness.

Both Mr. and Mrs. Keenan went upstairs but their adoptive son Edmond stayed in the kitchen. He was all ready for his day. He had a quick start to it when he suddenly put his clothes on upon hearing someone at the door. Edmond didn't want to be caught in his pyjamas, even though it was so early in the morning.

"I have about one more week until school is finished for the year. Then it's off to Fiona's Fine Restaurant where I will be working."

"Oh, is that right? Fiona's?" Barbara repeated, thinking it to be an elegant name for a restaurant.

"Yeah. It's gonna be great."

"Glad to hear it." Jacques was eloquent with his words.

"I'm feeling two-hundred percent today." Edmond mentioned.

"By any stretch of the imagination I would say so." Jacques chuckled.

Mark arrived back in the kitchen ten minutes later. He had put his clothes on. A pink T-shirt, khaki beige pants and grey sneakers. After getting dressed he spent time washing his face and otherwise sprucing up before the interview.

He knew he would be on camera. It looked as though the newspaper reporter and cameraman were ready to begin filming the second he approached them nearby the kitchen table. His wife Doris was there wearing a green T-shirt along with checkered brown and white shorts. Additionally, she had on a pair of light taupe sandals that had a new style of stretchy laces that fastened up with a little clip. She was watching with Edmond close by.

"Please, sit down Mr. Keenan." Barbara said.

"Sure." He pulled up a chair.

"Mark Keenan, you as one of the neighbours of Sunlit Avenue are probably familiar with what has been going on around your street. First of all, what goals are you currently working on?"

"I'm contributing a nice T-shirt slogan for my wife's business that she is going to start in town four weeks from now. I'd rather not say what it is at this point."

"A business you say?" Barbara leaned forward for more effect in the camera shot.

"Yes. She's working on her business that she has already named Kokomoz. A clothing company. They will be opening shop in town soon."

"Your son has told us that he will be working at a local restaurant after he finishes his eleventh year of school later this month." Barbara seemed to be taking note of what Mark was saying to her while the camera was running. "Very informative. And what are all of your neighbours working on?"

"Well, I don't know what Cullen Dangsi is working on but I do know that his girlfriend Rain Woodrow is writing a book about the rainforest. Rita Young is still taking pictures and getting them published in magazines. The Hemley family we'll still have to see. Brooke Akira is very quiet and secretive. I know he is a very productive person though. Let's see. There's Aleisha Forbes. She's developing her latest woodcarvings of a whale and a dolphin. Ralph and Zoey Holiday are both retired and are spending more time with their grandchildren. Sid Mathison is developing a strategy for selling more Happy Face Heaven artworks possibly. Hazel and Cora are preparing for the Neat Street line of robots to be made. Sven is making up wisdom quotes and his brother Vic has been keeping busy at his job just like the rest of the people on Sunlit."

"Then you each are still working on getting there in regards to the goals I have heard so much about lately." The newspaper reporter said.

"Yes. The only thing is now we have decided to work on our goals together. That way we can see just what to do to get them accomplished." Mark gently swept his hand across his hair. "Check back at the end of the year and you should see a lot of progress happening."

"Yes. A sort of year end progress report. I will possibly do that. In the meantime, the article I'll be including in the newspaper will inform our readers that you are still making good progress toward reaching your goals together." Barbara waved as a sort of signal to Jacques to stop the camera for now. "It has been great talking with you today Mark. Jacques and I are pleased about your progress so far."

"Thanks for the information. We should be going now." Jacques nodded.

Within minutes they were back in their car and were pulling away from the curbside and moving down the street.

They headed back to Fredericton again to the location of the newspaper office. Soon Barbara would be putting the article in the paper once it was typed up. She knew the crowds were buying newspapers left and right with the coverage of the last article. What's more, she guessed that people around Fredericton would begin to calm down again with the news that the Sunlit Avenue neighbours were still making good progress and that there should be a progress report by the end of the year.

The Keenans still didn't know why they hadn't thought of year end progress reports before Barbara went ahead to talk about it. That was part of goal setting to them. Especially now. At any rate, the Keenans took it all in good stride and soon sat down to eat breakfast.

* * *

"Cullen...what are you writing?" Rain asked as she peered into the computer room with a quizzical look on her face.

"A project. Hmm...let's see."

"Whatever it is, you have been working on it for hours."

"Just give me a little bit of privacy. I've got some work to do." He tapped the computer desk with his finger as he sat thinking and thinking. Rain saw him staring at the computer screen and she wondered about him. "Just what are you up to Cullen Dangsi?"

"I've got to have more time to work on it. Then we can talk some more. Okay?"

"Anything you say." She cleared her throat, still caught off guard by his definite answer. She could tell from his tone of voice that he sounded as though he was a man at work.

She closed the door to let him have his space. It wasn't like him to ignore his girlfriend by being so occupied in his work. She stood there behind the closed door for a moment and was puzzled. She scratched her head and walked away and went to go cut the grass with the battery powered lawnmower.

Once it was all mowed nicely she sat down to rest and ended up having a nap for an hour. After she awoke she then helped herself to a tall glass of iced tea with a little bit of lemon flavour. She sipped it and then guzzled it down. After she quenched her thirst she found a note on the sofa that had a single word on it. Alazaner. She was curious to know more about it to get a clue as to what he had been working on all day, so she went upstairs to talk to him. "I found a note with the word Alazaner written on it. What does that mean? Is it part of your project?"

"Where did you get that?" He asked with a gaze of fixed attention.

"On the sofa." Miss Woodrow answered.

He stared at her and then began. "Oh, I misplaced that note. I was trying to remember Alazaner's name because I didn't have the note and then I remembered it." Cullen grabbed the piece of paper from her. "Thanks though. Now I can put the note in safe keeping. Anyway, well, Alazaner? He's a character I'm writing about."

"A character? Are you going to give me a hint about what you're writing?"

"I just did."

"Cullen. What's the matter?"

"I don't know what you mean. I just have to get this done, okay?"

"Alright. But tell me about it later." She closed the door again and went to go design some cards in the living room. She had to finish about fifty cards of different sorts before the end of the day.

While she was doing so, she kept busy for about an hour before she realized that Cullen seemed to be keeping something from her for the first time and she didn't know what it was that he was keeping from her. Cullen wasn't usually like that and she was surprised. He was acting so peculiar that she wanted to know what was causing him to act so unlike his usual jokester self. Finally, she heard him coming downstairs to where she was sitting at her creative corner and noticed him pulling some more notes from under the cushions of the sofa. There were three of them. Rain laughed at him when she saw how he had them tucked away from her.

"Here." He sighed, passing them to her.

She read them. "Shopkeeper." "Isaiek Sheer." "Mr. Ten." She thought the names were pretty peculiar. "What is this?" She looked up at Cullen still standing beside her.

"My project. Like I said." He sat down on the sofa.

"Okay." Rain filled a rubber stamp with some blue ink and pressed it on the front page of a card. After that she wiped the rubber stamp clean and pressed the next stamp on it below where she had pressed the last stamp.

"I'm going to grab lunch. Don't peek at what I'm working on. I'm going out to get a submarine sandwich."

"I'm busy anyway." She noticed him leaving in a hurry and hoped he would be careful when driving there in his car. "To what end, Cullen. To what end." She said aloud as she heard him walking out the door.

When Cullen got to his car he found a bright yellow sticky note taped to his windshield. On the sticky note, bad boy Cally Ryerson had written some threatening words to Cullen. He found it a few seconds after leaving the house. After glancing around a little, Cullen was in a rush to get in his car and drive away quickly. The note read, "I spotted what you've been up to lately Dangsi. You're suddenly serious. So am I. Don't spill the beans like Cora. Or else."

* * *

Aleisha was at home working away at her latest woodcarving idea of a Fin whale named Bubbles and a Bottlenose dolphin named Swirl. To her it was a superb idea. She hoped it would make a splash and people would be admiring her carving skills. Bubbles and Swirl was the latest woodcarving she came up with after the outing to the zoo. She had written a story to go along with it to show the buyer of the product how far she would go to get the message across about the intelligence of whales and dolphins. She was just finishing up the very last details of applying the paint sealer to the painting job of the turquoise and blue seascape water surrounding the two sea creatures. The painted sculpture of the whale was already brownish-grey on the top and white on the bottom. While the painted sculpture of the dolphin was grey on the top and white on the bottom. Bubbles the whale appeared to be ten times larger than Swirl the dolphin. It all made for an eye catching appeal that showed Aleisha's years of experience in woodcarving. The lamp was painted a sandy beige color and the lampshade was white. There were also touches of white and black throughout the majestic section where the ocean surrounded Bubbles and

Swirl in layers of painted water to give the appearance of more depth. From plain view, the tabletop lamp was wider around its base and thinner near the lampshade. And to the talented Aleisha, it was the perfect homemade lamp. And on the back of each lamp would be found written in red paint - Aleisha Forbes.

After she placed her paintbrush in a glass of water she looked at it again and was very pleased with her efforts. Before wrapping it up in plastic wrap to be ready for delivery, she first had to let the paint sealer air dry a little. So she read the poster-sized page that would be mailed along with the carving to the next buyer. As she went ahead to read it she thought of how each customer who would be buying a Bubbles and Swirl homemade lamp would receive one with their order.

Bubbles and Swirl

One day when the sun was brightly shining in a cloudless sky over both land and sea, a whale named Bubbles and a dolphin named Swirl swam together. They rose to the surface of the water as whales and dolphins so often do, and once again breathed in the fresh air above the open ocean. They felt the warmth of the sunrays and made sounds to one another in celebration of the beauty of nature all around them. It was a day filled with awe and wonder. For the many sea creatures from the shimmering sands to the sparkling seas, such a time quite simply meant that it was time to play. From the looks that Bubbles and Swirl gave to each other, it seemed they were both more than ready to begin. And so once again they dove in the water to play their favourite game. The seconds went by and soon they were already deep enough in the ocean for the fun to take place. Then with a sweet smile, the whale opened her mouth and released a great number of bubbles. Up, up, up went the bubbles. As she did so, the dolphin made a sudden dash and followed after them. The dolphin swirled around and around and around the bubbles and then travelled with them back to the air above the water. When Swirl lifted her head above the surface again she waited with curiosity to see where her friend Bubbles would soon be seen in the waves. Whether the whale would be in front, behind, to the left side or to the right side of her, Swirl could not tell for sure. Each time it was different. For the moment she could only guess. A few seconds went by and the whale appeared to the right side of the dolphin. It was one of the playful games they grew so fond of during their three years together. For the two female friends had seen many other sea creatures watch their game and they each enjoyed it in their own way. They knew the whale and dolphin were playful and intelligent by how they had discovered an interesting way to play. Just seeing a dolphin and a whale together was exciting enough for the many sea creatures. To see them in a great friendship with each other was something else. The friendship between Bubbles the Fin Whale and Swirl the Bottlenose Dolphin was something that ran deeper. From season to season, they had followed each other's lead and learned how to become experts at their own particular game. A game known as Friendly Fins.

Sincerely,
Aleisha Forbes. Carver of fine wood products.
P.S. Enjoy.

"Wait a second. I should get this turned into a children's book instead of mailing it along with the woodcarvings in each order. Who am I kidding? I've got to do this." She said out loud to hear herself. "An illustrator could do the drawings of Bubbles and Swirl for the story too. Oh, this is so great."

Aleisha tested the lamp one more time to see if it would light up and it did. She felt relieved and went over to the dining room to take two pictures of it for her website. Looking at the photographs on her digital camera, she was delighted how they turned out with the lighting from the window in the dining room. It was mid-afternoon outside and still bright. The homemade lamp was there in the dining room in a cabinet where she would store it until someone placed an order to buy it on her website.

Aleisha went to her desktop computer with her camera and posted the photos. Soon the pictures were on her website. The price for the lamp was set at four-hundred dollars.

"Alright, it shouldn't be too long before someone buys that." Aleisha usually brought in one-hundred dollars a day on average with her woodcarvings. After keeping busy for a total of four days on the Bubbles and Swirl piece, her hands were tired. It was time to rest. And time for a break. She went over to see her pet chinchilla in the living room.

"Hi Orom. Good day to ya." He was perched on a lava rock chew stick used to help grind his teeth down as they continuously grew.

All of a sudden Aleisha heard someone knocking at the front door and ringing the doorbell. It was Cullen. He was glad she was home. "Hi, I've been meaning to give this letter to you. The mailman put it in my mailbox instead." He said.

"Oh? It's just a bill. I'm grateful you brought it to me though. What's new? What have you been up to?"

"It's my day off and I have been working on my project all day. It's a secret. Don't tell anyone but I've been writing a lot lately."

"You have been writing? What about?"

"I'd rather not say at the moment. Anyway, I just had lunch at Kaiser Subs. I bought a veggie sandwich. When I was eating it I thought of the letter I had of yours in my car."

"Cullen look at the lamp I just finished over here. It's of Bubbles the whale and Swirl the dolphin." She took it out of the cabinet and showed him the fine details.

"Oh my. What you've got there is certainly creative. Have you listed it for sale?"

"Yes. I just finished it a little while ago. I've got so many bills to pay. I have to start the next lamp."

"It all goes with owning a house."

"That's for sure. I'm always working away though. Hey, has Rain been writing her mini-book?"

"Yeah, all week. I'm going to go home and work some more on my project. I figured out a thing or two about writing. With enough practice you can write even more easily as you keep refining the work. My project is coming along good."

"I just hope I can carve the next one quicker. I'm running a business after all."

"I know you are. And I hope I can finish what I'm working on quicker by working on it a lot." Cullen sounded as though he was in a mellow mood to Aleisha but he was as determined as could be and he was glad there was a neighbour close by that he could talk to who would share in his passion. What he didn't realize was that she too had a secret. "You motivate me even more. After all, there's a lot to do."

"You can say that again." Aleisha laughed.

"This is going to be nice for Rain to read. Isaiek Sheer is the name of the main character. It shouldn't be long now before it's done. Well, I should be going."

"Thanks for dropping by. Great talking to you."

"Have a good day."

"Thanks, I will. Let this day be one to remember." She laughed again. "Do you think that in the year 2020 people will be buying a lot of glasses? Get it? 2020 vision?"

Cullen shrugged his shoulders. He didn't seem to be in the mood for joking. Aleisha could tell right away when he quickly waved as he headed out the door and said, "Bye."

"See ya. Until next time."

Aleisha was filled with excitement at the prospect of turning her story into a children's book. It wasn't long before she contacted a guy on the telephone about finding an illustrator for the children's book. They talked things over and made the right arrangements. Everything was going as planned. And for the moment there was nothing for Aleisha to do but sit back and relax.

* * *

Having reasoned with herself all day about Cullen's sudden writing frenzy, Rain went over to the kitchen sink and washed a few utensils in soapy water. The water was hot to the touch when she tested its temperature. After she set down a handful of forks, knives and spoons that she had been rinsing under the water tap, she remembered there was something she had been meaning to tell her boyfriend. Since he was making a mozzarella cheese sandwich with whole grain bread on top of a bamboo cutting board and humming to himself happily right beside her she went ahead to say, "This character of yours named Isaiek Sheer sounds like he's out of sight. Just like those notes were. You kept them hidden. He must be pretty special to you. Whoever he is."

"I love you girl. Thanks for saying that. He is special to me."

"Good. Anytime you're ready to tell me who he is, you can. I love you too."

He topped the sandwich off with a green olive on the side of the plate and after eating it to whet his appetite he headed for the computer room. He already had a bottle of water handy that was still sitting on his workspace desk. When he got to the room, he stared at the screensaver of tiny grey and orange squares bouncing around the sides and corners of the computer screen and watched them go in no particular pattern, at least not at first. After about ten seconds of seeing them bouncing to and fro he began to see the pattern. He ate his sandwich while staring at the screensaver for a while longer.

"I'm glad that I sell computers." He spoke softly to himself. He finished off his sandwich with the entire bottle of water and rolled the seat that he was sitting on closer to the screen. "This will be ready in no time. The rate I'm going at with it." He clicked the mouse buttons and the words on the screen came on again. "I should remind Rain thanks for being patient with me."

CHAPTER 11

Sunday, June 19, 2011

Sven and Vic Nicolos both had a day off work. They were sitting on the sofa sipping some grape juice that they had been keeping in the refrigerator for a few hours. As Sven talked about his idea of wisdom quotes, Vic finally decided that he would have original quotes that he had not heard of before. It was a new idea. Vic wondered what Sven would think about the new idea.

"Today's weather is turning out to be a real dicer. We're supposed to get a thunderstorm but it looks like it's going to be a sunny day out." Vic said with a gritty coarseness.

"A dicer? I haven't heard that word before."

"Yeah, call it a shake of the dice. I guess since you picked Sven's wisdom quotes, I'll pick Vic's original quotes."

"Whatever gets ya going." Sven stared out the window.

The two men were sitting down on a tan colored sofa and the walls of their living room was of a light taupe color. All around them were small eighteen inch by twenty four inch tapestry weavings of an assortment of different color schemes that Vic had purchased. The tapestry weavings added depth to the room décor that accentuated everything else in the room. There was a long, rectangular coffee table in front of the sofa with some white and green square shaped peppermints in a gold candy dish to the left side of the table that belonged to Vic and on the right side there was a magazine about home decorating that belonged to Sven. There was a matching chair facing the sofa. Their place also had beautiful dark oak bamboo flooring.

Vic turned on the radio and not a minute later he heard an announcement from the radio host.

"We're going to play a hip new song that you are sure to like. Next up – a Peace-eba song that is one of our favourites. Dream Chasers. I love it, man."

Sven heard Vic chuckle. So he said, "You're on to something Mid-town."

The song began to play. "Hey, it's starting. Turn it up. It's my favourite band. The boys and I listen to their music on occasion.

"Got it."

"*Hurry-hurry, hup-hup-hup. You said you have the feeling. The inspiration. Like a sudden change in the weather that moves across the nation. And now the feeling is with you, so get up, up, up. Now, just what are you gonna do? Let your talents, your gifts and your abilities guide you through and through. Stand tall, get ready for the time is near to go after that special something that is what I hear. Oh yeah, I'll tell you what I've got to say. Oh, by the way, it's also how you are as you live each day. You've got it, you surely do. The words that will help bring you there are both simple and true. I'll say them and you can be reminded of them after each day is done, and that is - let that feeling be a lasting one. That feeling of yours is with you, you're perfectly fit. It truly is amazing that you are going after it. So*" *there you are, as easy as it may seem. You are going after your dream. You've said to me just a moment ago that you're calling that feeling Wave Motion. You astound me and I'm all filled with emotion. Remember, yes remember, that it's in every way that you live each day. It's all about who you are that will get you far. And as far as I'm concerned, since the day I met you, our friendship has been earned. The fact is, I love you man. From the moment we met, we both have said we can. We are chasing our dreams. Chasing our dreams. Chasing our dreams. We are Dream Chasers."*

"God, what a song. What do you think of that?"

"It truly is amazing."

"Make way for my goals too, Flare." Vic smiled from ear to ear and bellowed a laugh that left him feeling unusual yet fresh and ready for more goal setting. Sven only listened for the moment but his brother was actually preparing himself for what was to come. It was so noticeable that Sven held back a smile with his hand. Vic's body language said it all. He was pumping his fists in the air and moving his feet back and forth at a fast rate cheering himself on and it appeared as though he was out on a jog.

Sven finally said, "Hey Vic. Go for it."

* * *

The Hemleys were busy playing a game of family soccer with one another at a local minor league baseball field. The game was going along nicely when the unexpected occurred. A dog suddenly ran off with their soccer ball. It was a greyhound, a popular breed of dog well known for an ability to run at very fast speeds after whatsoever they are intent on chasing.

No sooner did Damien begin running after the dog to get the soccer ball did he go and slip on a big mud puddle in the grass. He lay down in it with a sore elbow after skimming across it. Within seconds he was all covered in mud. Damien lost his patience and got upset as he lay there in the mud after his sudden mishap. He caught a glimpse of the dog running along with the soccer ball down the street at the other end of the ball field.

"I couldn't get the ball." He told his family after they approached him and he wiped some mud off his face with his right sleeve.

Lulu stared toward the place where she last saw the dog. "Buy a new one."

"I couldn't get the ball." He only repeated.

Mavis looked at him funny and said, "Then get a new ball."

Mavis drove home with the family and on the way there everyone except Damien talked about how smart the dog was to roll the ball like he did as he quickly ran away with it. When they got back home Sid Mathison walked over to them as they got out of the car and asked some questions. He saw Damien rush into the house looking embarrassed and found out from Mavis that her husband was headed to the shower to wash away any remaining mud left over from his mishap with the greyhound that ran away with the family soccer ball.

"He was frustrated but he's alright now." She assured Sid.

"That's a relief."

"He scraped his elbow on the ground. He has a sore elbow."

"I'm glad that you and the kids are safe and sound."

"That's for sure. That dog looked like he was pretty fast even with the ball. Damien kept saying to himself that he couldn't get the ball. I think it's better to let the dog keep it instead of having to chase after him."

"Geez."

Sid Mathison was intrigued. "Speaking of dogs, I visited the pet store the other day and saw a dog there that I thought I should buy. It's a Chihuahua. Maybe I could go and see if he's still there. Or call them and ask to put him on hold."

"You could do that. It's up to you."

"Yeah." Sid assuredly spoke in his regular tone of voice.

"See you later. I've got to go get that Chihuahua. It's a co-incidence. Me seeing a dog I would like as a pet and now this."

"Yup." Mavis nodded. She crossed her fingers and sat down on the front steps of her house to see if Sid would soon be leaving for the pet store. Five minutes passed by and sure enough, Mavis noticed Sid leaving his house to head for the pet store. He waved when he saw Mavis and gave her the thumbs up.

An hour later Sid Mathison showed up with the Chihuahua at the Hemley family's house.

"Isn't he a dream? His name is Oazic. My new pet Chihuahua." The dog was tan colored and was a long haired Chihuahua. Sid was holding him but had a blue leash on him.

"A Chihuahua I can handle." Damien cleared his throat. "Funny how things turn out. You buying a dog after one took our ball. That wasn't any ball. That ball had been with us since my kids were babies. They wrote on it. They learned how to spell their names on it."

"Jeez, I can understand why you wanted that ball. Oh, I'm so glad I got this dog."

"I lost a ball. You gained a dog. Go figure."

"Maybe it was time for a new ball anyway."

"What? Sid. Are you trying to smooth things over? I'll remember that next time you make me a smoothie. Ha."

"Whatever you say. Man."

"Dad...telephone." Francis hollered out to Damien. He was standing near the curb at the edge of his front yard with Sid and Oazic.

"Okay. I'm coming."

"Take care Mister Hemley." Sid waved a hand in the air to Damien as he headed back home with his new pet. The dog looked as though he was already getting used to Sid as they walked away together.

"Yup. Later."

Once Damien got to the telephone he soon discovered who was calling him. "Hi...don't hang up...it's Griffin. What I have to say is important. Please don't worry that I'm calling you."

"Alright, Griffin. What is it? I'm listening." Damien was caught in the moment. All he could do was listen.

"The other day I went ahead and started a business with Lenny. We came up with something exceptional. Woodcarvings that are saber toothed tiger heads made of western red cedar wood. Do you know why it's important to use cedar wood?"

"No, Griffin, I don't. Do tell."

"It's because cedar wood is weatherproof. These are not the usual kind of woodcarvings you have heard of before. They are woodcarvings that are fastened by a screw to front doors of people's houses much like a door knocker is fastened on. But you can cover your door in them. I call them woodcarving tattoos for front doors."

"Geez. Saber toothed tigers eh? How many other front door tattoo styles will there be?"

"You mean other than the saber toothed tiger style?"

"Yeah."

"Well, many. I have to tell you something now. I, along with Lenny, have some investors who are funding me and Lenny and dozens of other woodcarvers that I hired and we put together an online business selling our door tattoos."

"I hear you." Damien gulped between breaths. He was sitting on a recliner chair that had a floral design of pink, blue and green on it. He picked up a black pen that was on a small, round mahogany table by the telephone and dropped it on the floor because he felt fidgety. He bent over in his seat to get it. "Go on."

"Please, Damien. Don't tell the investors that I kidnapped you in the past. Please my boy. The last thing I want is for them to find out."

"Gee. I guess it really is important to you. Just don't kidnap me again."

"I won't. Each woodcarving tattoo is going for one thousand dollars because we think it will be one of those ideas that spark people to want to buy them."

"Uh-huh."

"Oh, if you only knew how I have been doing lately since I started the business with Lenny. The basement apartment is going to be filled with boxes of door tattoos from all the people that were hired to make them by the investors."

"Geez." Damien covered his eyes with his hand in response to hearing Griffin talking to him.

"Do you mean to say that the same place where I was kidnapped will now be filled with boxes of woodcarvings just waiting to be shipped to customers? And are you sure I won't be kidnapped again?"

"I won't kidnap you again. Got it?"

"Yes, okay then. That's a relief."

"I hope the rest of your group won't tell the investors either."

"I will mention to them not to tell then. Was that everything you wanted to discuss?"

"Yep."

"Happy woodcarving then. Bye. I gotta go."

"Have one splendid evening."

"Yes. See ya." Damien hung up the phone as soon as he said it. He felt uneasy about staying on the telephone with the same person who had kidnapped him. Only a matter of days had since passed by from when that had taken place and Damien wanted to focus on something else other than being reminded that he was held captive.

Griffin still listened on the line after Damien was through talking and whispered silently to himself, "Bye, my boy."

* * *

At seven forty-five pm, a man parked a red delivery truck by the curb outside Hazel and Cora Pepper's house. The truck contained one of the first Catchy Petunia robots from Neat Street Robots. It was packaged nicely in a metallic grey mesh fabric with a yellow ribbon tied around its midsection and neckline. Along with it was a gorgeous bow to finish the glamorously giftwrapped item. The man went around to the back of the truck and slid the fifty pound present off the truck and into his arms when he noticed not one but two cars in the driveway which meant someone was home. He carried the life-size, six-foot robot to the door and hoped it was Cora he would be speaking to upon delivery of the package.

Cora was sitting in her favourite black leather easy chair at home doing some channel surfing when the doorbell rang. She got up to answer the door and saw a man holding out a six-foot giftwrapped package and she knew what it was right away. There it was right in front of her. Cora was filled with elation because it was manufactured by the crew at Neat Street Robots only very recently. Cora invited the man into her house and he set the packaged robot down in the hallway by the door. He watched her happily unwrap her present from Neat Street Robots and after she did so, she held her hand up to her mouth and couldn't help but gasp. "Oh my gosh. Mom, come and see this."

"It's one of the first Catchy Petunia robots sent to you via Neat Street Robots I'm proud to say." The man said. There was a certain sound of vim and vigor to his voice. He was wearing a pair of circular glasses, a light grey suit, a black shirt, a white tie and black shoes.

"I'm going to see what he sounds like." Cora found five buttons on each shoulder to press to hear the words of inspiration he might soon be saying.

She pressed the first one. *"Take it to the Max, Robot. Neat Street Robots."* Followed by the second. *"Life, live it. Take it to the Max. When you are making good traction you are taking good action. My name is Catchy Petunia."* And the third. *"The fun has begun."* The fourth. *"Zim Zim. Look, I'm gleaming. Does my appearance look unusual to you? Look at you. You look radiant."* Then the fifth. *"I can tell by the way that you look at yourself that you are a stargazer. Stargazer."* Over on the other shoulder to the sixth button. *"Nature. It is a breath of fresh air."* The seventh. *"Have you guessed by now that I like to be able to talk to you? I'm listening. Always listening."* The eighth. *"Robots are the face of technology."* The ninth. *"It's all so dramatic. I have been shaped by humans and now I'm helping you to get it going on. You may be just filled with excitement to hear me say what I'm saying."* And finally the tenth. *"If I do say so myself, certain qualities about you have not gone unnoticed dear stargazer. Remember though, I'm different than you and you're different than me and it all makes it that much easier to learn how to be. We're talking stellar proportions here."*

"Awesome-o." Cora smiled a smile so perfect that the professional photographer Rita Young would have taken a great picture by the look of astonishment that was on her face.

"Isn't it though?" The man with the circular glasses said.

"He sounds like a gentle man. The guy that is the voice for Catchy Petunia."

"Indeed. I think so too. Here comes your Mom now."

Hazel Pepper walked by and took one look at the robot and said, "My… my…my."

"Did you hear him?" Cora asked with a wrinkled forehead, not sure what her mother was about to say.

"Yes, where are you going to keep him?" Hazel quizzed.

"Where else but in the living room beside the little curio cabinet in the corner?" Cora put her hands together. "I've got to hand it to you Mom, they sure make them well." Miss Pepper looked at the delivery man. "Are the other robots that they made so far similar to this robot too?"

"They are. You're going to prize him. I mean, he's your invention. Hey, I have a letter for you too."

"A letter? You mean the second letter from the company?"

"That's what this is." He passed the letter to her from out of his suit coat pocket. The letter was addressed to her from the company she founded. Neat Street Robots.

"I've got to read that." She opened the envelope and held the letter out so she could see the words clearly.

Dear Miss Cora Pepper;

The launch of the Catchy Petunia robots has so far proven to be a success. The building of the prototype robot is ongoing which means the new type of robot will hopefully hit the market within days. You will be happy to hear that Neat Street Robots has a Chief Executive Officer named Jett Black. A quick-witted kind of guy who has helped us focus on our work in order to get the robots built efficiently and in our efforts to begin selling them at the Neat Street Robots store that is already open. There was a minor setback regarding one detail at the factory. One or more factory worker(s) decided to spray paint the following on the upper right arm of each robot built. *The factory workers were here. Cora, are you shocked and amused?* While that may be so, we have allowed the words to continue to be spray painted on each robot as long as work will indeed speed along in a productive way. Perhaps some feedback from customers will give us the solution as to whether the spray painted words should be kept on the robots upon making our greatly anticipated Catchy Petunia sales.

Please feel free to contact Neat Street Robots CEO Jett Black at any time.

Kind Regards,
Donna Koji
Neat Street Robots Sales Manager

Cora had to see for herself just what the spray painted words looked like. "The words that the factory workers spray painted on the robot are still readable."

"Yes, I heard about what has been happening in regards to that. On one hand it may affect sales and on the other hand the idea may just jazz up the appeal of the prototype robot."

The six-foot tall robot was lime green, black and light grey in color. He had short black hair with finely trimmed bangs along his forehead and green streaks throughout the hairdo to give some contrast to his almost human-like look, green eyes, a grey face including a nose, two ears, and a mouth that were also grey. He had a grey neck, two shoulders and a midsection that were green which appeared as though he wore a short sleeved shirt. Grey arms and hands, green legs down to just past the knees that appeared to be a pair of knee length shorts. Grey legs that ran below the knees, and black sandals with green laces that hid his grey feet and most of his toes. He was standing on a wide, black, three-foot wide platform that displayed him in an upright manner that was his own kind of flooring to stand on containing a foot-wide grey border around it. There on the black platform was a small sized company logo of a vertical black and white oval shape surrounding the words Neat Street Robots that were finely arranged in a circle and designed with sharp pointed edges on the capital letters to give a futuristic appearance. The logo suited the company and when Miss Pepper saw it she felt the ambition to start designing an entirely new kind of robot from the one she was seeing. A female robot. Being part of team ON-ST certainly had its benefits. She guessed that her team was so focused on selling the new and fantastic male Catchy Petunia robots, they hadn't yet mentioned to her anything about another robot design. Or even a female robot. After all, the company was a company that would specialize in selling robots to the public. But if Cora sat and thought up the details of the second line of robots before the rest of her team mentioned anything about it to her, she first had to think of the name for it.

"I'm pleased with how it turned out. Thank you for delivering the robot to me."

He gave her a wink followed by a friendly nod. "You're welcome. Sure, nothing like delivering a talking robot to someone who helped to get it all going. Whatever you're doing to make things better, keep doing it. That's my motto."

"That's assuring. I mean, ah, nice motto."

"Gotta go. Maybe someday we will have robots that are in fact able to learn from us."

"Maybe."

"One thing is for sure, you've got a taste for robots. It's been cool meeting you."

"Same here."

And with that, he headed out the door to the red delivery truck. He revved the engine and set out for his drive back to the Neat Street Robots company parking lot where he would be calling it a day. His work was done for the evening. He turned on some rock and roll tunes during the drive home but nothing rang so clear to him as the words that she had said to him. "Thank you for delivering the robot to me." It made his day mean all that much more to him. He had only heard of Cora before. Now he had been given the opportunity to meet her. And he especially liked how he had been carefully selected from a number of staff to deliver the one prototype of robot that he hoped everyone would soon be talking about. It had already hit the media. 'This is shaping out to be one good company to work for.' He thought. 'Neat Street Robots is sure to be a success, isn't it? After what I've seen, it could very possibly be anyway.'

CHAPTER 12

Thursday, June 23, 2011

'That Cora is driving me crazy. Gee, like it hadn't already occurred to me that robots may one day learn from us. I liked finding that out from her but of course I'm aware of that. I mean we have to start somewhere and that is why I'm interested in working on this television commercial for her. To advertise for her company. I will make an advertisement about Catchy Petunia that she alone would go for. So that people can envision robots being an inspiration to us. That's my goal as far as I'm concerned.' Vic Nicolos thought to himself how to put it in writing. 'I could secretly write out a commercial for Cora. I'll go from there. I have to make the commercial so that it will be out of the norm and I have to fit it all in a span of thirty seconds at the most.'

Vic began by doing some scribbles to let out his frustrations. After that his ideas began to pour. He wrote the following down on paper.

Maybe someday humans and robots will go far together. Who knows? I would like to see Catchy Petunia going for a shopping trip to a high-end mall with a lady he lives with, a person he has come to know as a friend. Catchy Petunia will not only be walking and talking with the lady but will be deciding a thing or two about humans.

Vic had heard through the grapevine that Cullen had been keeping his writing project a secret until the time it would be all done up. He not only heard that but he also received some news that Cullen was not behaving like his usual self lately. There was a noticeable change in his personality that Vic found so bizarre it kept him on high alert towards Mr. Cullen Dangsi for one reason. He was acting so serious. It's no wonder the neighbours were talking to each other about him. Rain had said not to worry and that he's just been finding out what being totally motivated can do to a person. But motivation can take a person only so far, it's also the contents of what they're achieving that can take it further. Only Cullen knew about the contents of his project. The real question for Vic wasn't how often he had been writing but more like discovering what had he been writing in the first place.

Vic spent his day off work grinding away at his ideas until they began to take on a completely new meaning. The flow of words in the commercial was going in the direction that Vic thought it should and the scene was right. After four hours of writing and doodling pictures of the lady and the yet to be seen Catchy Petunia, Mr. Nicolos took a rest from his work on the half a minute long television commercial and read over what he had been writing all afternoon.

Shawnee Leeta and her robot Catchy Petunia had just arrived in a department store when Catchy said, "The sun is bright today. I can't imagine a world without robots. Can you?"

"No, not without robots like you." The lady laughed as she found what the robot said to be funny.

"How far can you make your credit card budget stretch this month, Shawnee?"

"Why do you ask?"

"Because I'm all for exploring the city in your car right there alongside you while we talk together until I'm left to say this. Take it away, Shawnee. I'm ready for what's next."

"Oh my goodness." The twenty-eight year old Miss Shawnee Leeta said, as she reached for a bottle of sunblock lotion sitting on the shelf in front of her. She wanted to keep the sunburns away while she was out in the sunlight.

"Oh my intellect." Catchy Petunia answered her with a degree of emotion to his voice.

"Keep it real." Shawnee assured the robot.

"It's easy if you try." Catchy clapped his metallic hands.

It was brilliance. Pure brilliance. Vic saw that the lady and the robot had a close friendship that indicated they were ready to get more acquainted with each other. Just what they would be later discussing, no one knew. But one thing was for sure. Shawnee and Catchy were on to something. And that meant, quite literally, that there was room for Shawnee to practice being the ideal philosopher and for Catchy to be the ideal student.

If made into a television commercial, it would appear to be a simple scene from a day in the life of one human and one robot in the not too distant future when both humans and robots alike learned from one another. It hit home for Vic. He had a feeling that Cora might go for it and mention it to team ON-ST. There was a chance it could be made into a commercial. Vic had to find out for sure. He had to show Cora what he had written. So that she could decide for herself if it was a good television commercial idea. And take it from there.

* * *

Edmond Keenan waited on a young family at a table for four. They each were in the process of ordering potato salad, steamed baby carrots, a whole wheat bun and a spicy peppered steak drenched in the house's secret recipe barbeque sauce. A sauce that perfectly suited the sirloin cut of meat. The young couple and two kids picked the menu item called Sizzling Summer Steak from their menus that they had been holding in front of themselves and reading for a while shortly after arriving. They ordered their supper plates and sat looking around as Edmond poured four glasses of water from a cooled pitcher of iced water. Some of the ice cubes in the pitcher tumbled into their drinking glasses and Edmond was careful not to spill any water in front of them as they reached for their drinks. He was getting a bit more experienced at his job after being a waiter for an hour or so. It was pretty busy and the chefs were cooking up a storm but Edmond kept his cool by serving one customer at a time.

"We can't decide whether to have peppered salt or salted pepper on our steaks, isn't that right kids?"

"That's funny alright. Good one." Edmond chuckled.

"Dad, I want what the cook thinks is right to have on our meat."

"Okay. Can you fill our glasses again in a few minutes?" The man said, sitting back in his chair in relaxed mode. "Hey, what can I tell ya? I'm a comedian."

"I can do that." Edmond was caught off guard for a second. "A comedian?"

"Sure. Been travelling around from city to city for several weeks and now that summer is here, I'm taking a vacation by staying at home. Get it? I'm on vacation so I'm spending some quality time with the wife and kids here in our hometown."

"Oh. Yes, that's hilarious." Edmond held the pitcher with both hands.

"I kid you not. Combine five words. Look Oh Gosh I Can. And by gosh, you've got five letters. L…O…G…I…C. That spells logic."

One of the kids yawned. "You practice your jokes all the time dad."

"It's what I do."

"Of course dear." The children's mom said. "He's making a living one way at a time. I hope each way makes you laugh."

The handsome Edmond set the pitcher of water down and leaned a little on the table. "I can take those menus for you." After Edmond held all four menus in one hand and picked up the pitcher with the other, he soon walked to the open countertop area where the restaurant chefs were standing nearby. He gave them a note indicating what dishes to prepare.

"What do you think of Fiona's Restaurant?" A fellow waiter asked Edmond.

"The food here is pretty good from what I've heard Blake."

"Isn't it though? And the people you meet here keep coming back. This restaurant has so far been in business for over five years."

"I haven't eaten at Fiona's before but now that I've seen the food they serve, I'm sure to bring some friends and dine out with them sooner or later."

"Glad to hear it."

"There's a real comedian over at one of the tables that I'm looking after. Funny, isn't it?"

"I'd say."

"He's been traveling around a bit but now he's staying in town for a while."

Edmond's co-worker turned to face the three chefs who were in the little kitchen area situated out in the open for anybody to see what is involved in preparing the meals. "It shouldn't be too long before they're done. There's one thing about Fiona's. They always seem to have enough chefs cooking in the kitchen."

Edmond found himself getting used to hearing all the noises of the restaurant and seeing the vibrant color schemes that brought drama to an already happening place. Edmond was realizing how much the welcoming atmosphere of the place had an effect of moving people. There was a dark purple carpet with light blue and yellow squares all throughout it. The walls that surrounded the interior of the restaurant were painted with two distinct colors. Dark blue cobalt and medium purple violet. The mural-like art on the walls gave such an eye catching edge it was as though they made up a vivid tapestry. There were sketched outlines of people all enjoying themselves. It was surreal.

Soon Edmond carried two full plates of food to the family of four. The fresh faced young man then carried the other two supper plates following them. To him the meals he had in front of him looked so delicious he reasoned that he should always go to work with a full belly or else spend long hours running on empty while serving savory plates of food that only a high quality western style restaurant such as Fiona's could produce. He also reasoned that packing a lunch would be well worth it, all things considered.

At the end of the day, Edmond made a good amount of money from tips in addition to his hourly wage. He went home and called a couple of his friends to let them know what a good job he did on his first day of work at Fiona's Restaurant. After the phone conversations, Edmond decided to buy a desktop computer with the money he would be making from his new job at the restaurant. Then he would go online where a good source of information would be readily available to him. He had a hunger for knowledge.

CHAPTER 13

Sunday, July 17, 2011

Rita strolled around her yard and listened to the trees blowing ever so slightly in the wind around her. She heard someone coughing repeatedly from somewhere close by but didn't look to see where the coughing was coming from. The wind current picked up and it caught her attention as she found the sudden pick up in speed of the long drawn out gust of wind reminded her of Cally's band Wind Spontaneous. The change in the wind's direction made her heart pound for a few beats as she realized with a renewed ambition all her own that she had been feeling jealousy toward Rain Woodrow for months. The jealousy was becoming more and more apparent to her as she listened to the air flowing by her. It was only now that she decided to let any harsh feelings subside long enough to go talk to Rain. She had to so that she could vent her frustrations to her. Or at least hint of them. She was determined to go over to Rain's house if she happened to be home but as the wind died down the coughing persisted. Someone was coughing repeatedly somewhere nearby the right side of her house. It was Rain. Rita spotted her standing around the flowers in her garden and assumed that Rain had breathed in some dust from the air current moving overhead. The perfect opportunity to talk to Rain had presented itself to her and she responded by quickly stepping over her own lawn that was yellowish-brown in some parts over to Rain's green grass to say hello.

"Hi Rain. How have you been lately?" Rita Young inquired.

"I'm good. And how may I say are you?" Miss Woodrow questioned.

"Good. I heard you coughing. Are you okay?" Rita paused for a moment.

"It's just my allergies. When I go outside and there's any wind at all, I end up with a cough and a runny nose. But that's fine. Oh, guess what? I've finished writing the mini-book." Rain coughed some more.

"Have you? Did you send it off to get published?"

"Yes. Someone should be notifying me pretty soon."

"That's great. I'll have to read it sometime soon."

"Yes, please do."

"Like soon soon."

"Okay, I'll let you read a copy of it in a few minutes."

"Yeeha. Looking forward to it." Rita noticed Rain had been weeding her garden. Loose weeds were strewn about on top of the grass in piles. The flowers were in full view. When Rita saw the work that her neighbour had done on the garden there in the front yard where they were, it wasn't long before she asked, "What have you got there? What kind of flowers are those?"

"Delphiniums." Rain pointed. "I'm growing some yellow and white delphiniums." She was standing beside Rain and peering at her flower garden that ran the length of the driveway.

"Yeah?"

"As in sunshine and clouds, Rita."

"That's nice." Rita cleared her throat. "I have to admit. I wouldn't have thought of that one myself. Guess it goes with having the name Rain."

"Funny. My mom named me that because she was aware that water is important to have, just as a daughter such as myself is also important."

"That's pretty clever." Rita was listening intently.

"That's right."

"You remind me of my aunt. She cooks up a storm on the barbeque in the summer. Shish kabobs, chicken burgers, stuffed peppers, corn cobs, you name it. After it's all cooked she says, "The hurricane has ended. It's time to dine sunshines."

"She says that, huh?"

"And now's the time to gather 'round. She says that too."

"Where does she live?"

"In a house not far from here."

"Sounds like she's happy to entertain."

"She is." Rita laughed as she thought of the barbeques. "She's good at entertaining her guests. Anyhow. To change the subject, I'm still getting up early each morning for more sunrise photographs."

"How many sunrises have you photographed lately?"

"About ten. I have it on digital camera. Sometimes I go for an early morning drive to places up on a hill where I can see for miles. That's how to get the best photos."

"Gee." Rain replied. "Hear that beeping sound from a truck? It's the construction crew working away on the houses they are building over on the next street."

"I haven't seen what the houses look like so far. I keep forgetting to look at them."

"Oh, I have. The other day I went on a walk with Cullen and we saw the framework going up on several of them. They're putting the roofs up on a few of the houses." Rain listened. "That's the sound of the roofing nails being nailed in."

"I can hear it."

"Do you want a drink Rita? We can talk some more about it over a glass of lemonade, pink lemonade actually. You can come in and I will read my book to you."

"That would be fun."

"Okay."

"My boyfriend has been on a writing frenzy lately. You probably have heard."

"Yes, I've heard. But in the process you're discovering that there is more to this guy than you thought, right? I mean, this guy has been at a steady pace for weeks now hasn't he?"

"Yes he has."

"I have a crush on him. I mean the guy goes from being the jokester who really knows how to cheer people up with his jokes to someone that is now so serious and getting lots of work done. It makes me wonder what he is going to do next. Maybe he will put the effort into writing joke books so that people all over the place can read lots of his funny jokes. I'm so attracted to Cullen. Is he home?" Rita paused, unsure of whether or not she would see Cullen in the middle of his writing frenzy. She wondered if she might find herself watching him with his hair all messed up and three days growth of beard stubble still to be shaved as he searched for some mouthwash to disguise his morning breath before he would be sitting down to talk to her and Rain.

"He's shopping." Rain looked at Rita. "I didn't think that you had a crush on my boyfriend."

"Well, I'm certainly fond of the guy. You picked a good one my dear."

"Let's go in the house."

Minutes passed by and once the two ladies were settled on the couch with their pink lemonades in their hands, Cullen arrived home with some grocery bags at the door. He set them down and when he came into the house he heard and Rain and Rita's voices right away. Cullen caught the two ladies in the middle of their chat.

"I have a new card for the card store." Rain had already picked it off the coffee table in the living room and held it up close so that she could read it. "It has a space theme."

"Space eh?"

"Yep."

"It's a card I'm going to put on display in one of the birthday card sections called 'Friend.'

Here it is.

Happy Birthday

I hope that the stars and moon in space
Work their magic to put a smile on your face
With knowledge that there is always something new
        to be
By looking up and seeing the grand scheme of things
That exists between you and me."

"Nifty." Cullen sighed. "Hi Rita."

"Hi sexy. How is it going?"

"It's going good." Cullen scratched his head for a moment. "Sexy?"

"I have a crush on you. I was just telling Rain about you."

"Oh you were, were you?" Cullen folded his arms. His face was turning red. A few seconds went by and he continued on with what he was saying. "Anyway, Rain is going to read the mini-book to me that she wrote. Would you like to hear it being read?"

"Yes. She was just telling me that she would read a copy of it to me. This should be fun."

"Oh, you've got that right. Wait until you find out what I've been writing." Cullen hurried upstairs to get his printed pages of the mini-book he was keeping in the computer room. Rita took a few sips from her glass of pink lemonade as he came down the stairs again shortly afterwards.

"Alright. Here it is." He said.

"I'm going to read my mini-book first and then you can read your mini-book. Okay Cullen?"

She cleared her throat. He nodded and Rain proceeded to read it for them.

"A mini-book about the great and tall rainforest.
By Rain Woodrow

Let the Sun shine forth and the rain tickle. The tall trees climb and the dewdrops trickle. The green grass grow and the flowers bloom. As we continue to give the rainforest more room. The rainforest. It is alive. Yes, the rainforest is a natural living rainforest. What is more, it produces oxygen. You got it, the air we breathe. The trees in the rainforest are so large that they alone make up a very big amount of the clean air supply in the world. It has taken many years for them to get to the point of filtering out high volumes of carbon dioxide and releasing a plentiful amount of fresh, clean oxygen for us all to breathe. We can certainly breathe easier as long as this is happening.

Only recently have people been cutting down the giant rainforest trees to make space available for farming. We have often heard about the burning of the trees that sometimes goes on. That is bad news. The good news is the current generations of people alive on the planet now can be the ones to help put a stop to that from occurring any longer by turning things in a positive direction. We should work together to do our part in ensuring that the rainforest stays intact for not only humanity but all life on the planet.

One way we can do that is by building centres of employment nearby the rainforest where the farmers live so they have a source of income by hand-crafting items with a theme relating to the rainforest. They could range anywhere from simple watercolor paintings to clothing that contain a company name sewn on them. The company where they would be working at could ship the products around the world internationally for purchase and the communities of people living near the rainforest, including the farmers, would have more than adequate funds coming in for a good living.

And hopefully this should put a stop to the harming of the rainforest. We could be helping it to grow instead.

We're right on topic here. Think ever so green. These rainforest items ranging from paintings to clothing with a special company name displayed on them would soon be part of the latest trends of their kind. Trends well worth keeping up to date and noticed by many. With designs so eye catching that people would be coming back for more and ordering for friends, family, and the list goes on.

At the company, there may very well possibly be piles of stock up for sale every day and even though the company workers located nearby the rainforest may be doing what is out of the ordinary, it might come naturally to them because it will be all about something that is local and familiar to them and part of their surroundings. That's right, we're talking about the oxygen producing rainforest that they have already come to know. Yet people may come from miles around to meet the workers as more people help to put new products on the market. Getting new ones out is important to put more in stock when the international orders are being placed from across the world. Whole communities could start developing little by little. And that is what we would be pleased to see, isn't it? Think ever so green again.

Recognize we are reaching for it. That is the roadmap plan for action we can use as we go about the business for keeping the rainforest intact. To me it can start in South America at the Amazon rainforest and as business grows we could work on the other rainforests across the world. It can also start as the funds begin coming in from any sales that are made by the centres of employment. Of course it can start as a plan is made to carry out a successful business. Fine Point Rainforest Incorporated is the name of the business and at the time of this writing I can tell you that I will be making sure there are generous proceeds from the sales of copies of this mini- book going towards developing it. I know it's quite a plan. But it's one that is very real and easy to work on if we take one step after another. My hope is that it will be just the answer we've been waiting for. If we do what we can it will be a successful endeavor. All made possible so that we can keep breathing clean, crisp air for years to come.

The great and tall rainforest stretches across the planet and in some countries it reaches for many miles and you can especially find yourself starting to wonder how the fine balance of nature will respond by having room to grow and flourish. Along with helping creatures such as the sloth, gorilla, jaguar and anteater to name just a few examples of the creatures inhabiting the rainforest, the reasons to stop people from cutting the huge trees down is of course endless. The beauty of nature surrounds us. If we can spend time with nature around us and breathe a lot easier with fresh, clean rainforest filtered air, it can be even more beautiful still.

Think of how peaceful and serene it can be to hear the birds singing away high in the treetops after a shower of rain. And as we listen, may we hear the sounds of nature play out with a renewed sense of peace as we discover firsthand how refreshing it can be to watch the birds enjoying the shelter of the great and tall trees. Some of the trees are really high up there at the rainforest canopy with their branches and leaves reaching many metres toward the clouds. They are ready to absorb rain and sunlight and, all the while, are continually cleansing the world's air supply. So let's do what we can to help them. We will be helping ourselves in the process.

The rain streams across the rainforest. It is there where the waterfalls are some of the beautiful scenery and the medicines are thankfully ever so green. The trees, oh how they grow. And the animals are all about. Their calls echo into the distance. The sounds of the rainforest include showers and birds singing for hours. The sights of the rainforest include vines that are climbing and trees so ancient you will be chiming. Think of it today. Think of it tomorrow. It will definitely get you thinking. As you learn more about it, you will know about its flora and fauna, or more simply, plants and animals.

Think rainforest.

Soil + Trees + Animals + Rain = STAR
Kindness + Enriched + Earth + People = KEEP
Oxygen + New = ON

Society + May + Invest + Like + Ivy + Near +
    Ground = SMILING.
Limbs + Air + U + Grow + Happy = LAUGH.

Are you smiling yet? How about laughing?

I hope this mini-book has been a fun and informative read for you. Just think of all the people that would benefit by you simply reading this mini-book and then buying one or perhaps two of the products up for sale at the first Fine Point Rainforest Inc. employment centre once it is built and established and the local farmers living nearby there begin making the products. Fine Point Rainforest Incorporated. It is sure to please. Look for the company website in the near future. Nature in all its glory includes a rainforest left undisturbed and left to grow and flourish in order to enhance the present time into being naturally a wonder to the world."

"That is outstanding. What a lovely story." Rita was all smiles.

"Yeah, it's something special. And to top it off, it's written by someone named Rain Woodrow. Great." Cullen gave Rita and Rain each a high five.

"It's quite something, isn't it?" Rain said.

"Yes it is." Cullen said. "It sure is, naturally."

"What are you going to do once they put your book up for sale? You've got a lot of work to do." Cullen asked.

"We'll see. That is if they do sell my mini-book."

"They will. I just know it." Cullen winked. "What say you hear my mini-book now? I'll read it to you. Okay?"

"Please do." Rita went on. "I want to hear your story."

"It's actually Isaiek Sheer's story. Here goes." Cullen lifted his typed pages closer so he could see the words.

"The Twenty-Fifth Year With Isaiek Sheer
By Cullen Dangsi

I can remember the day it all happened. Early one morning on January 25 of this year I was celebrating my 25th birthday with a morning cup of green tea. To my surprise, a mysterious man named Mr. Ten and I had been sending letters to each other every few minutes through the use of my own mailbox outside the door of my house. Mr. Ten explained that superpowers were being given to me and he brought to my attention how to charge these superpowers up. I soon found myself saying aloud before bed eight days in a row the following words, TED = Time, Experience and Determination. And I would be doing so each month, unless I forgot to say the words and then I would have to wait until the next month.

That was nine months ago. So much has happened since then. At the Glass, Metal and Wood shop, the place where I work, the customers keep on buying specially created items such as glass pendants, iron artwork, and wooden designs and noticing my bizarre looking hair done up with fresh, new colors daily. They seem to get just as much enjoyment out of seeing me from one day to the next as they do shopping in the store. Not only that, but the three craftsmen that I hired to make the various works of art are very inspired now to make never before seen new touches to their creations by combining their talents to make for some pretty nice items that have all three materials of glass, iron metal and wood in them. They just know I'm onto something here with my change in appearance and behaviour at work. I'm fond of how they spend time working alongside each other for hours when they are making more of the creations that people love. They can find it rewarding and can share in the excitement when their stuff is on display in my shop. By producing these items with their own talented workmanship using excellent choices of materials, they keep improving their artwork skills as they do so.

I haven't told a single person about me being a superhero. Only a few people have heard that my superpowers are to color my hair the most spectacular colors by merely imagining what colors I would like my hair to be. After saying those special words I already mentioned to you, of course.

Don't mind me I'm just sporting a new style. It's really me too. Yes it is. And it's shaping out to be another one of those things that draw the curiosity of people that I talk to. It's no laughing matter. Simply put, I'm tapping into something here. Thanks to Mr. Alazanar Ten. And it has left me feeling a bit unusual at times. At least that's how I feel when people look at me in a funny way but then that's bound to happen sometimes. Especially when I'm away from the shop and people ask me where I got my hair done. I did it myself, I say. That's for sure. I won't go into any details but I did it myself. What is more worthwhile to mention than the fact that it is supernatural? Yes it is. I know that to be true. I'll keep that to myself though.

This letter is going to be given to Mr. Ten so he can plaster it against a brick interior wall of someone's secluded place in a building somewhere. Even I don't know exactly where. At any rate, they will have heard my story soon enough. So I say, hello to you.

Mr. Ten hasn't told me about any other superheroes yet other than himself. What he did tell me about himself was that he is going to live to a ripe old age of one-hundred and fifty as unusual as that may sound to you. Yes, it seems Mr. Ten has a superpower after all. He happened to tell me a couple of months after we met. From what I gather, he has an amazing tendency to talk with an Asian accent, to look at me sometimes while holding his glasses in his hands and saying, "Yes, yes."; to sweep back his fairly short black windswept hair with a comb on occasion and to reach an arm up to me and pat me on the shoulder when the timing is right. Perhaps he does it partly because I have sudden outbursts of laughter for such the slightest reasons in front of him. Maybe because I dress with a sweater on warm days and just a shirt on cold days and he's the reverse opposite.

Often he says to me, "You've got to dress with the weather my North American friend." And I respond by saying, "That's right, Alazaner. But it's sometimes hard to keep track of the temperature."

Mr. Ten is the owner of a grape vineyard in France. His sister lives there and uses the grapevines to create all kinds of dried grapevine wreaths. He gets half the profits that she earns for merely letting her have access to the vineyard. Vines among us. That is the name of the business she operates online. So Mr. Ten has plenty of time to spend roaming about with me being his casual self, as he calls it.

Where I live is in the city of Edmonton, Alberta. I'm a Canadian. Between talking to my friends who are the woodworker and glass blower and metal finisher while exchanging ideas or cozying up for some drinks of herbal tea with them and Mr. Ten and listening to some music, there is a lot to do on any given day. I like to relax and think.

When I'm out and about I'm starting to see a few of the glass pendants that I sold through my shop being worn by people passing by my workplace. They come into the store to see me again and to say hello and to tell me that when they wear their necklaces, they often remember who they bought them from. I think they look flashy themselves and that's extraordinary itself. Such is life.

I'm one dynamo of a worker for a shop. A little girl who comes to visit me at work every now and then can vouch for that being so. She admires the range of pendants on display under glass and says her classroom at school is always abuzz with the latest on the photographs she brings of my splendid hairstyles. She is only twelve years old but already she adores taking the paintbrush to long pieces of string going every which way that are painted a variety of colors and then pressed against her canvasses. She says pictures of space give her the inspiration to create them. She is getting so good at making them I'm sure it won't be long before she will start saving for an RRSP and then later collect the compound interest even at a young age too. Thanks to my advice to her on the matter. She calls her pieces of art Bazundoos. I think of her as the kind of kid who sets some time of her own to make her mark if you get my drift. Her name is Alexis. Maybe one day Alexis' fine detailed works of art will go very far. That would be out of the norm for her as far as I'm concerned.

Let's take it from there and remember to live our daily lives in extraordinary ways so we may find tomorrow to bring with it new profound examples for us each to live by. With a combination of chance and positive results we will one day look ahead at ourselves and smile.

Isaiek Sheer, a.k.a. Straight Eights the Superhero."

"Oh my God. I like it. Do you like Cullen's mini-book Rain?"

"Do I? Why it's just the story my rascal Cullen would come up with after working on it secretly for so long like he did. I sure do like it."

"Hey, why don't you each go get your mini-books published now that you are done working on them?" Rita asked boldly. "You two really have something here."

"We already have sent them in earlier today."

"Well I'm glad to hear it because what you've got there is special. If you get my drift."

"Oh, we get it. Point taken. I have to get my message across so that we can take care of the world's rainforests."

Rita yawned and tapped her fingers to her mouth and noticed that after doing so, Rain was caught off guard. Rain was about to say something. She began, "Gee…"

Rita couldn't help being a little embarrassed as she sat in front of her. So she burst out with saying, "Excuse me." Rita declared. "Looks like I could use a good nap."

"A nap?" Rain shrugged her shoulders.

Rita didn't want to tell Rain she was envious of her. Rita knew she still had to look after herself and attend to her own goals. And it was especially being made clear to her now that it appeared Rain and Cullen had come so close to accomplishing theirs already. She had yet to strive towards any new goals to the likes that the rest of the neighbours were reaching. She had procrastinated. Even though that may be the case, Rita was aware the rainforest mini-book was part of the process of taking one more step towards getting a company established in the first place. But after hearing Rain read the words to her, it was apparent that there would be a brighter future for the planet if the rainforests were looked after by humans. At least that was the way that the mini-book had outlined it.

"You have the solution. Plain and simple." Rita stretched out her arms and rolled back in her seat. "Excuse me again. I'm sore from taking those photographs at work lately."

"I'm glad you think so. We're all part of the solution if we want to be."

"Wow. Sven would be jealous. That's a wisdom quote right there."

"I'd say." Cullen blurted out loud.

Rita had to say it. "Why don't you contact them and ask them to put that at the end of your mini-book?"

"It's going to be a pocketbook." Miss Woodrow said.

"Suddenly you're calling it a pocketbook?" She answered.

"It was going to be a pocketbook all along."

"Aha." Rita gulped.

Cullen bit one of his nails, "My mini-book is going to be mini-sized. As soon as it's up for sale and in bookstores. Isn't that right, Rainy?" He sat quietly and seemed to be waiting for some kind of response from his girlfriend.

"Sure, sure." She said.

"It's Sunshine not Rainy."

"Sunshine? It is?"

"Yeah. It is."

"C'mon guys. Just call me Rain okay?"

"Okay." Her boyfriend answered.

"You got it." Rita spoke outright.

"Alright. I'll go email them again and ask them to put that at the end of the book like you suggested." Rain looked at Rita.

Rita acknowledged Rain by giving her a quick nod. "Now we're talking."

"They're sure to like it." Rain went on.

"So…what do you think Akira has been up to lately anyway?" Rita mentioned.

"I don't know. He's so quiet. I guess he has probably been busy with both of his jobs and enjoying the fact that he is a bachelor. That's Brooke for you."

Rain paused and finally gave an answer. "Everyone on the street is supposed to be working on their goals though. Big or small. Who can tell with Akira. Maybe he's developing a new series of automobile designs at work. I'd only be guessing. There is only one way to find out. And that is by asking."

Cullen was caught by surprise and he went ahead by saying, "We've got to ask him. Let's write him a letter and put it into his mailbox."

Rain burst out laughing at Cullen's remark. "Nah, I'll phone him instead."

"Better yet, I'll go visit him. He's home. I would like to say more to you guys about my book about Isaiek Sheer but I think that going on a walk instead would be a good idea. But first, seeing Akira and discussing some details about stuff that he's been up to lately is what I'm keen on doing. Yes, I'll have a nice little visit at Akira's house. If he's home that is."

"Okay then." Rita said with a bit of pep.

"Bye darling." Rain waved as Cullen stepped toward the door.

Soon Cullen was out the door and on the way to his neighbour's house but the closer he got to Akira's house the more he thought about the possibility of Cally being nearby. After all, his car was in his parents' driveway. When he reached Akira's yard across the street from where Cally's car was located something unexpected happened. Suddenly from out of nowhere, Cally ran toward Cullen and gripped him by his shirt collar firmly and held it with a good grip. Cullen's voice trembled, "Let me go."

"I won't, not until you tell me what you're up to mister."

"Okay, okay. I've written a superhero mini-book."

"Tell me more."

"It's a short letter describing stuff about what goes on in the life of Isaiek Sheer. A guy that can change his hair color by thinking of whatever colors he imagines and then his hair will be those colors."

"What the heck? Is that it?"

Cullen gulped. "Yeah."

"I'll show you what a superhero can do." Cally lifted Cullen up off the ground by the strength in his arms while holding him upright and clinging to his sides. Cally gritted his teeth and snarled in anger at Cullen. "You're going to answer me when I ask you something. Here it is." Cally had slowly been moving him across the yard toward Akira's place as soon as he lifted him a foot up in the air. He now had him propped up against the side of Akira's house and had placed him on the ground again. "Who is that guy that I saw walking through my parents' yard today? I confronted him and he said that he knows you Cullen."

"Oh, that guy. He looks pretty suspicious doesn't he? Walking around like that. He told me he is keeping an eye on the neighbourhood. I can't figure out why."

"Yeah, but who is he?"

"Just some guy sneaking around I figure."

"Just a second." Still gripping onto Cullen, Cally took a handful of green grass off of Akira's lawn and put it on Cullen's head. "Now you have green hair. How's that?"

"I don't know what you're talking about. Now please let me go." At that second, Cally loosened his grip on Cullen and let him go. 'Jeez. I'm getting out of here.' Cullen thought to himself and approached Akira's front door and rang the doorbell a few times. By then, Cally was walking back to his parents' house.

Every second that went by, Cullen felt more and more relieved of danger. And then a moment later Brooke Akira answered the door. Brooke was glad to see Cullen.

"Can I come in?"

"Sure. Hi, how have you been?"

"Good but I have to tell you Brooke, you know Zoey and Ralph Holiday?"

"Yeah."

"Their bad boy son just put a few wrestling moves on me. Freaky stuff, man."

"Don't worry about it."

"That's what Sven says." Cullen straightened his shirt and caught his breath and soon came out with what he had been meaning to say. "I thought I'd visit you and see what is new with you."

"Same ole same ole. Just kidding. Actually I've invented something new. It's what I've called "The sport of goal setting." Cool, isn't it?"

"I guess so. That's nifty."

"Yep. Each person is represented as having a car of the future or a flying car to ride. Instead of looking at the road ahead as you do with the cars of today, you see your life in terms of reaching new heights with the cars of tomorrow."

"Reaching new heights. That's cool. I like the sound of that."

"When you go after your goals, your flying car takes you higher and higher up each time you complete a goal. To new heights."

"Brooke, this adds a whole new dimension to things."

"That's right. Your goals can take you there. The futuristic flying car is the example I use for you to get to where you're going. An example of what you can do." Brooke motioned toward the kitchen where his computer was set up. "C'mon over here and read my new website. You can learn all about it. I'm going to make it available to the public in a matter of days."

"Really cool."

Cullen sat down on a wooden chair beside Brooke's office chair located at the kitchen table on which his desktop computer was set up. It wasn't long before Brooke sat on the office chair beside him and he saw the first webpage. It read; Brooke Akira's fantastic site on the Sport of Goal Setting. See the potential. Goal setting is a sport that brings a greater life picture into perspective for you. When a goal is set – you do what you think you can. When a goal is met – you think about what you do. Goal setting is great because it involves you from the first step of each goal and what you will soon accomplish, to the final step and what you just accomplished. Goal after goal. It is something that can continue to play a part in your life as you complete one goal at a time. Goals can take you in a positive direction. Goals are opportunities that are just waiting for you to take the steps necessary to progress along far enough with them until one day they are met and become reality. I call this meeting your goals. First you've got to write them down. That's the first step on your way to goal setting. By doing the steps that are part of every goal and working on them from day to day, you can begin to achieve results. You will be doing so if you enjoy it. That much is clear to me. Start today by making a goal list of five to ten goals that you would like to achieve. Be specific when you are listing them. For example, Buy a two storey brick house with nice curb appeal before the year 2018 with a one-hundred and seventy thousand dollar mortgage somewhere in the same city as where I currently live.'

Cullen clicked on a button on the screen and went on to read the next webpage. He read on and he felt excited as he discovered how having goals can add more to each day. As he did so, Akira rubbed his hands together feeling good about the information he had put on it. It read, 'Also, telling people what your goals are is a good idea to make them more real to you. And by letting the right people in on what they are, those same people may even help you to achieve them.

Once each one is achieved, you can make new goals to keep reaching new heights. Goal achievement can be represented by picturing your car of the future being there to guide you to your next goal and each one after that too. As you finish each new goal you can be positively uplifted with the help of your car of the future. These futuristic cars are there for you to help you get a better view of where you are going. Each goal is represented by a different color helium filled balloon that you are trying to reach as markers for finishing each goal. They go higher up in the air as you complete each of your goals to give you a good view of how far you are to reach before you get to the next helium filled balloon. They are each tied down by a string and are there for you but still flying high in the air up above. When you reach them you can take the card off it that tells you that you reached your specific goal. You can decide for yourself what ones you may then work on with each new goal that is met or achieved. That is how to play the sport of goal setting.

"This website is amazing."

"I'm putting it in the search engines this week. Hooray."

"Hip hip hooray for Brooke. So that is your goal. Did you think of your next goal yet?"

"That's a very good question. I haven't determined what it will be yet. Let me see. Maybe it will be to start an online mailing list on my website in a few days for people to share their stories of the results they are having."

"Good for you." Cullen shook hands with Brooke. "I invented a character named Isaiek Sheer who can color his hair vivid colors by just imagining it. My girlfriend Rain wrote a few pages about preserving the rainforest. Good stuff."

"Congrats. Onward and upward."

"You and your cars. Vroom."

Brooke laughed a little. "Hey and shoes too, don't forget."

"Oh yes, your other workplace. A shoe store."

"Yes, as it so happens, my days are filled watching people try on new shoes."

"Yup." Cullen rubbed his sides that were still sore from where Cally grabbed him.

"Yet still, I'm bewildered by how many pairs of shoes can be stacked into one shoe store."

"I hear you. Sounds like they should have a big shoe sale."

"That's exactly it." Brooke rubbed his hands together. "Did you hear that Cora's CEO Jett Black is due to arrive early tomorrow morning?"

"What? No, I haven't. That's the first I've heard of it."

"He also goes by the name Midnight."

"Gee. I wonder what new information she will be telling us."

"Yeah. And get this – I'm beginning to find Cora all the more attractive too."

Cullen put his hand over his forehead and felt the wrinkles as he thought about Brooke Akira's surprising comment. "You find her attractive? You and a lady like her? I mean…"

"What? I'm only twenty-four and I found out recently that she's twenty-one."

"But I thought you wanted to stay a bachelor."

"Come on, a girl like her? She's reaching new heights. She even has a robot in her house. From the Neat Street Robots factory. I saw it too."

"When?"

"The other day."

"This comes as a surprise. And you know what? I like surprises. The neighbours are going to talk."

"About what? She put her hand on my shoulder and leaned on me."

"Huh? Was she flirting?"

"Maybe. Or she could have wanted to show me how dreamy this is all starting to be. Her company is selling more of those robots that they have up for sale."

"This all comes as news to me."

"Doesn't it though?"

"Yes."

"She told me my idea of the sport of goal setting is great."

"She did, did she?

"Yes."

They were both silent for a minute. Cullen was closing his eyes and imagining the two of them together. Brooke was staring at the new website he created.

"Oh my God. Do you know what this means?"

"What?"

"You have a lady friend."

Brooke slapped his face to exaggerate and said, "You don't say."

CHAPTER 14

Monday, July 18, 2011

Cora booked off a week from work for some vacation time. It had been only four days since Jett Black, a guy working as Chief Executive Officer for Neat Street Robots, had talked to her over the telephone to set up a specific date to meet with her at a local café in regards to the developing of a new line of robots - Sizel Coolbeans. He wanted to find out for himself what information she had on the new female robot that she would be introducing to the company.

Cora rushed over to Pasa Streenies Café to get there early enough so that she would have enough time to gather her thoughts before Jett arrived to meet her. It wasn't twenty minutes later when he came by to see her and sat down at her table. Jett spotted her right away from the description that she gave him over the telephone regarding what she looked like. She herself was attired in a business suit. She wore a checkered brown and mustard toned jacket buttoned up to the neckline with matching round buttons and identical skirt along with a pair of brown slip-on dress shoes. Even so, the description that he himself gave her proved accurate. He was white but had black hair that looked freshly trimmed short and he had a thin goatee. Wearing a suave and sophisticated black and white suit, Jett Black appeared to be pleased to have a chance to discuss some business with her. Just as she herself had a look of exhilaration on her face when she first saw him. Finally they had encountered one another and their meeting had already begun by the time they both stood together to shake hands before sitting down opposite each other at their table for two.

"Feel free to call me Midnight too. Some folks do."

"I hear you, Midnight."

"I've been meaning to tell you something. You and The Sunlit Avenue Group seem to have the makings of not only goal setters but instead goal inspirers. Do you find that knowledge especially amazing? Because, I find the thought of goal setters that are inspirational so neat-o in fact that I can honestly say...you and The Sunlit Avenue Group are one great team."

"Gee, Midnight, goal inspirers? That's possibly the nicest comment I have heard in a while. You have a way with words." She replied.

"That's true. But I have to tell you, a female robot name Sizel Coolbeans? What will you think of next?"

"I guess I'll just have to wait and see." Cora smiled.

"For a second there I thought you were about to reveal something. Yes, I'll just wait and see." Jett Black winked as he looked into her eyes.

"The Sunlit Avenue Group...I like the sound of that. Maybe we'll call ourselves that from now on."

"Oh, you've got to. Right. Cora, I would also like to be a goal inspirer too."

"Cool".

"Yes it is. And remember Cora, it is way cool."

The waitress was an older woman about fifty years of age with a beige colored uniform on, including white dress shoes. She greeted them. "How are you both? Would you like to have some water before you order?"

"No thank you. I'll just have a glass of iced tea for now. Jett, do you like iced tea?"

"Why yes."

"Their iced teas are pretty good here."

"An iced tea it is then. One for me also." He nodded at the waitress.

"Would you like some menus?" She asked.

"Yes, please." Jett Black answered. The waitress nodded and went to go get their drinks.

By then, Cora went ahead to say, "Wait until you hear about this new prototype robot I came up with. What makes Sizel great is that she can shake your hand and say, "Hello again." She also is pink and black. I was thinking that we could work on gathering more workers for the company in the near future. People that are professional experts with the most up-to-date knowledge at building robots and making them move around, wave and talk. What do you make of it?"

"Oh, that's certainly something we could work on. Finding more experts in the field of robotics. Alright. You want robots waving their hands and saying "Hello again?" For sure. I'll see if we can do that. We at Neat Street Robots might have to put some offers on the table for funding such workers as those but I'll see what we can do. What else were you imagining they might do?"

"How about nodding their heads by the push of a button when we ask if they missed us?"

Cora mentioned.

"Curious. Would they still say a number of inspirational messages? Like Catchy Petunia does?"

"Yes. If possible."

"Okay. I'll see what we can do then. Cora, I have a question for you about Neat Street Robots."

Jett folded his hands together on the table. He paused. He then tapped his fingertips together and it was as though he was getting ready for the right moment to arrive.

"What is it Midnight?" Cora drew a blank for a couple of seconds and then adjusted her posture at the table and all at once she gave the CEO a glance that had a look of alertness so definite that if she were in school she would be graded an A+ for attentiveness.

Jett waited a little while longer and then out it came. "Where do you see the company going in five years and ten years from now?"

"I see people talking about robots as being a major topic of discussion in general. And after enough robots have been purchased by people from Neat Street Robots, by five years from now it will have been thought to be smart to have robots because they spark the imagination in people. And ten years from now they will have made an apparent mark in society that will move people. Many more will be built possibly by then."

"Sounds like you thought that one through already."

"I was ready for that one." Cora eyed the waitress approaching them with their drinks.

Before long, they were sipping on their iced teas that the waitress had brought out to them. That is when Cora ordered a roast beef sandwich and Jett ordered a tomato, lettuce and cheddar vegetarian sandwich.

"It's been a while since I came to this city. I'm glad to have been given the chance to meet with you."

"Same here."

"I bet you're wondering how business is going. Ask me how business is going."

"How is business going?" Cora felt amazed.

"Business is very good, as expected."

"Good to hear it."

"Every robot that comes out of the factory is made with the utmost care and people are dropping into the store and purchasing them. Word of mouth is spreading fast."

"Yeah. That's what I like to hear."

"Great news so far. Have you received your first pay cheque yet?"

"Indeed I have. Which reminds me Midnight, one of the people in the Sunlit Avenue Group showed me a thirty second television commercial that they had written for me to see. Here it is." Cora gave him a folded piece of paper from her brown purse.

Jett cleared his throat. "A commercial for Neat Street Robots?" Jett proceeded to unfold it and read the note. It took him over half a minute but he was pretty convinced it was something they could indeed consider as a television commercial. Its content was the Catchy Petunia of the future. Jett hummed and hawed for a minute as he was thinking it through. Soon he said, "Yes. This is good material. It may just bring in more customers to our store."

"Vic Nicolos is the guy who came up with the advertisement."

"It's pretty clever for a commercial. I'll say that. I guess that having robots thinking for themselves would be the next step after what I've been hearing about robotics."

"Same here. Right on."

"Right on alright. You have been thinking about what's next and I assumed you might. Do you have extra copies of it?"

"Yes."

"Good."

"I guess this is the next step for Neat Street Robots then. Later we may generate more than enough sales to pay for Sizel Coolbeans to be made."

"As a matter of fact, you're right. We'll go from there."

The waitress came back to the table and set down their sandwiches for them. "Roast beef club for you ma'am and tomato, lettuce and cheddar for you sir."

"Thank you." Cora replied.

"Thank you Cora for meeting with me today like this."

"You're welcome Midnight."

"This looks like a good sandwich. I've gotta try it."

"I haven't had roast beef in a while."

When Cora and Jett finished their food and handed the waitress the money to pay for their meal and got up from the table, Cora gazed at the CEO. "It's rare for a girl like me at the age of twenty-one to have a CEO like you to be there for me to talk with about business. And at the same time having a CEO so intent on improving and shaping up business for the company by making goals just like The Sunlit Avenue Group have been doing. It's great we met today."

"I found the meeting to be very informative." Jett said just after he and Cora left the café. "Yup. Thanks for the info."

"You're very welcome. I should be talking to you again soon to let you know about Sizel Coolbeans and the television commercial about Catchy Petunia."

"Great. Thanks again Midnight."

They were ready for another day. As Cora Pepper walked him to his car, Jett Black turned toward her with a few more words to mention. "I hope my visit with you will soon be proven to have been a mysterious turn for the better."

"Alright. Take care Midnight."

"You too Miss Pepper."

CHAPTER 15

Tuesday, October 18, 2011

Three months had passed since the day Cora met with Jett at the café. But then a lot had changed with The Sunlit Avenue Group and the situations they had been encountering from day to day. Each person had been seeing a certain amount of success and even challenges. Mark and Doris Keenan had been tending to their jobs and watching to see how many people would find their new clothing store called Kokomoz just the thing they were looking for in the line of clothing. At first, it had its ups and downs. But now things were picking up and moving along for the entrepreneurs. The T-shirts were a hit. Their slogans included, "Kokomoz is like strawberry sherbet." And even more that read, "On a breezy day may you have smooth sailing." And yet another, "This is turning out to be a sweet awesome turn of events. Kokomoz."

Within two months Doris sold so many T-shirts that people across the country were wearing them. Doris was very pleased, to say the least. That was until consumer demand for the T-shirts jacked up the prices for them skyward until they were considered designer clothes. Because of this, Kokomoz customers were becoming upset because they found out each T-shirt was running upwards of eighty dollars a shirt after the price adjustment. Doris had been spending hours each day wondering about the simple Kokomoz T-shirts that had ended up as designer wear clothing. With everything that had occurred she was prepared to put the money she had accumulated toward expanding the company in the future so that hopefully many more people would share in the fun. The fun of Kokomoz.

Mr. and Mrs. Keenan, including their son Edmond, were developing a distinguished edge as they were getting more experienced in respect to their work. It was becoming apparent to the rest of The Sunlit Avenue Group how much the improvements they were undergoing were taking them in the right direction. The goals they set only months earlier had moved them so far, yet so quickly, toward shaping their everyday lives and they were meeting the sure signs of success.

Doris invited Rita over to her house to look at some photographs she had taken. Doris had already hired some models to wear Kokomoz T-shirts who had their pictures taken at the studio where Rita worked so that there would be some photographs on The Sunlit Avenue Group's website for anyone to see. The two women were now involved in a discussion about it.

"So Doris, I took the photo shots that you wanted of the men and women wearing the Kokomoz T-shirts. Here they are." Rita opened her black leather briefcase and handed them to her.

"Great." Doris began to check them over.

"Tell me if you like those ones. I took them the other day in front of the painted background of a sunrise."

"These ones are keepers. I can say that for sure."

"It really does seem as if we are taking it all to a new level now for some reason. Ever since Cora's CEO Jett Black came up with the idea of the phrase "The Sunlit Avenue Group" we have been working on our projects more like a group of people set on accomplishing a team project. Haven't we?"

"Why yes." Doris acknowledged Rita. "How true."

"I especially like how Cora is going to use Sven's wisdom quotes and Vic's original quotes as the inspirational messages for the next robot series named Sizel Coolbeans. We're really working together on this now."

"Yes."

"So Doris, do you have anything to say about how things are going for us?"

"I guess it would be to mention the real meaning of our latest new motto given to us by Rain Woodrow. 'Let's keep goaling strong.' I mean, do you even understand how that four word phrase can work to change lives? Think Rita. I mean, geez."

"It's no wonder it's going to be something that Rain can use for the company Fine Point Rainforest Incorporated. Use it Rain. That's what I told her."

"And she did."

"That's for sure. Now that her book was published last month, she should be working to build her company anytime soon."

"So true. Let's talk more about these nice photographs that you took the other day."

"Do you want them on the Sunlit Avenue Group's website? It will advertise your business."

"Yes. Let's see. Put this one and this one and these three on the website. Please, as soon as possible."

"Okay. It may take a few days but they will be there." Rita assured her.

"It's good thinking to have our own website so that when the news crew comes back to interview Mark at the end of the year for that year end progress report they will have some material to access. And guess what we can say?"

"Log on to our website and you can read all the progress that we the neighbours of Sunlit Avenue have made."

"That's right. Wasn't it a creative idea Mark had?" Doris beamed a sly smile.

"I should say so. That reminds me. Cora went and told her company's employees about the Sunlit Avenue Group's special website two weeks ago because they were wondering about what type of stuff we have been keeping busy on."

"No way."

"Yes, she did."

"But we were supposed to keep it a secret until the end of the year when they do the next newspaper article on us." Doris gasped, feeling a bit concerned about the apparent change in their plans. She shook her head, not knowing what to make of it.

"I'm aware of that. Anyway, she's stirred up a ruckus at her company and I mean the people there appreciate being familiar with Cora's story enough let alone her telling them what all the neighbours on the rest of Sunlit Avenue are doing. On top of that, word is spreading fast with the news stories around the country."

"There are news stories? For goodness sakes."

"Haven't you heard that they mentioned on television on a news station how everyone is logging online to check out the website?"

"No, can't say I have."

"Are you kidding? Well, from what I gather people around the country are hearing about us and it's making Cally Ryerson angry." Rita folded her arms all at once. She tensed up for a moment and then relaxed again and let it go.

"Angry?" Doris wrinkled her forehead.

"He didn't think it would spread nationwide as quickly as it has. But it did."

"I wonder why he is angry."

"Who knows. But you can bet Cally will be keeping watch on it all down to the fine details by the way he has been affected by bigger audiences during his rock and roll band's shows at the Fen Fen nightclub."

"Bigger audiences?"

"Way bigger. And that is because Cally Ryerson is mentioned on our very informative website as being the only child of Zoey and Ralph Holiday who happens to be a drummer in a band named Wind Spontaneous. And it even mentions that they live in Moncton." Rita waved her hand in the air while feeling stirred with emotion.

"So their music is drawing more crowds?"

"Yes."

"I think Cally is over-reacting."

"That, my dear, is something Cally is famous for."

* * *

"Well if it isn't Mr. Dangsi. Guess what Dangsi? My parents saw the new Catchy Petunia commercial on television. You can begin by telling Cora that I said those robots are expensive." "She put them at a fair price." Cullen gulped.

Cally went on to say, "And your superhero mini-book? Gee, what an amazing idea. Are you going to put some color on your hair?"

"No comment. Other than it's already colorful."

Cally paused for a long breath. "It's starting to get colder out these days."

"If you dress for the weather it won't be as cold."

"I knew that."

"I'm just saying." Cullen shrugged his shoulders. "Cally, are you after me? 'Cause if you are I'm not scared of you."

"I knew that too."

"You did? Or, I mean, you do?"

"Yep. Ever since you kept your cool when I held you off the ground even though you were worried."

"Yeah. I did keep calm."

"You don't have to worry about me roughing you over anymore. I get it. Get it, Dangsi? Let's not give each other the old cold shoulder now. By the way, I liked reading your mini-book on Isaiek Sheer."

"You did?"

"He's talented and a babe magnet."

"Oh, is that why?"

"It's more than that Dangsi. He's got a real go at things."

"Incredibly so."

"And my daughter Dance likes the mini-book."

"She read it?"

"Yup. Let me shake your hand." Cally said.

"Alright." He slowly lifted his hand for Cally to shake while wondering if he was to be trusted or not. For the time being, Cullen thought he should trust him. So Cally lifted his hand up to his and they did a quick shaking of hands in the evening air. It was dusk and the sun was setting over on the western horizon behind Cullen's house. It was clear out and the stars would be coming out as night approached.

"Thanks." Cullen said.

Cally coughed. "Thanks? What for?"

"Just thanks."

"Anytime, Dangsi." They savoured the moment and then out of nowhere Cally teased Cullen's bangs with his fingers so that it stood up on end.

"What are you doing?" Cullen asked, putting up with it.

Cally kept teasing Cullen's bangs until his hair was all spiked up. Then Cally yelled out loud to Cullen. "You look star struck!"

That is when Cullen began to shed some tears. It hit home with him. Cally noticed the tears and couldn't help but saying, "You're crying Dangsi. But is it because of your hair or something else?"

"Crying? You can say that again. I'm star struck. So much stuff has been happening on Sunlit Avenue that I forgot to take a real breather from it." So he took a big sigh to let it all out. "Phew."

"Dang it Dangsi, you sure nailed that one. It is healthy taking a breather every now and then."

CHAPTER 16

Wednesday, October 19, 2011

"Remember that gift card you gave me a few months ago?" Sven asked.

"Sure, I remember." Cullen answered.

"I finally used it. I ordered tossed salad and spaghetti with meatballs."

"Hey, glad to hear it."

"Uh-huh. My brother ordered the same as me."

"Oh, that's good." Cullen nodded. "Yep."

"So, what's new?"

"Oh yeah, that reminds me. I've been meaning to tell you about Cally. He let me in on something. He isn't going to be rough on me anymore. I was relieved to find out."

"Don't worry about him."

"You said that to me before." Cullen replied, rubbing his fingers across some overgrown stubble along his chin. "I guess he wanted to see what kind of person I am. He wrestled me and I was trying to get away. Now everything's cool."

"That would be a great title for a song. Don't you think? Everything's cool."

"You're telling me. I wonder if I should be the one to write it or Cally."

"Definitely you." Sven brushed his hair away from his eyes. "Surprise him."

"I'll write the song and he can put the words into music."

"And possibly play for the crowds at the nightclub where they perform."

"God, I hope he will go for the idea."

"Me too, my good neighbour, me too."

"Everything's cool is the name of the song after all so why shouldn't he?"

"That's right."

Sven and Cullen high fived each other and strolled up the street and down the next only to discover that the new street one street over was now named Russet Street. They continued on their way for an hour long walk together, going down the main road toward a major shopping area of town. During their walk they planned out an upcoming barbeque that most of The Sunlit Avenue Group would be attending at Cullen and Rain's house in only two days.

A few more hours went by. Cullen had been busy at home writing the song and had finished it, so he dropped by at Sven's to announce his success. Strangely enough, Vic wasn't home. Cullen figured he must be out running errands. Cullen thought Vic might like to read the song too, so he told Sven to keep the page he had written the song on to show Vic because he had more pages of it on hand. He gave Sven the page that he had written it on. And as he was reading the words, Cullen was filled with glee at the sight of Sven's eyes studying the page over so closely.

Everything's cool.

*A song by Cullen Dangsi for the band Wind
	Spontaneous.*

"Hot tabasco sauce, corn cobs, and a pinch of rosehips

*What exactly will be the next few words coming from
	your lips?*

Nothing too plain I hope.

Nothing too lame I hope."

"Is it lemon tea for two or two for lemon tea?

There's some for you and there's some for me.

*Enough with the tasting of food that's bursting with
	flavor.*

*Now how about putting me at ease with some words
	I can savor?"*

You said to me, "You're in for it tonight.

Now how about getting this recipe right?"

I said to you, "It has bite and a punch of all its own.

I'm thankful my stomach won't soon groan."

"No matter how this food has turned out,

While I eat it I won't have to scream and shout."

You see, I've learned from you already the reason why.

And that is because you're my food taster guy.

My food taster, food taster, food taster guy.

*"Oh, what sensational dishes you have there, oh me
	and oh my."*

"Each food tasting session was made from a lot of wit,

And recently I noticed I have a worn oven mitt.

A worn oven mitt, a worn oven mitt." I begin to say.

*"Is how I can measure how much experience I have
	gathered today."*

"I can honestly say that between us two,
Everything's cool for me and for you."
"With that it seems very fine.
And everything's perfectly alright as we dine."

Sven nodded his head. "Yep, way to go. I bet Cally could get a rhythm for this in no time." Sven began humming away the first few words of the song.

"He's sure to get some kind of music going for it." Cullen replied.

"He could very well play it at one of his shows with his band."

"Maybe. I hope he does."

CHAPTER 17

Friday, October 21, 2011

Everyone had arrived at the barbeque around six-thirty pm. It was the first one of its kind held on Sunlit Avenue since the street had been built. Rain and Cullen were more than glad to hold the barbeque at their house and use their new barbeque grill to do some cooking outside on the back deck.

Rain was helping herself to a blue plastic party cup of lemonade in the kitchen when Rita approached her. She had just finished filling Sven's party cup with lemonade too and then set the pitcher on the table for the other neighbours to help themselves to it. The neighbours were in the living room relaxing and talking or on the back deck eating some food.

"Guess what the Peace-eba band said when Vic emailed them explaining how the mini-book has an answer to preserving the rainforest?" Rain asked Aleisha.

"You tell me. What?" Aleisha responded.

"We're on it. You can count us in. Let's see about making the laser line show like you were saying." Rain was clearly more than happy to talk about it. "They said they will donate a lot of the profits to Fine Point Rainforest Inc. so it can have some earning potential."

"You don't say. That, my dear, is how you do it. Make a laser line show. You can bet I'll go see it." Rita adjusted her posture. She had been slouching for hours. It was as though she was just waiting to hear the announcement. All at once she was attentive.

"Talk about improvements or what eh? Not just for us but for other people too." Rain giggled.

She looked at her neighbour Rain open her arms to hug her and once she did she tightly held her in her arms. Just then, Vic walked by and winked at Rain. After that he headed for the bathroom upstairs.

Rita sighed, "Do you think Vic could help me get my photographs of Kokomoz in the media?"

"Only one way to find out. Ask him."

"Yeah. I will." Rain freely let go of her grip on Rita. Seconds later Rita went to the living room and found an empty space on the sofa beside Sven and Aleisha and thumped down on it. In that moment she thought of a fantastic idea. She thought, 'I will be the one who photographs The Sunlit Avenue Group with the help of another photographer I could hire.' Then she turned to look at Sven and Aleisha while feeling proud that she thought of it. "Well my dears, I have it. I will be The Sunlit Avenue Group's photographer."

"How ingenius." Brooke said, facing her from a nearby dining room chair across the living room.

"Me and maybe another guy I know of could take some pictures of the group."

A second later Ralph walked into the room and looked around. He was trying to find Vic.

"Do you know where Vic is?" He asked.

"Yeah, he went to the washroom." Rita eyed him until he answered her.

"I just heard Vic is the guy who helped get the laser line show started. The guy is one clever events planner. He's an example of how one good thing leads to another."

"And another and another." Rita giggled.

Sven passed some chocolate balls to Rita on a circular glass candy dish. "Want some?"

"Sure." She took a handful and munched on them. By then Vic was walking down the stairs back to the living room.

"Hey, there's Vic now." Ralph hollered.

"Guys, did you miss me?" He asked, looking at Ralph and then noticing Rita was sitting in his spot he had only a minute ago on the couch.

Sven spoke up to his brother and said, "When you were gone Rita decided something."

"And that is...I'm going to be the photographer for our group."

"Well alright. Way to go." Vic replied.

"These chocolates are good. Have some." Rita handed the candy dish to Vic.

Rain was nearby. She overheard the conversation and was standing in the doorway to the living room. She said, "There's more where that came from. I have a big bunch of those chocolates. Help yourselves."

Vic walked like a robot toward Rita to mimic Sizel Coolbeans. "Did you hear some of my original sayings are going to be some of the messages that Sizel says, Rita?"

"Sure did."

Vic and Sven were smiling. Sven turned to Rita with a fixed gaze and said, "I wonder just where we'll be in a month from now."

"We'll have to wait and see." Rita cleared her throat and stood up beside Vic. Then she asked him the all-important question. At least to her it was the all-important question. "Hey, ah, can you help me get my Kokomoz photographs in the media?" She paused and rubbed her chin, waiting for his answer.

Rain cleared her throat and announced, "The hamburgers are done. Does anybody want theirs right now?"

"Me." Aleisha stood up.

"I do." Brooke hurried outside to get his.

"What about you, Zoey?" Rain asked with her hands on her hips, as Zoey was rocked in the recliner in the corner.

"I already had a hotdog."

"Oh." Rain answered back to her.

"Think I'll sit here for a while. I'll have some lemonade though."

"I'll get some for you."

Vic had been thinking the question through that he had been asked only a moment ago. "I can see what I can do. I wonder where we should start?"

"Your guess is as good as mine." Rita gulped.

"Rita, guess what?" Rain went on. "Aleisha said she and Cullen both like secrets."

"That's very curious."

"I mean it sounds like a co-incidence to me. Maybe they are in on something together."

A minute later almost everyone was outside getting some hamburgers and sitting on the lawn chairs they had brought with them. Inside the house Rain brought Zoey her cup of lemonade. "I can tell by the look on your face that you are thinking about something. What is it that you would like to say?"

Slowly but surely she said, "I've got to hand it to your Cullen. I heard he and my boy Cally have cooled it off." Zoey unfolded the printed page of a song from Cullen. "I hope my boy plays the song at one of his gigs. You've got a boyfriend who knows how to express his feelings in a song."

"Yes, I read the song. He's pretty good at that. For sure." Rain emphasized to Zoey. Rain gave Zoey her drink of lemonade and she guzzled it down.

"Now that's refreshing."

"I'm glad you liked your refreshment."

Rain took Zoey's empty blue plastic cup to the kitchen and listened to everyone talking outside. It was getting pretty dark out. But with the light bulb above the back deck already turned on, everyone was happily munching away while watching Cora. Almost everyone's eyes were on her. She was sitting beside Damien, Francis and Lulu while noticing Brooke. There he was in plain sight of her and waving at her from where he was sitting on a lawn chair while eating a hamburger with lots of toppings. Brooke held the hamburger so that the toppings would stay in place. There was a slice of a pickle, a slice of tomato, a piece of lettuce, ketchup, mayonnaise, relish and barbeque sauce.

Cora had been so dreamy ever since she began seeing Brooke. After all, the two had so far been boyfriend and girlfriend for two months. He liked that and all the neighbours knew it too. No one said much once Brooke stepped over to the barbeque grill to get his meal only a few minutes beforehand. Most of the potato salad left on the stove in the kitchen had been eaten and it was now down to the last minutes of eating before everyone would be going inside the house again.

The crowd of neighbours were spending the time taking it all in. Finally, everyone did a cheer. They shouted, "Progress, progress here we go. One day after another, how we love it so."

The time came for them to go inside the house and Cullen had closed the back door to warm up the house once they were inside. It was chilly outside. Rain gathered around the group that were either sitting or standing together in the living room and got everyone's attention. "I have an announcement to make. The special song by Peace-eba and my mini-book along with the lightshow display will be held in a week at the Amplitude Theatre. I will be getting thirty percent of the proceeds from it."

"That's incredible news." Damien exclaimed.

"Your company? That means you can start it now."

"I already got permission to build a workshop in a small town near the Amazon rainforest. That's where we're starting."

"Yeeha." Cullen cheered. "Was it easy to get the workshop?"

"Well, when they heard about the mini-book they said I can set up the workshop. We can build the workshop once the proceeds are in. By next year we could be seeing the first homemade crafts being sold internationally. Made by the craftsmen that live near the Amazon. And a few other people who volunteer to travel to the Amazon to work there and get things going."

"Wonderful. That is if everything turns out for your company." Brooke looked pretty mellow to Rain. "There are probably going to be many steps involved before they will be selling the hand crafted artworks. But good luck with it."

There was a short pause but Cullen broke the silence. "Anyway, Sven and I went for a walk the other day to see how the houses were coming along one street over and we found out the street is now called Russet Street."

"Wait a minute." Cora interrupted. "Russet Street? I thought they were going to call it Starlight Street. Aww, too bad."

"What made you think that?" Rita asked.

"I spoke to some of the construction workers and after they heard about the line of robots my company sells, they said they might call it that. Anyway."

"Thems the breaks, Cora." Damien shrugged his shoulders. "Tough toodles." He went on. "You can't win 'em all."

"Yeah, yeah." She was sulking a little.

"C'mon and smell the roses." Brooke smiled.

Cora's thoughts began stirring about her new boyfriend again. She walked over to him and held his hand in hers. "I love you Mr. Akira."

"I love you too." He blushed shyly. Having a girlfriend was still so new to him. It had been a while since he dated anyone. And Cora was a girl he was definitely compatible with.

"I'm going to move out of my Mom's house as soon as I can. Yup. It won't be long now. I'm moving into a nice apartment somewhere close to work."

"You are?" Sven confirmed.

"Yes. My mom can have a roommate."

"That's good." Brooke said.

"You're my miracle." Cora said while winking at Brooke. Her comment was totally out of the blue but the sound of her voice came to him as plain as day.

"Gee, I wasn't expecting that one." Brooke kidded and blew her a kiss. "To top it off, how about I say baby you've said it all. Or something to that effect. Can I fix a kiss on you?"

"Fix a kiss? Okay."

"Life is a miracle." Brooke calmly spoke back to her. Then he placed one on her cheek. She touched her hand to her cheek where he had kissed her.

"Such is life." Damien's words sounded somewhat all too familiar.

"Yeah, especially when you have goals. They take you places. You should have heard my friend Laurence when I told him that I had a meeting with the CEO of Neat Street Robots. He said, "Are you kidding me?" He likes how I'm getting lots of business experience these days."

"Tell me about it. Business experience is valuable." Damien commented confidently. "Take it from me as the co-owner of Hemley's Great Fountains Alive. I get so much out of running that business that Mavis and I have decided to focus on how to run it even better so that people from all over will have those peaceful fountains to listen to and watch. That is our new goal or aspiration."

Rain stated keenly. "Those fountains definitely are peaceful sounding. I went to go see them again a few weeks ago when I had some free time. You and Mavis weren't there that day."

"Oh really?"

"Yeah. But there were a lot of shoppers there."

Most of the Group was sitting down on the variety of wooden dining room chairs and other chairs that had been arranged around the room. The rest of them were standing around half expecting something else to be revealed by one of the neighbours. They were all mingling to a certain extent.

Then all of a sudden there was a blackout. As soon as it started, Rain was out in the kitchen fiddling around for some matches in one of the cabinet drawers and pulled them out along with a big, wide lemon scented candle that would burn for hours. It could be placed on the living room table in front of everyone. She set it in front of her neighbours and they sat there staring at each other in the dim light.

"Well folks, it looks like we've really done it this time." Ralph couldn't help it. "To me, this is when the party actually starts when it comes down to it. I feel excited all over."

"Pay your power bill lately?" Damien joked to Cullen.

"Yes."

"It would happen at a time like this." Zoey slowly said.

Ralph said with a loud tone of voice. "Just when you least expect it."

"I like surprises." Aleisha said.

"We heard about that earlier." Sven said.

Cullen crossed his arms over his chest to get comfortable. "Maybe we should cool it for a while. I mean, just relax here and enjoy ourselves. Francis, can you look out the window to see if the power has gone out on the whole street?"

She walked over to the window and pushed the drapes to one side. She answered, sounding bewildered. "No, it hasn't Mr. Dangsi."

"Shucks." Ralph said.

Francis kept looking out the window. "But there is a guy with a big truck in your driveway."

"What?" Cullen peered out the window to see what she was talking about. "Is that Cally Ryerson?"

"What's he doing?" Damien frowned.

"I'll go find out. Man." Cullen stepped out the front door and walked over to where Cally was standing by the house. There was a small sized black monster truck covered in mud parked in the driveway close to the walkway leading up to the house and Cullen could tell right away that Cally was up to something.

Cally had managed to cover his rugged looking truck in mud while out off-roading. He had gone over to talk to Hazel at her place and to show her his big truck. She mentioned that she thought it was nice that he had a off-roading vehicle to ride in but what caught her attention the most was all the mud that was still on it. She asked him to wash it with some soap and water and a sponge and bucket and told him that she makes a lot of effort to keep a clean and tidy house. All the muck was unsightly to her. She even went so far as to grill Cally on washing his monster truck regularly and this had caused Cally to go overboard. He went home to get a bright spotlight stage prop that he had for his rock band's shows and brought it to Cullen's driveway along with the truck to shine on his vehicle while he washed it in the twilight of the evening outside. He aimed to have a clean off-road vehicle to show all the people at the barbeque so they would see it when it was clean and in the spotlight.

"What are you doing?"

"Well, uh, the spotlights I have here aren't lighting up now. I plugged them into your outside outlet and I put them on super bright setting to shine on my truck. I was going to wash it. See how much mud is on it?"

Cullen noticed a bucket of soapy water with a sponge in it and another bucket of water right beside it. "There is a blackout at my house. Your spotlights must have overloaded one of the fuses in the basement. A lot of the neighbours are at my house. I was having a barbeque. A party."

"Yes, I'm aware of that. I was going to show you guys my new truck once I finished washing it here. I went over to Hazel's and got the buckets and sponge. I went off-roading today."

"You should ask me next time. Okay Cally?"

"I didn't think you would mind." He went on. "I don't have to do a show tonight. But tomorrow my band and I are doing two shows. One in the afternoon and one in the evening. If you can believe that."

"Hmm. So when did you get the truck?"

"Yesterday. Oh, guess what? I'm moving into Hazel's house. Yeah, Cora's mom. I'm her new roommate."

"You are?"

"That's right. Cora's moving out."

"Yeah, I heard. She's at the party right now. Along with Brooke."

"Her boyfriend. Yep." Cally scratched some stubble on his cheek.

"I wonder if she heard you were going to move in."

"Hazel said she planned on telling her after the party."

"Gee, welcome to Sunlit Avenue, neighbour." Cullen wiped his brow.

"Thanks. Don't worry, next time I'll ask you before I use your outside outlet again."

"I hope so. I'm going to go to the store to get a new fuse as soon as I look at what one blew."

"What about the party?"

"It's alright."

"You sure?"

"It won't take too long to go get a new fuse."

"I'll drive you to the store."

"Um, alright. Be right back."

Cally waited outside while Cullen went inside the house to tell everyone that a fuse blew and that he was going to the store to get a new one. He told them that if they wanted to they could stay until he returned. Everyone decided to do just that. Cullen went down in the basement with a flashlight to do a quick check on the fuse before heading out for the store. Within minutes he was traveling down the road in the small sized monster truck with Cally at the wheel driving.

"Nice truck, isn't it?" Cally said.

"Yes. Nice truck." Cullen repeated.

"I thought of a nickname for you. It's Cullen the beautius."

"Cullen the beautius?"

"You handsome guy you." Cally pursed his mouth. He smirked at Cullen for several seconds.

"Lovely. Or shall I say, aw shucks."

"I'm guessing your guests are going home?"

"No, they're staying while I replace the fuse."

"That's music to the ears because I have to tell Cora a few things."

"Like?"

"Oh, good luck and keep on with the robot company. I think they're still a bit expensive though. How much are they again? Twelve thousand each?"

"Yeah."

"She's original. I'll tell you that much. And Rain too."

"Uh-huh."

"How's her card company going lately?"

"Well, she's been making pop out cards."

"Are they selling?"

"Yeah. She's been so busy making them too. I think she should hire a helper to make cards for her. She often works on piles of them for fourteen hours, getting them just right."

"Is Rain the only one who makes the cards?"

"Yep."

"I think she should do that then. Hire somebody."

"I'd say. I'll talk to her some more about it."

They approached an intersection and Cally swerved the small sized monster truck to a left turn and Cullen watched with a look of astonishment on his face. He felt a jolt of power coming from it as they sped ahead. Cullen had been listening to the engine roar on the way there and had spent the minutes getting used to the experience of travelling in the fancy truck.

"Although the engine is loud, I can understand why people would buy such a vehicle. It seems to give you a feeling of being adventurous." He said.

Before they said anything else to each other, Cally found a parking space in the hardware store parking lot.

"By the way, I can be described as the kind of person who finds out information about what a person is like by misbehaving in front of them and seeing how they respond. Then I can see how they are themselves."

"I kind of figured that about you."

"I just don't tell people that about me very much."

"Can I call you Cal?"

"My band members call me Cal. You can too. Alright?"

"Sure. Let's go shopping."

Cullen Dangsi found the fuse he was looking for while he was shopping around the store with his new neighbour and Cally found a light brown mug that said in yellow lettering, "You're one cool dood." Soon after purchasing their items they were exiting the checkout and ready to leave the place. Cally unwrapped the white tissue paper that the cashier had put around it. He showed it to Cullen and said, "Hazel's gonna get a kick out of seeing this."

In a short while they were back at the house. Cullen walked to the basement with a flashlight in his hand again and installed the fuse. By the time the lights went back on, everyone in the living room stopped to notice Cally Ryerson. He was standing there in front of them. His short, spiky brown hair and six-foot-two build brought out a few gasps from the group of neighbours.

"Look, it's Cally." Rita finally said. "We were talking about you. Your parents here were talking about you too."

"Oh gee." He started. Then he changed the subject. "I have an announcement to make. I'm moving in with Hazel Pepper."

The neighbours of The Sunlit Avenue Group went silent, as though they were thinking through a mathematical problem. They didn't seem to have the answer to it until Cally said, "Huh? Why so quiet?"

Everyone blurted at once to him after that moment. And he soon found out what it was like to meet an entire roomful of people who were now his neighbours. He stared at their faces one by one.

"He's here." Damien uttered.

"Hi mister." Francis said.

"Look, it's him." Sven mischievously stated.

"It is." Brooke said as though he was a little too relaxed.

From out of nowhere, Rain came out with it and said in a merry tone, "Come and join the party." Her words were welcoming. After that she looked around the room and the neighbours put two and two together and spoke up.

"You mean you're her new roommate?" Cora gasped.

"Yeah, welcome to the party." Lulu smiled. She pinched out the candle flame on the big candle on the coffee table all by herself because the lights had since come on.

"Jeez. Is that true?" Sven asked. He wanted to make sure what he was being told was correct.

That is when Cullen came up the stairs from the basement and stepped into the living room just as Cally noticed Cora sitting on a chair from the dining room. "There's the girl I've been meaning to talk to."

"Me? What would you like to say?" Cora asked.

"I'd like to tell you good luck and keep on with the robot company. But man, I've got to say. You sure have a way of bringing in crowds. My band is doing two shows on

Saturdays now and…what else can I say? You've got me and my band rocking on."

"Well, gee thanks."

"No, you've got to realize what I'm saying."

"I realize exactly what you're saying. I help bring in the crowds so they can hear your rhythm."

"But it feels like it's to the beat of a different drum. And I'm like…"Can we do this guys?" And they're like…"As long as we keep our taste in music alive." I hope you know what you're doing Cora."

"I'm perfectly aware of what I'm doing. I'm attracting your listeners. As long as you provide the entertainment those crowds of people will keep coming to your shows."

"Entertainment? Yeah, that's what it is. But remember I'm keeping it real and I will be doing my best. And when you find an apartment I will be moving into your old room."

"Man, I should look for one pretty soon then."

"Yes." Rain said.

Cullen winked at Zoey. That is when she remembered about the paper in her hand. "He's got a song for you, Cullen has."

"Thanks Zoey." Cullen passed a typed page to Cally over from Zoey's hand. "I wanted to be first to show you the song I had written. This is for you. Maybe you and your band can play it. I hope you like it."

After he read it he nodded. "My food taster guy. Did you come up with this?"

"Yup. It was me and Sven. He thought I should write you a song."

"Everything's cool. That's the name of it. I like it." Cally folded it up in his wallet. "I will show it to my band."

"We all sat listening to Zoey read the song while you guys went out to the store." Damien mentioned.

"Fancy that." Cullen smiled cheek to cheek.

"Anybody else for some pink lemonade?" Rain questioned to her quests.

"Me." Lulu raised her hand.

"No, no. It's your bedtime. Too much sugar." Damien suggested.

"Okay." Francis declared while watching her sister pout.

"I'll have some water." Cally approached Rain and followed her into the kitchen. She gave him a bottle of water and he drank down the beverage as though he was very thirsty.

Brooke stood nearby and saw Cally drinking it down. "Quenching your thirst?"

"Yup. Hey, cool party Rain." Cally set the empty water bottle down on the counter top.

"Thanks." She answered.

"You can call me Cal. You and Cullen both."

"Okay. Got it."

CHAPTER 18

Monday, October 24, 2011

The following Monday at about ten-thirty am, Zoey checked to see if there was any mail in the mailbox for either her or her husband Ralph. Among a few bills was a letter that she had to open right away because she wanted to see what it contained. On the envelope was written Gosh o' Golly Studios. She brought the mail in the house and opened the letter that was addressed to her and Ralph and shouted out loud, "Look at this!" But no one else heard her. She was at home by herself. Ralph had gone to the dentist to get his teeth cleaned only ten minutes earlier.

She stared at it closely. She held it up to her face and kissed it. She was holding a cheque for two hundred thousand dollars. To her great amazement, receiving a cheque from Gosh o' Golly Studios was just what she and Ralph had recently been dreaming a lot about ever since they and the grandchildren came up with a new game show together over the past few weeks. It was called Names For Words. The rules of the game were to take a specific word such as the word car. With that word the contestants have to think of words that go along with it such as car wax, car wash, car engine, car dealership, car company, etc. Four other main words other than car would soon be next; one after the other, such as animal, telephone, farm, ice. Each contestant would write a number from one to fifty and the person whose number is closest to the chosen number gets to have their turn first and so on to the next person. The main words are called out one at a time to see how many words can be matched with it and every time a contestant thinks of a word that goes along with one of the main words with a ten second time limit they get one thousand points. Near the end of the game show the contestant with the most points can go on to win the bonus round. If the contestant can correctly guess the Sentence of the Day which is made with the day's selected main words from a list of three possible sentences composed of them, he or she wins the game. Some of the prizes can include free groceries for a year, new stylish makeovers, new vehicles, trips to places around the world, and cash prizes.

Zoey pulled a note out of the envelope after she had a good look at the cheque amount and read it.

Dear Ralph, Zoey and grandchildren Xavier and Dance,

Congrats on coming up with a new game show. The first airing on television will be on November 15 of this year. Be sure to watch to find out how Names For Words can make you shout words of joy.

All the best,
Timothy Benton
Game Show Host of Names For Words

"Well, I'm enticed enough." She brought the letter and cheque to her bedroom and put them on her night table. It would be another hour or so before Ralph arrived home and they could go to the bank to deposit the money into their bank accounts. A few minutes later she decided to give Xavier and Dance each fifty thousand dollars with the money from the cheque. Mrs. Holiday would be asking her husband to write a cheque to Xavier later when they got home from the bank. She would write a cheque to Dance. They would deliver the cheques to them personally and bring the grandchildren to the bank at a later time to make sure they got the money. That is if Ralph went for the idea.

By the time Ralph arrived back home Zoey stood by with her hands on her hips. "So…" She said while she was grinning from ear to ear. She waited for him to say something about it.

He finally said, "What?"

"Hi dear, we received a two hundred thousand dollar cheque from Gosh o' Golly Studios today."

"Oh my, oh my, oh my. That means they are going ahead with the game show. Right?"

"Yes. But some of the money should be given to Xavier and Dance. Fifty thousand dollars for each of our grandchildren and fifty thousand dollars for each of us. Are you all for it?"

"Are you kidding? That sounds about right to me. They helped plan it out. They are the ones who thought of naming the winning sentence The Sentence of the Day."

"I'd say." Zoey patted her husband on the shoulder. "Ready to go to the bank with me?"

"Yup."

"Just a minute." She grabbed the cheque from her night table in her bedroom and walked back to Ralph who was standing at the front door. After doing so, she grabbed her purse and put the cheque in it. "And away we go."

CHAPTER 19

Tuesday, October 25, 2011

Rain wiped the tears from her eyes that were welling up as though they were from an unknown stream. What she had been working on held a meaning that was dear to her and she couldn't help but to cry. After staying up all night to make four dozen copies of one of the most thoughtful types of cards she has ever created for her store customers, she was putting the finishing touches on the final card out of the forty eight cards and read the words on the front of the last one out loud. "Life is like a concert." Upon reading the words she proceeded to open the card and read the words that followed inside the card. "You set the stage. People arrive. And then you Rock and Roll." What made her cry was the knowledge that people would be buying them since they would soon be ready to be brought to her store. 'If enough of these cards were sold,' she reasoned to herself, 'the store may surely stay in business for many years to come.' What exactly was hitting home to her was how such a card could touch the lives of the people who would be reading it for years to come. 'Cards and More in Store' was a store where many people purchased hand crafted cards to celebrate special events and occasions in their lives and in the lives of people they know. Although that may be so, people of all ages just might be coming back for more cards in the future if they held a significant meaning to the events they were celebrating.

Rain had worked hard all night on them and now that it was morning she wanted to make sure they would get to the store before the day was through. She realized that after getting enough sleep during the morning and afternoon, she would drop them off at her store in the evening when she had rested enough. So she headed upstairs and rolled into bed right beside her boyfriend. He awoke when she pulled on the tan wool blankets that had been wrapped around him.

"Rain?"

"What?"

"Can you tell me what time it is?"

"Five fifteen. Almost time for you to get up."

"Already?" He yawned an over-exaggerated yawn. "I noticed at three o'clock in the morning you weren't in bed. What were you doing?"

"Working on some cards. I pulled an all-nighter."

"Why?"

"Because the cards were so great, that's why."

"You should have gone to bed."

"I didn't want to go to bed. I had to stay up all night. If you read the cards you would understand why."

"Why? What could they possibly say to keep you up all night?"

"The cards read, "Life is like a concert. You set the stage. People arrive. And then you Rock and Roll." Pretty good, right?"

"Rain, make a lot of them and keep making them."

"I will darling." She turned to her side to kissed him on the cheek.

"Guess what?"

"What?"

"I have a good card idea. Ah, okay here goes." Cullen went on. "May we joke someday about how we made it all happen."

"Oh, that's a good one. I can put it with the 'Just Because' cards."

"I like the sound of that. I thought of it yesterday."

"Darling, you know how you and I were talking about hiring an extra person to make cards for me? I think I should hire someone to help out with some of the card making now that we talked it over. I have really been putting in the hours lately. It's time to hire someone. You may be just the person to help make the cards for me. I'll pay you twelve dollars an hour."

"Okay. Can I make some of what I just mentioned to you?"

"Sure."

"That will be the first kind of card I'll design then."

Rain yawned and decided to reset the alarm clock for five o'clock p.m. When she finished resetting it she said, "Get up and have a fun time at work today." She was so tired she still had her clothes on under the covers.

"Yeah, I'll get up now. See you later sweetie."

Before long, Cullen was out of bed and was cooking some blueberry pancakes for breakfast. While he stood there in the kitchen cooking them at the stove and slid two cooked pancakes on his plate, he heard a loud sound of a motorcycle engine revving up and winding down again only to rev up and wind down again. This happened over and over somewhere at the front of the house. Cullen had to see who was outside. After opening the front door, he peered through it and saw that it was the same guy he saw sneaking around before. He was wearing the brown leather vest again and some jean shorts and a pair of blue sneakers. He was sitting on a red motorcycle in Sven and Vic's driveway turning the handle on the motorbike a number of times to hear it revving up loudly. He continued to do so until Cullen marched over to see him after first shutting off the stove burners so his pancakes wouldn't burn.

"I'm getting a headache from wondering about this guy's strange behavior." Cullen said to himself.

By the time he went across the road to Sven and Vic's house, the man was still sitting on his motorcycle and was taking a rest from all the engine revving he had been doing.

"What are you up to mister?" Cullen didn't like to be impolite but he just had to find out what the guy was doing.

"God I love that engine noise." The man told Cullen while looking in his direction.

"So early in the morning?"

"Well, as long as I'm up before the birds I'm okay. That's my motto. I love to have a good time." The man stroked his fingers against the motorcycle's gas tank. "Beautiful isn't she?"

"I guess so." Cullen had to get down to business. "Say, I keep seeing you around here every so often. Just what have you been up to anyway? I'm getting curious."

"Hop on."

"There's no way I'm getting on that thing."

"Suit yourself."

"So, what are you doing here?"

"I'm checking up on the neighbourhood. That's what I'm doing."

"Oh, you are?"

"I'll be seeing you around."

"You will? Have you come to check up on me and my neighbours?"

"Bye for now." He accelerated his motorcycle again and he was off and rolling up the street at the drop of a hat. The motorcycle sped onward somewhere in the distance soon afterward. It left Cullen's mouth agape with surprise.

"God that guy is mysterious." Cullen headed home to get ready for work. He was having a real eye opening start to his day as it was, let alone hearing him fire up the loud humming noise of the motorbike like he had. It was so unexpected.

"I should catch that guy's name next time. I'm starting to take a liking to the guy's tendency to be so mysterious. I wonder where I will find him next time. Whenever that might be."

CHAPTER 20

Friday, October 28, 2011

Vic Nicolos called Rain Woodrow on the telephone. "Hey sweet ums, today is your big day. The laser line show is tonight. Are you ready for it?" He had to see what kind of mood she was in because the day had arrived. The day of the first laser line show playing Rain's book words and a new Peace-eba song to go along with it.

"Yes, I'm ready. I hope there will be lots of people watching the show. I'm going to meet Peace-eba in the audience and sit with them tonight. Cullen is going too. I'm going to sit beside him too. He is making sure of that."

"You're sitting beside the Peace-eba band? You have got to be kidding. You should get there early and get talking with them about your business."

"I could do that. In fact, I will."

"Splendid."

"Hey Vic, one of the Peace-eba band members called me to say that the new song they wrote is brilliant."

"No way. They called you?"

"That's right Vic. Thanks for contacting them like you did. Tonight will be great. I'm crossing my fingers."

"I should think so."

"Yes."

"What percentage of the proceeds are you going to get again?"

"Thirty percent."

"Amazing. Well, I'll let you go and talk to you later. I'm on my lunch break. We're putting some brown siding on a house today."

"Okay, have a nice time. Bye."

"Bye."

The hours sped by one after the other and before they knew it, Rain and Cullen were leaving the house to go to the Amplitude Theatre. Rain decided that Cullen should drive them there in his car because she was very excited about the event whereas he was more relaxed. It was nearly time to meet Peace-eba. Rain was getting all wound up as it was and seeing the laser line show based on her own story of keeping the rainforest intact meant so much to her.

Once they got there they saw only a few people waiting in line for their tickets. But Rain and Cullen were relieved when they remembered the reason for that. They were early. The Peace-eba band members stood close by patiently awaiting their two guests to arrive and as soon as they saw them they approached to get a closer look at them.

"Are you Miss Woodrow and Mister Dangsi?" One bright eyed fellow asked, taking into consideration the description he had been given over the telephone of what Rain and Cullen would be wearing.

"Yeah. You guys are Peace-eba right?" Rain asked the four guys that had circled both her and her boyfriend.

"That's us. Gosh sakes. It's great to meet you. The name's Jules." Jules had chestnut blonde hair and was about six-foot-three. He was cleanly shaved and had a pair of yellow and orange sunglasses sitting on top of his head.

"And I'm Peter." A red haired guy with a beard said. He looked five-foot-six.

"Yes and I'm Nolan." A bald man with a blonde mustache had said. He appeared to be around five-foot-eight.

"Yvonne." A guy with dark hair nodded at them. He looked around six feet tall.

"Nice to meet you." Cullen quickly said, finding that he was now getting more excited about the meeting.

"Yes it is. Sweet." Jules answered. He winked at Rain and put his yellow and orange sunglasses on.

Nolan, the bald man, put his arm over Cullen's shoulder and spoke quite assuredly. "Let's go and sit down in the theatre now. In forty-five minutes the show will begin. And just as we mentioned to you earlier Rain, here's the tickets." Nolan smiled, giving Rain and Cullen their tickets.

"Thanks. Nice shirts by the way." Rain said. Each of the Peace-eba boys were wearing long sleeved shirts which were gold with blue lettering that said, 'How can you tell Ritz is Ritz?' And along with them, they had black jeans and blue sneakers on. They were all dressed alike.

"Do you like our choice in clothing? No, there wasn't a sale on. Our fashion designer just thought we should wear these clothes tonight." Jules said.

"Pretty nifty." Cullen was staring at the band members. Then he looked at Jules' yellow and orange sunglasses some more.

Cullen was wearing a white, long sleeved dress shirt with a pointy triangular collar along with yellow pants and white dress shoes while Rain was wearing a grey long sleeved shirt and a green vest over it along with beige pants and black dress shoes. Rain also had a medium sized black purse slung over her shoulder.

Rain had a tone of appreciation in her voice. "Okay. We can go find our seats and wait for it to begin."

"I'm with you." Nolan said.

They went up some stairs and approached a man who was there to check if they had tickets before letting them in to see the show. The man took their tickets and tore off the stubs and soon gave the tickets back to them before they headed into the high tech theatre. When they arrived they had a look around and then sat down in the back row. Rain and Cullen sat together just as they had planned. Cullen was to the right of Rain. To the left of Rain sat Jules. Beside him sat Nolan, Peter and Yvonne. The first exchanges between one another had already been made. The group of four were trying to contain their enthusiasm so as to ensure they didn't get overcome by emotion in front of the young couple.

"This is going to be incredible." The energy in Jules' voice was building.

"You've been saying that for an hour now."

"Yes, I have Yvonne. I'm feeling great." Jules tipped his sunglasses to the end of his nose.

"That's brilliant."

"Guys, we could actually save the rainforest by contributing to Rain's company."

"Yes, we could."

"In that case, why don't we donate ten percent of all our concert profits to Rain so that she will have the funding for Fine Point Incorporated?"

"Oh, we have got to do that. We have just got to."

"Are we up for it guys?"

"I am."

"Same here."

"Sure, sure."

"Then that's what we'll do. Contribute ten percent of our concert money."

"Sounds like a nice idea." Rain concluded. She was focusing on living her dream. She still had to make sure she could get the company started. One step after another of her goal was being completed and she knew it and Cullen knew it just as the Peace-eba band boys knew it too.

Jules put his fingers to his mouth and out came a shrill whistle. It stirred Rain's and Cullen's attention. "Let the show go on. C'mon." He hollered. He was revving himself up even more as he waited for the laser line show to start.

"I read about these laser line shows and they are really something." Rain said.

"And they are the latest in film technology too. Let me tell ya." Cullen continued.

"This is so exciting." Rain shook her fists in the air. As the minutes went by they each were becoming more and more lively now that the time for the laser line show to begin was fast approaching.

A few minutes later the crowd began pouring into the theatre. One by one they found their seats and sat down. Some people sat in front of Rain, Cullen and the Peace-eba band who were seated at the back of the theatre. When that happened they spoke more quietly to each other in case anyone found out that it was actually Rain Woodrow along with her boyfriend Cullen and the Peace-eba band themselves who were sitting there nearby. The very same people who helped put the laser line show together.

"Gee. I think it's going to be a hit. Here's my business card with my phone number. Give me a call so we can talk some more about your new company, okay?"

"Okay. Nolan, right?" Rain looked at the name on the business card closely.

"That's me."

Nolan watched Rain put the business card in her wallet in her purse. She in turn had her name and phone number already written down on a sheet of notepad paper that was tucked away in her jacket pocket. She passed it to Nolan. "Here's my phone number."

"Thanks. What a sheer delight this is going to be." He said.

The show was beginning. The laser line show was called *A Rainforest Mini Book Film.* Rain and Cullen looked at each other and held hands.

"They picked a different name for the show?" Cullen look puzzled. His puzzled look only lasted a few seconds and then he put his arm around Rain and said, "I've been meaning to bring you to a laser line show for a while now darling. Looks like we are finally going to see what one of these is like."

"That's right. And you could say we brought each other to this one."

"Cool." Peter replied.

It was right then and there that a blue laser beam from the left of the movie screen and a red laser beam from the right of the movie screen moved toward each other and met at the centre of the screen. The two laser beams were each dozens of feet in length from one end to the other. Strange sound effects boomed from the loud speakers. They had a futuristic kind of ring to them.

A second later the laser beams moved in dozens of different angles over the span of several seconds as a fast paced and continuous drum beat sound played. Some words appeared on the screen. It read, *A New Song by the popular Peace-eba band*. A few seconds later some more words appeared after the first ones disappeared. It read *The Special Song*.

The song began playing from the loud speakers on each side of the theatre. Unusual sounding drum beats sounded and it seemed as though it was a hollow rap tap tap rhythm at first. Then a fast triple beat sounded four times in a row followed by five slower drum beats. It repeated over and over as an electric guitar generated some wild sounds. The guitar howled and roared and did wavy patterns of an odd sort of tone. They were high pitched at first. Then they started sounding like bursts of rhythms that surfaced and flowed in skillful highs and lows like waves of music that emanated from the electric guitar strings in perfect unison to two maracas.

The blue and red laser beams multiplied into ten altogether. There were five red ones and five blue ones and they danced across the room in a beautiful way that was all created by the original talents of someone that had already made up the light display. One moment later the lyrics to the song appeared on the screen line by line as a recording by the singer Jules began.

> *"I'm going where life takes me and here's the reason*
>   *for it man.*
> *Someday is now so I'm saying I can.*
> *Just where it will lead me I do not yet know.*
> *One thing is clear to me and I'm telling you so.*
> *I'm going in the direction of my greatest dreams.*
> *That's one notch further as funny as it seems.*
> *What I've got to live for is very apparent to me.*
> *This day is the day that I've been waiting to see.*
> *The excitement behind every word that I say.*
> *Is all because of how I was shaped by today.*
> *No longer will life be misleading, unfortunate and*
>   *unkind.*
> *It's all about self-discovery and how there's something*
>   *in you to find.*
> *As I go on my way towards shaping it even more,*
> *There's something about this idea of another notch*
>   *further that I can't ignore.*
> *By now you've probably figured out one thing is true.*
> *You've got to be real to the person that is you.*
> *Gawk at me, stare at me or look me straight in the eyes.*
> *This one notch further reasoning is so assuring that I*
>   *am sometimes a person who cries.*
> *Now that you've heard this exciting new idea of mine,*
> *I'm hoping you will soon see how it makes you shine.*
> *Teach yourself how exhilarating life is to live.*
> *When you already have learned about what reaching*
>   *for more may give.*

I'm hoping my words will help make it all refreshing
and new,
As you see how life changing that hearing them can be
even though they are few.
And with every word that I say,
May you have one gorgeous day."
Peace-eba

Lights flashed at all angles around the borders of the movie screen. The futuristic sounds played once again from the speakers. Then Rain's words from her mini book were shown line by line on the movie screen. *A mini book about the great and tall rainforest. By Rain Woodrow.*

Let the Sun shine forth and the rain tickle. The tall trees climb and the dewdrops trickle. The green grass grow and the flowers bloom. As we continue to give the rainforest more room. The rainforest. It is alive. Yes, the rainforest is a natural living rainforest. What is more, it produces oxygen. You got it, the air we breathe. The trees in the rainforest are so large that they alone make up a very big amount of the clean air supply in the world. It has taken many years for them to get to the point of filtering out high volumes of carbon dioxide and releasing a plentiful amount of fresh, clean oxygen for us all to breathe. We can certainly breathe easier as long as this is happening.

Only recently have people been cutting down the giant rainforest trees to make space available for farming. We have often heard about the burning of the trees that sometimes goes on. That is bad news. The good news is the current generations of people alive on the planet now can be the ones to help put a stop to that from occurring any longer by turning things in a positive direction.

We should work together to do our part in ensuring that the rainforest stays intact for not only humanity but all life on the planet. One way we can do that is by building centres of employment nearby the rainforest where the farmers live so they have a source of income by hand-crafting items with a theme relating to the rainforest. They could range anywhere from simple watercolor paintings to clothing that contain a company name sewn on them. The company where they would be working at could ship the products around the world internationally for purchase and the communities of people living near the rainforest, including the farmers, would have more than adequate funds coming in for a good living. And hopefully this should put a stop to the harming of the rainforest. We could be helping it to grow instead.

We're right on topic here. Think ever so green. These rainforest items ranging from paintings to clothing with a special company name displayed on them would soon be part of the latest trends of their kind. Trends well worth keeping up to date and noticed by many. With designs so eye catching that people would be coming back for more and ordering for friends, family, and the list goes on.

At the company, there may very well possibly be piles of stock up for sale every day and even though the company workers located nearby the rainforest *may be doing what is out of the ordinary, it might come naturally to them because it will be all about something that is local and familiar to them and part of their surroundings. That's right, we're talking about the oxygen producing rainforest that they have already come to know. Yet people may come from miles around to meet the workers as more people help to put new products on the market. Getting new ones out is important to put more in stock when the international orders are being placed from across the world. Whole communities could start developing little by little. And that is what we would be pleased to see, isn't it? Think ever so green again.*

Recognize we are reaching for it. That is the roadmap plan for action we can use as we go about the business for keeping the rainforest intact. To me it can start in South America at the Amazon rainforest and as business grows we could work on the other rainforests across the world. It can also start as the funds begin coming in from any sales that are made by the centres of employment. Of course it can start as a plan is made to carry out a successful business.

Fine Point Rainforest Incorporated is the name of the business and at the time of this writing I can tell you that I will be making sure there will be generous proceeds from the sales of copies of this mini book going towards developing it. I know it's quite a plan. But it's one that is very real and easy to work on if we take one step after another. My hope is that it will be just the answer we've been waiting for. If we do what we can it will be a successful endeavor. All made possible so that we can keep breathing clean, crisp air for years to come.

The great and tall rainforest stretches across the planet and in some countries it reaches for many miles and you can especially find yourself starting to wonder how the fine balance of nature will respond by having room to grow and flourish. Along with helping creatures such as the sloth, gorilla, jaguar and anteater, to name just a few examples of the creatures inhabiting the rainforest, the reasons to stop people from cutting the huge trees down is of course endless. The beauty of nature surrounds us. If we can spend time with nature around us and breathe a lot easier with fresh, clean rainforest filtered air, it can be even more beautiful still.

Think of how peaceful and serene it can be to hear the birds singing away high in the treetops after a shower of rain. And as we listen, may we hear the sounds of nature play out with a renewed sense of peace as we discover firsthand how refreshing it can be to watch the birds enjoying the shelter of the great and tall trees. Some of the trees are really high up there at the rainforest canopy with their branches and leaves reaching many metres toward the clouds. They are ready to absorb rain and sunlight and, all the while, are continually cleansing the world's air supply. So let's do what we can to help them. We will be helping ourselves in the process.

The rain streams across the rainforest. It is there where the waterfalls are some of the beautiful scenery and the medicines are thankfully ever so green. The trees, oh how they grow. And the animals are all about. Their calls echo into the distance. The sounds of the rainforest include showers and birds singing for hours. The sights of the rainforest include vines that are climbing and trees so ancient you will be chiming. Think of it today. Think of it tomorrow. It will definitely get you thinking. As you learn more about it, you will know about its flora and fauna, or more simply, plants and animals.

Think rainforest.
Soil + Trees + Animals + Rain = STAR
Kindness + Enriched + Earth + People = KEEP
Oxygen + New = ON
Society + May + Invest + Like + Ivy + Near + Ground = SMILING.
Limbs + Air + U + Grow + Happy = LAUGH.

Are you smiling yet? How about laughing?

I hope this mini book has been a fun and informative read for you. Just think of all the people that would benefit by you simply reading this mini book and then buying one or perhaps two of the products up for sale at the first Fine Point Rainforest Inc. employment centre once it is built and established and the local farmers living nearby there begin making the products. Fine Point Rainforest Incorporated. It is sure to please. Look for the company website in the near future. Nature in all its glory includes a rainforest left undisturbed and left to grow and flourish in order to enhance the present time into being naturally a wonder to the world. We're all part of the solution if we want to be.

The laser beams did some beautiful patterns of light beam displays for a couple of minutes. The sound of rain came from the speakers for a tranquil effect. It marked the end of the laser line show. The audience sat mesmerized by what they had seen even after the lights came back on.

"Droplets at peace." Nolan said following the laser line show, "Did you know that eba means life or animal? So peace-eba means peace-life or peace-animal."

"Oh, it does eh? How perfect." Rain smiled. "That was breathtaking!"

"No it wasn't. It was a breath of fresh air darling. Such is the rainforest." Cullen winked at her.

Everyone proceeded to get up out of their seats and the crowd left the theatre within a few minutes. Rain, Cullen and the Peace-eba band spent a short while talking in the hallway outside the theatre.

Jules said, "Rain, from what I gather, you are going to be the hottest sensation. That is if they keep playing the laser line show for a few weeks or so."

Yvonne said, "She sure will be." He soon high-fived Rain and Cullen.

"That has the makings of a mighty fine start to your company. The theatre was packed. Pretty near every seat was taken."

"Stay in touch you two. We'll see how Fine Point Rainforest Inc. works out. Here's hoping you keep getting the necessary funds to build your company."

"I have to buy a couple of airplanes to ship the handmade items made by the workers to a warehouse here in Moncton." Rain said with enthusiasm.

"Is that neat or what?" Jules said to Rain. Then he watched as Rain waved her hand across Cullen's eyes to get his attention.

"Cullen?" Jules asked before Rain did.

"Sorry, I was daydreaming there for a second. Are you telling me that head office for Fine Point is going to be in Moncton?" He asked.

"Why, yes it is going to be here in Moncton."

"Oh."

"That's what the plan is anyway."

"Rain, I'm sure whatever plan you have for Fine Point Rainforest Inc. it will be pretty nice. Rain gets credit for thinking of the details for making the laser line show possible." Jules said.

"And you guys get credit for your totally awesome song to add to the laser line show."

"Let's get down to business. Rain, you should expect the first payment of funds next Friday. After that it should be monthly. Sound good?" Peter knew that Rain would be wondering how much money she would be receiving. He couldn't yet tell her the exact amount but he had hoped she would have keen interest in hearing about the first payment for her new company.

"Sounds like we're doing good." She stated with a more serious tone.

"Yes, that's right. Phone me, we can talk about business." Nolan waved and the Peace-eba band was off to their fancy hotel to celebrate. "Nice seeing you two tonight. Bye."

"Talk to you soon." Rain said.

"This has been great. Bye." Cullen was ready to call it a night.

They left in the car and headed back home to the house. Once there, they both sat on the sofa and Rain noticed Cullen's book about Straight Eights the Superhero on the coffee table in front of her.

"What a super story you have too Cullen."

"The world needs more superheroes. That's why I wrote it."

"You're telling me."

"Anyway, it's been a super evening."

"Yes, it has. Whew. What a laser line show that was. Let's just sit here and take some time to reflect."

"I'm with you, Rainy."

CHAPTER 21

Sunday, October 30, 2011

"So Hazel, I think this is what we should do for Fine Point Rainforest Inc. I told Rain my idea and she's all pepped up about it. Here goes. Okay now. The products that are sold at Fine Point Rainforest Inc. will be called the "Great Emotion" series. These products or items will portray people with cheerful expressions of all kinds. Possibly…a type of painting of a woman with her arms stretched and raised high up in the air. Several different woodcarving types of a man posing with his arms and legs held in a certain way so that it portrays a great expression of some sort. A waterproof jacket with a sewn on piece that says the company name on the upper left on the front side. An umbrella that says on it "Clouds above but plenty of love." Sid felt curious to find out what Hazel thought of the product ideas he had come up with himself. "What do you think of it so far?"

"You are setting it into motion."

"So true. So very true." He answered back to her with glee and a finger pointed in the air. It was as if he was going to say something. He opened his mouth to speak but no words came out. Then he closed his mouth again and kept pointing his finger in the air.

"What? Tell me what is on your mind."

"You're going to like this. Listen to this. "There is a world of opportunity out there. Let that way of thinking help give you faith to keep looking on the bright side of life." Yeah. That's how it goes. Rain said she will see if she can get people to paint those words on canvas and sell them too."

Hazel gasped. "Are you going to work for her company?"

"Yeah, you guessed it." Sid zipped up his black fleece sweater. "I'm the Product Developer."

"I would like to help design the products along with you."

"Well, now that you mention it Rain did say she would like to hire someone to make the company catalogue. I have already put in a good word for you."

"You did?" Hazel shrieked.

"Remember how you said we have to catch up with the other neighbours and come up with an action plan too? Well, Hazel, I told you we'd think of something. Working for a company such as this one that Rain started certainly has its benefits. Fresher, cleaner air to breathe is one. Prosperity for those who make the products near the rainforest is another."

"Yeah, yeah. There are many benefits." Hazel put her hands together to warm them. "It's getting so cold these days."

"Uh-huh. That's fall for you. It's getting close to winter."

It was three thirty pm. They were both standing in Hazel's brightly lit sunroom that was surrounded by windows along three of its four walls. The room was painted a mocha brown color. The blinds were made of wood and were also a brown color but of a lighter shade. Sid kept staring at the ceiling light fixture which was a simple dusty rose colored flat, round shape with frills around the edges that reminded Sid of pinched pie crust edges. Pie crust edges he remembered seeing when he was a child.

His attention was brought into focus again when Hazel took a deep breath. With each passing second, Sid was becoming filled with more and more anticipation and eagerness to begin. He got out his cell phone and looked up Rain's phone number. Then he dialed it.

"Who are you phoning?"

Sid remained focused and didn't answer. "Hi Cullen. Is Rain there? She is? Great."

A second or two later she greeted Sid. "Hello Mr. Sid."

"Hello. I have a question for you. Would it be possible for Hazel to be the one who is in charge of making your company's catalogues for people to read?"

"Designing the catalogues is an endeavor I hope we will soon be aiming for. Yes, she can if she has an interest in the job. It's just part time though."

"Oh, she definitely would like to have the job. Please consider she still would be working her tiling career in addition to designing the company catalogues."

"Yes, that's right. She can work on both her tiling career and the job I'm offering."

"Good." Sid spoke to Hazel while holding his cell phone in his hand. "Hazel would you like the job? She's offering it to you."

"Do I? Why yes. I would be glad to work for her making the catalogues for the company."

"She says she will take the job."

"She will?" Rain sounded on the telephone line.

"Yes. She will."

"Pass the phone to me. I want to talk to her." Hazel said.

"Okay Hazel. Here ya go."

"Rain…do I have the job?"

"Yes, you do."

"I'm delighted to be working for you. Thanks so much. When do I start?"

"Hmm. I'd say after everything is given the green light you can start on the catalogue designing."

"Excellent. We'll keep in touch. Thanks again."

"Bye. Tell Sid bye for me too. Thanks for taking the job."

Hazel closed the cell phone and passed it to Sid. Where there is success, there is Sid and Hazel at the drawing board."

"Yeah, there is Sid and Hazel staying focused too."

Hazel rubbed an eye. "Oh, I hope the company starts moving along soon."

"It will. Fingers crossed." Sid crossed his fingers.

"Oh, Sid." Hazel was trying her best to stay calm but she kept picturing the appeal of the finished product that the catalogues may have. "We each have two jobs now."

"Hey, pretty neat eh?"

"I can just picture it now. Being paid by Fine Point Rainforest Inc."

"We have to see if we can sell some products online first. That's what is in store for the near future if everything runs smoothly."

"I'm so looking forward to this. What about you?"

"Myself included." Sid sighed.

"Good. Because with both our efforts combined we'll be working on it in no time."

"Great Emotion Products. It's catchy alright. It'll take teamwork. That I've got to say. I can't over emphasize the importance of that enough."

"You just did."

"Wow eh?"

"Alright." Hazel reasoned. "It's going to take some talent and a lot of patience."

"And waiting and watching."

"I would say so." She sighed loudly and rather dreamily.

"You're all dreamy eyed Hazel."

"Yes. I'm daydreaming. What do you think my job title is?"

"Catalogue Designer?"

"That sounds about right."

CHAPTER 22

Tuesday, November 8, 2011

Mavis and Damien arrived back home on Sunlit Avenue to see several neighbours gathered around their front yard. The neighbours had been expecting their arrival after Mavis told them that she and Damien were headed home. They had spent part of the day in a courtroom in a case against Griffin and Lenny. Mavis had said she would meet with the neighbours to tell them what the verdict had been. Guilty or Not Guilty. She wasn't prepared to tell them on the phone after having just walked out of the courtroom. She only told them Cally Ryerson was one of the witnesses, including herself and her husband Damien.

It wasn't long before she stepped out of the car and walked over to where four of the neighbours were standing. Zoey, Ralph, Aleisha and Rain appeared to be all ears as she approached them. They circled her to hear every word she was about to say while they watched as Damien strolled into the house to relax after being in court.

"What was the verdict? You've got to tell us."

"They were found guilty. They were sentenced five years in jail with one year of community work." Mavis wiped her brow. She had a look of astonishment on her face. "You should have heard what Cally said in court. He was one of the witnesses and he said that Damien was concerned about what the kidnappers were going to do next. And that they kidnapped Damien and a few other people too. Griffin had called Cally on the phone one time and told him about it to get a reaction out of him. "Let's face the facts here." He said in court. He wanted to make sure that Griffin would not get away with it. The police traced the last call that Griffin made to Damien."

"What about Damien? Is he alright?" Zoey asked.

"Yes, he is. He's feeling a lot better after hearing the verdict." Mavis noticed that Zoey was wearing a Kokomoz T-shirt under her unzipped jacket that read, "On a breezy day may you have smooth sailing."

"I'm just glad Damien finally decided to press charges. What did Griffin and Lenny do when they made the announcement that they had been sentenced five years in jail?" Aleisha asked with hesitation.

"Griffin was in tears when he heard the announcement and stood up suddenly. Lenny covered his face in disbelief and then stood up too. Then they took them away." Mavis went on to say, "Damien told the cops at the police station a few weeks ago that he was on high alert the whole time they held him hostage. But he held himself together."

Rain was holding a bouquet of flowers behind her back and held them out in her hand to her neighbour. "These are for you and your family."

"Thanks Rain."

Ralph waited until Mavis received the bouquet from Rain and then went ahead to pat her on the shoulder. "I'm glad everything turned out for the best, neighbour."

"Me too." Aleisha smiled.

"Same here." Zoey gave her a quick nod.

"Well, I must go home and talk to my kids. The babysitter is expecting me to pay her."

"Yup, talk to you later then neighbour." Ralph said.

The babysitter, known as Cindy, was soon given forty dollars for taking care of Francis and Lulu for a few hours. She was glad to receive the money. Within a minute she was out the door and went to go get her bicycle around the back and hopped on it and left.

Mavis noticed the babysitter leaving on her bike and commented to her daughter Francis.

"We're in for quite a windstorm tonight, honey."

"Really Mom?"

"Yeah, I heard it on the weather report a minute ago."

"We haven't had a windstorm in a while."

"That's right. Now, go work on your homework and I will give you some chocolate ice cream."

"Okay Mom."

"Lulu can have some ice cream too." She said, still staring out the window.

"Lulu." Francis said as she was walking down the hallway toward where Lulu was sitting in her bedroom. "Mom told me that you and I can have some chocolate ice cream after a while."

"Oh boy, I love chocolate ice cream."

"That's for sure. You love anything that's chocolate."

"You guessed it."

* * *

The windstorm came and went during the early morning hours but Damien had a sleepless night. He tossed and turned in his bed thinking of the band known as Wind Spontaneous. Cally Ryerson's band. He heard that Cora found an apartment and had moved into it only two days beforehand and Cally had already moved into Cora's old bedroom and was now Hazel's new roommate. Damien had guessed the reason why Cally wanted to move in with Hazel was because it was the new and famous Sunlit Avenue. Although that was so, he kept wondering all night long if there was going to be anything between Cally and Hazel now that they were roommates.

When his wife awoke from sleeping, he asked her, "Did you happen to find out why Cally decided to move to Sunlit Avenue? Did you hear the neighbours talking about it?"

She answered, "Yes, they said that Hazel was looking for a roommate and Cally was looking for a house for rent."

"Quite possibly. Anyway, I was up the entire night thinking about the reason for it and you know how your mind can wander at night when you think about stuff. I just couldn't sleep."

"Why don't you take the day off work today and relax? Maybe you can catch up on your sleep."

"Yup. Can you open shop for me?"

"Sure, no problem."

"I'm going to go get a lemon ginger tea and go back to bed."

"Yes and there's some oranges and grapes in the fridge."

"Right." He yawned. "I wonder what Cullen's up to today. He told me he has the day off."

"Why don't you go find out?"

"I should catch up on my sleep but I think I should ask him if he would like to go shopping for cars with me."

"That's something different."

"Yeah, it is. I've got to get up and ask him." He looked at his digital watch. "Let me see. It's eight fifteen."

Mavis walked to the bathroom and began washing her face to freshen up for her day and wondered when Damien was going to catch up on his sleep. Damien went to his dresser where his cell phone was sitting and he reached for it. He opened his cell phone and found Cullen's number in his call list and dialed it.

"Hi Cullen?"

"Yes, that's me."

"This is Damien. I was wondering if you would like to go car shopping with me today. How about it?"

"Sounds fun. What time do you want to go?"

"Like eleven-ish."

"Eleven-ish?" Cullen repeated. "Meet me at my house then."

"Sure. Let's go look at some cars."

"I haven't gone car shopping for a while. Maybe it's time for me to buy a new car too. Are you looking to buy one soon?"

"Maybe. We'll see what cars they have around town."

"Sounds good. Wait until you read the article I read yesterday in the newspaper. It's about Cally Ryerson. C'mon over and you can read it."

"Sure. See you soon." Damien's eyes were suddenly wide open at the thought of what the article could say.

"See ya."

Two hours later Cullen had greeted Damien at the front door with a friendly handshake.

"Hello." Cullen said.

"Hey man." He grinned.

By that time Damien had noticed Cullen holding a newspaper in his hand. He was pointing to the article about Cally Ryerson. "This is the one I was telling you about. Go ahead and read it."

"Sure." He held the newspaper in his hands and began to read to himself what it said.

Motivated group of neighbours shape goals for success

The latest story we have on what has been going on with The Sunlit Avenue Group is that Cally Ryerson, a drummer in a local rock and roll band, has come up with something new called "The Combination Effect." He has explained it simply as having some popular rock bands teaming up so that they could possibly work on producing some really amazing songs together. More simply, it is an overall combining of creativity so to speak. From what he saw so far from the combined efforts of his fellow neighbours of Sunlit Avenue in achieving their own goals, he has claimed this would be a good way for more people to create goals to make outstanding music of their own. Cally Ryerson does seem to be on to something here. Cally would tell you that his fellow neighbours of Sunlit Avenue are definitely not in rock and roll bands of their own like he is but they are indeed entrepreneurs working together in business. And Cally has said he has been picturing what would happen if a whole street of neighbours in rock bands were to work together with the same get up and go ambition that those entrepreneurs on Sunlit Avenue in Moncton have been famous for on their goal achievements. He said maybe some rock bands will hear him out and have some really radical results with music from his insight.

Damien couldn't believe it. "You don't say. Cally actually said that?"

"What do you think of it?" Cullen took the newspaper from Damien and set it on the hall table while awaiting his reply.

"I think he has something here. People putting their talents together the way we have been doing, except now it's rock bands."

"Exciting to hear anyway."

"I can imagine."

"Yeah, that Cally has been up to something lately."

"I'd say he has." Damien said as he noted Cullen reaching for the door already.

"Okay, let's go look at some cars. Are you ready?"

"Oh, I'm ready. Hey, uh, did you hear that Mavis and I and our employees at the fountain store have been wearing shirts that have the Chinese symbols for strength, wisdom and love written on them? It's our newest goal to wear them to go more worldly with the Asian population of the world since we are international now with all those people who have heard about us. We keep appearing in the news."

"I heard about that. Word has been spreading fast about us. It's amazing what happens when teamwork is involved between neighbours. I guess people like that."

"Yes they do. You're right about that." Damien high-fived him.

* * *

"Flare?"

"What is it Vic?"

"Did you check the voicemail on our telephone yet today? I'm expecting a call from Cora."

"No, I haven't Vic. I mean Midtown." Sven was watching the pet lovebirds Fizz and Bizz preening their feathers in their birdcage as he stood near the living room windows. He noticed a steady flow of traffic going down the street and wondered if it was some of the people that have heard of him and his fellow neighbours from listening to the media lately.

"You haven't?"

"How about I'll let you do that?"

"Whatever." Vic picked up the telephone and proceeded to dial for voicemail. He heard a message from Cora right away. He felt relieved.

The message stated the following, "Hi Vic, it's Cora again. I'm calling to tell you that the CEO of Neat Street Robots has talked to some robotics experts and he has decided that hiring some more people to make Sizel Coolbeans wave her hand and nod her head like we had intended would cost way too much money at this point. So we are just going to go with Sizel saying the inspirational messages. With your original quotes of course and Sven's wisdom quotes. Gotta go. Bye for now."

"That's different."

"What?"

"Cora said Sizel Coolbeans won't be waving her hand or nodding like she thought. But she is keeping our quotes as messages for the robot to say."

"Well that's good to hear."

"Yeah."

"It means she will pay us each five thousand dollars like she mentioned for thinking of the robot's messages." Sven mentioned. "And don't forget. People will be hearing the messages too."

"I heard that Cora's company has been selling dozens of those Take it to the Max robots a month."

"Oh, I'm glad there are some nice paychecks in it for her. I wonder what she's going to do with the money."

"I don't know. I still find it neat how more people have robots now, just like how they pictured there would be back in the olden days."

"It's thankfully all because of a young girl's idea that started it all."

"Yeah, thanks to Cora Pepper."

CHAPTER 23

Thursday, November 10, 2011

During the middle of the night there was a loud screeching of brakes followed by horn blasts on Sunlit Avenue. Most of the neighbours were already awake by the time the vehicle making the sounds finally sped away into the night. It woke them up and kept them on alert. Just as it happened months ago, it happened once again. The neighbours that had heard the noise outside became very concerned because they wondered who it could be. Especially Sid Mathison. He jumped out of bed and thought "Cora."

He remembered the day he received the letter in the mail from Cora stating that all the commotion with the car noises was probably due to the people at Neat Street Robots finding out what goes on at Sunlit Avenue from day to day. He wondered who exactly it could be. And then he wondered if and when he was going to find out who it had been.

After he calmed down a bit more he finally crawled back into bed and fell asleep for the night. He slept soundly. It was quiet on the Avenue once more.

The other neighbours were also sleeping soundly in their own homes. But when morning came around, the neighbours began calling each other on the telephone about what had happened only hours ago. First Sid called Doris. And after that Doris called Rita and so on. Word spread about Sid being more concerned than the other neighbours until everyone knew about it. It appeared to be no cause for alarm at first but when Sid had said his say about the event everyone began to gossip.

That is when Cally decided to drive to Neat Street Robots to discover for himself who it had been. At the factory he made quite the ruckus by insisting he find out which one of the factory workers it might have been and confronting all the workers one by one until he felt that maybe it was someone else that had made the loud noises in the middle of the night. Cally Ryerson's visit to the factory halted production of the robots for about half an hour. The workers insisted they get back on schedule because a shipment of robots was due by the end of the month. So when he patted some of the factory workers on the back and said that he was convinced it wasn't anyone there at the factory that had made the noises in the middle of the night he told them he was leaving. When he was saying his goodbyes to the people at the factory, he noticed a switch on the base of a gigantic cooling fan. He felt curious to see what would happen if he pressed the switch and once he did there was a loud explosion that sounded throughout the manufacturing room in which they stood. Cally put his hand over his mouth when he saw that the gigantic cooling fan used to cool down the entire room was now in pieces all over the floor in front of him. After he got over the loud sound caused by the explosion, he and the workers were both shocked and stunned. Upon seeing the mess on the floor, one of the workers mentioned that it would be difficult to work in the heat without the cooling fan because it was nearby the part of the room where they poured the intensely heated up liquid metal used for pouring molds to make the Catchy Petunia robots. Cally claimed all he did was flick a switch. But he was told by another factory worker that the cooling fan was something that was supposed to be turned on gradually by pulling a lever located on a nearby wall. They escorted him out of the building before he could cause any further halts in the robot manufacturing process and Cally apologized for any damages to the factory.

Everything that Cally said at the robot factory helped to relieve him of any suspicions he had toward the factory workers about whether or not they did it. In Cally's view the factory workers now seemed to be a good and productive crew who cared enough to assure him that there was no cause for concern. He no longer felt alarmed. Instead he had high hopes for Cora's company Neat Street Robots. He would just have to be patient and wait and see if he could find out in the near future who was responsible for the loud car noises.

When he got back to Moncton he refueled his small sized Toyota Tundra monster truck at a gas station and headed to Sunlit Avenue. Once there, he walked into the new home that he shared with Hazel Pepper. Hazel was on the couch resting after a day's work of tiling houses with her co-worker Hugh. When Cally stepped into the entryway of the house, he jokingly waved his hand at Hazel mimicking how he thought Sizel Coolbeans would wave her hand if the female robot would be developed to do so like Cora had hoped. Hazel nodded in response.

"How is your day going?" Cally said.

"Whew. Let me tell you. Hugh, my co-worker, is one serious guy to work with."

"How so?"

"Well, when we are working away at tiling people's houses he often asks me to say "Hi" to all the neighbours for him."

"And?"

"And then he keeps asking me if I told them "Hi" yet. It happens every few days like that."

"Maybe he's waiting to hear back a "Hi" each time."

"Oh, he is. But he keeps it up. He's persistent. But he's usually fine to talk to other than when we are talking about that."

"Does he know what we've been up to lately?" Cally asked while taking off his autumn jacket and putting it on a coat hook fastened to the wall by the front door.

"Does he ever. He goes to The Sunlit Avenue Group website and reads up about us."

"He does, does he?"

"Yep. Uh, oh, by the way. I cleaned the mirrors around the house again. They're all cleaned up."

"Like you so often do."

"I like having spotless mirrors. That's why I clean them so often."

"Funny." Cally hinted. "Maybe the reason why Hugh talks about the neighbours so often is because he enjoys it just like you enjoy cleaning the mirrors around the house."

"What? Are you saying he and I both have different sorts of habits? I guess it goes along with working with him every day."

"Yeah. I guess." Cally pulled up his pants a bit and soon sat on the sofa beside her.

"I just like to keep a clean house though." Hazel insisted.

"I would say so."

There was a pause. And then Hazel asked, "How is your day going today?"

"I went to pay the Neat Street people a visit today at the factory."

"You did?"

"Yes, just to make sure none of the factory workers weren't driving that mysterious car up and down the Avenue last night."

"Oh my gosh. Cally."

"Don't worry. None of them did."

"Well that's nice to hear. We wouldn't want to cause an uproar at my daughter's company."

"Yup. But I had to go find out anyway."

"Did you know that Cora almost has enough money to buy a house of her own?"

"Really. That's something. At her age."

"That's Cora for ya."

"Cora the young business woman. Is she still cutting hair at the salon?"

"Why yes, she is. She likes it."

"That's good to know. Man, look at that Catchy Petunia robot in the corner. He's really great. What a team she has working at the factory to make something like that."

"Are they excellent or what? I had a chance to stop by there a month ago to see them in action. Excellent. I'd say."

"I met the CEO today while I was there. I saw him in the hallway on the way to the entrance to the manufacturing room. Jett Black sure seems cut out for being the company's CEO."

"Oh. You met the guy?"

"Yes, but I won't tell you what he said. It's a secret."

"Are you going to tell me the secret?"

"Okay I will. Jett Black told me that people are buying the Catchy Petunia robots as fast as they can make them. That's the secret."

"Oh dear. Do you know what this means? Cora's new business is a success."

"She should be receiving a letter from Neat Street Robots any day now."

"Woah. Wait until Cora hears the news."

"I'd say. Are you going to phone her soon?"

"Am I? You bet I will call her."

"That's good because I want to find out what she is going to do with all the money."

"You and me both will be hearing about it. That's for sure."

"So when are you going to call her?"

"Today." Hazel assured him.

CHAPTER 24

Thursday, November 24, 2011

Aleisha Forbes stopped by Rain and Cullen's house after three thirty pm to say hello. When she knocked on the door Rain answered it and gave her a hug when she saw it was her. Rain had been remembering the conversations that went on at the barbeque that she and Cullen had hosted earlier.

"Aleisha. I'm glad to see you."

"I'm glad to see you too Rain but wait until you hear what's new."

"Uh-huh. Go on."

"They are publishing my new children's book called Bubbles and Swirl and it's hitting the bookstands in a matter of days."

"I haven't heard anything about you writing a children's book."

"That's because I was keeping it a surprise. I like surprises. I remember that I mentioned so at the barbeque?"

"Oh. Hmm. Aleisha, be sure to tell me when your book is available so I can buy a copy."

"I will." She smiled and then scratched her head. "Could you tell Cullen about the children's book for me? Bubbles and Swirl, in case you forget."

"Yes. What is it about?"

"A whale and a dolphin that play and swim together in the open ocean."

"Alright. I will let him know."

"Thanks Rain. Gee, I've really gotta go. I'm going to go for a drive to the beach to walk on the sand one last time before the winter."

"Okay. But before you go I thought I should tell you that Cullen and Damien each bought new cars."

"How new are they?"

"They are this year's models. Cullen bought a silver 2011 Lincoln MKZ and Damien bought a blue one. There wasn't any to buy in Moncton so they had to drive to Saint John to get them."

"Well, gee. I'm glad they got new cars."

"It was time for Cullen to get a new car. His car was a 2004."

"Phenomenal. I really have to get going. Bye for now."

"See ya." Rain watched as Aleisha casually strolled up the Avenue back to her house.

Rain began to get a chill from the cold air outside. She quickly zipped back inside the house and closed the front door. She hadn't yet looked at the weather report online to find out what the temperature was but to her it seemed to be getting pretty cold out and winter was fast approaching.

Just then the telephone rang. When Rain answered it she was delighted to hear Doris talking to her. "Hi, it's Doris Keenan. I'm just calling to tell you that I retired from my job. I no longer work for the clothing manufacturer Reyonders. Kokomoz is doing such good business these days I decided to just focus on the Kokomoz company."

"Oh my."

"I also decided to donate five thousand dollars to your company Fine Point Rainforest Incorporated. I'll send you the cheque soon."

"That's terrific. It will certainly help Fine Point to get up and running."

"You're not the only one who would like fresher air for the future. So, how is everything going with it?"

"I received one-hundred and thirty thousand dollars recently from the proceeds from the laser line show. And the Peace-eba band gave me a lot of money from part of the proceeds from their concert. Ten percent each performance. Let's just say I have already met the start-up costs of the company. They are almost done building the warehouse close to the Amazon rainforest and I'm paying for the financing of an airplane to ship the goods to and from the warehouse once the business opens. I hired some people to fly an airplane and I just have to wait to hear back from someone by email to see if every one of the farmers that are going to be working at the factory is ready to begin."

"Yeah. Sounds like you are nearly ready for the business to begin."

"I have hired Sid to design the products and Hazel to design the catalogues for the company."

"Did they start yet?"

"Actually last week they did."

"Splendid Rain. Like I said, expect the cheque soon. I will give you the money in a couple of days."

"Well, it will sure play it's part to get it all rolling along sooner. Fine Point Rainforest Inc. is sure to be opening in a couple of months."

"Now that's nice to hear. Talk to you later neighbour."

"Yup. Later."

A few hours had passed by, and as Rain was putting aside some cards that she was working on for her homemade card company Cards and More in Store, she received another phone call. It rang a few times before she picked up the phone. And when she did she soon discovered that she was talking to Cora.

"Oh my dear. Cora, it's you. How are you?"

"Doing good. Actually really great in fact. I opened a letter from Neat Street Robots today that was a short note saying they have started making the female robots known as Sizel Coolbeans recently. Isn't it just marvelous?"

"Yeah, I would say so."

"And one of the inspirational messages that Sizel says was thought up by me. It's the first message of the ten. But the other nine quotes were still thought of by Sven and Vic though." Cora laughed with glee as she spoke about it on the telephone to Rain. "I even heard all about your company Fine Point today from Doris. She called me. I just happened to have a day off from the hair salon and she told me the latest news and then we gossiped about my boyfriend Brooke."

"What did you say about him?"

"His new website called "The Sport of Goal Setting" has been visited by over twenty-eight thousand people so far. He's quite content watching the number of visitors to his website increase day after day."

"And?"

"He has a message board so that people can comment on what he wrote and he likes to read about their own personal experiences that they write about online to him. He likes to hear people's personal stories about goal setting. A lot of people are going after their goals these days and Brooke tells me that they recognize the importance of their goals when they read something like a book or two on goals or Brooke's website. Yup. And he likes to kiss me and tell me how much he likes the Take it to the Max a.k.a. Catchy Petunia robot that is now in my apartment. That's what Doris and I were gossiping about."

"I bet that you are going to put a Sizel Coolbeans robot right beside the Catchy Petunia robot as soon as they make one for you. Isn't that right?"

"Oh maybe. And I have been saving up plenty of money for a new house with a garage thanks to all the robots they are building. Did you know I get five hundred dollars for each one they sell?"

"Darling, even Cally Ryerson, the newest neighbour on Sunlit Avenue knows about that."

"It's funny you mention Cally. I spoke to him and my mom on the phone two weeks ago. He told me that he met the CEO Jett Black and that he stopped by the factory to check up on the workers to make sure that it wasn't one of them who screeched some car tires and honked a car horn late at night again."

"I wonder who it could be."

"Couldn't say." Cora cleared her throat.

"Does Cally ever say what happened to that game show that his parents and grandchildren started? What was it now…Names for Words? Yeah, that's it. Is it still on television these days?"

"Names for Words only broadcasted one time in Canada and then they decided to air it in another country. I don't know which country for that matter."

"Well that explains it. I haven't heard anything about it ever since they told me it was going to be on television but that was months ago."

"It's still airing on television these days. At least I think so. Last month was when I last heard of it."

"Cora. Cullen told me last night that he thinks it's time to hire more people to help design homemade cards for my store. I talked it over with him and you know…he's right. So I put out an ad on the Sunlit Avenue Group website offering two job positions and today several people emailed me their phone numbers so I think I will call them and think about hiring two of them to make cards. I've been working twelve hours a day making cards."

"Rain, it sure does sound like it's time. Hire them. I sure would."

"I hope they like to work long hours."

"Probably."

"Well, I have to go. It was nice talking to you Cora. I wish you the best with those new Sizel Coolbean robots they have started making."

"Okay. And I'm looking forward to your company Fine Point Rainforest Incorporated opening soon. Bye for now."

"Bye."

CHAPTER 25

Friday, February 10, 2012

"I haven't heard anything about the year-end progress report that the reporter and camera man spoke of last year. It's been a while and I just happened to think of it." Edmond said while scratching his head. "Dad, did you hear back from them yet?"

"Sure did. We were on the front page of the newspaper. Remember when Rita hired a photographer guy to take a photo of our entire group? Well, they published it in the newspaper. That along with one line that stated to visit The Sunlit Avenue Group's website. And then they listed the website name for everyone to see."

"When was that?" Edmond gasped while picturing how many people may have read the newspaper.

"The last week of December." Mark let out a hearty bellowing laugh. "Why haven't you heard about it?"

"I just didn't. I guess I've been so busy talking to Rain lately that I forgot all about it. Did you hear that she made me Shipper Receiver at the Moncton warehouse they have in town?"

"Really? That company is making huge progress already since opening up shop last week."

"That's right dad. Mom already heard about it. She loves it." Edmond took a comb out of his pocket and combed his hair with it. "What are you reading dad?"

"I'm just seeing what boats are for sale here in the newspaper. But never mind that. Tell me when you start your job."

"I start this July. Hopefully I will have finished high school by then."

"Well your marks are usually in the ninety percent range. Give your studies a few more months and then you will graduate."

"Yes dad. I am doing good. Don't worry."

"So, your job duties will be shipping out packages from the warehouse to customers and receiving packages from the shop at the Amazon rainforest?"

"Yes. You guessed it."

"And Rain?"

"She hired a head boss to be in charge of stuff that goes on around the warehouse while she sits at home and works on her homemade cards. She can't forget about her card business."

"I guess not." Mark continued. "What drives that woman is she likes to reach out to lots of people. You can see it in the cards she makes. And now it's Fine Point Rainforest Inc."

"Yeah, that's her latest addition."

Neither Mark nor Edmond said anything more to each other for the moment until the doorbell at their house rang. It was unexpected. Edmond checked to see who it could be. He answered the door and saw that Cora Pepper and a delivery man were standing at the door. He could tell it was a delivery man by the big package he was holding onto.

"Hi Edmond." Cora said right away. "This is for you and your parents. A Sizel Coolbeans robot."

"Oh yeah? Wow, are you sure? I heard they are twelve thousand dollars."

"It's a gift as a thank you for your mom donating to the rainforest company that Rain started. Doris donated five thousand dollars to Rain to help her company run smoothly in its first few months of operating."

"My mom did that? Oh, I didn't hear about that. I'm awestruck. Let me see her. The robot I mean. Sizel. Let me see her."

"Okay then. I will bring her in the house for you first and then you can take a gander at her."

"Is it really the robot? I've got to see this!" Mark said with great excitement a few seconds later.

The delivery man picked up the robot in his strong arms and set her down in the middle of the hallway by the front door. He then pulled off some blue tape that fastened some neon green plastic mesh wrap that was around her and unveiled the robot.

"Oh my goodness. Look at her. Is that cool or what?"

"She looks entirely different than Catchy but she has something in common with him. She has ten inspirational messages that she says like Catchy does."

"How true." Edmond tapped Sizel on one of her metallic arms with absolute astonishment that the Neat Street robot was in front of him.

Edmond and Mark took a good look at her. The robot was pink, white and black. Her head down to her shoulders was pink and she had black outlined eyes as though it was a lady with eyeliner applied around her eyes. Her eyes looked almost human. So did her ears. She had a black mouth. She had a small bust line on her chest like a female robot should have. And it appeared as though she was wearing a white, long sleeved shirt and black pants. Her hands were pink just like her face. And on her feet were black sandals. She stood at a height of six-feet tall and under her sandals was a three-foot wide circular, flat stand to hold her steady in standing position. The cool looking Neat Street logo with an oval surrounding pointed capital letters in the name Neat Street Robots made the words look all that much more futuristic.

Cora finally came out with it. "So...do you guys think you would like to hear the inspirational messages now that you've seen her?"

"I sure would."

"Yeah, I would like to hear the messages alright. Let's play them now." Edmond remarked with heartfelt joy.

"Be my guest." Cora smiled.

Edmond proceeded to press the first one. *"Something special is in the works. My name is Sizel Coolbeans, an Enjoy it to the Max Robot. Here to inspire you and spark your imagination and to remind you to be creative. A little bit of positive creativity goes a long way."* He went on by pressing the second one. *"Love is wholesome, pure and true."* And the third. *"Think do. Think. Do. But do think. And remember it all takes time."* The fourth. *"The stuff that life is made of can help us all get up to speed."* The fifth. *"There is always an easier way of doing things. The key is to find it."*

"We just heard some of Sven's wisdom quotes and here we go with Vic's original quotes." Cora nodded with a fixed gaze on her face.

The sixth button. *"Know your biz."* The seventh. *"Stand the test of time and you won't go out of style."* The eight. *"If it's not nothing it's definitely something."* The ninth. *"Sometimes a mere hobby can lead to a great invention. That is the science of the matter."* And the tenth. *"Go beyond the odds."*

"I'm overwhelmed at the moment Cora."

"What?"

"Great, isn't she?" The delivery man asked with a convincing tone of voice.

"Yes, but I have to go sit down for a while."

"What's wrong Edmond?" She asked.

"I just realized how lucky I am to have such a gift from you Cora. I'm baffled, perplexed, mystified."

"Really?"

"Uh, yeah." His words were stated with an accentuated tone.

"Gee, son. Why for that?" Mark asked.

"Okay. I'm over it."

"What…just like that?"

"Yeah. I like the present you gave me and my family Cora. Thanks."

"You're surely welcome."

"Yes. Thank you."

The delivery man looked the robot over and said, "Well, I should be going. I still have to drive back to Fredericton to Neat Street Robots and tell them I delivered the Sizel Coolbeans robot."

"I hope they make many more of them." Mark added.

"I do too." The delivery man continued.

"What is your name, sir, before you go?" Mark questioned.

"Harry." The man said, wrinkling his forehead. "Oh fudge. I left the van engine running. I've got to go. Are you coming Cora? I'll bring you back to your apartment."

"Yup."

"Hey, thanks for stopping by." Mark waved as they were on their way out the door.

"See ya." Cora blew a kiss to them.

As they sped out the door they were met by dozens of cars that by mere co-incidence just happened to be driving down Sunlit Avenue. It appeared as though it was a parade of automobiles with people in the cars peering out at Cora and Harry. One person shouted through an open car window. "Look! Neat Street Robots!" The commotion caused the people in the cars behind them to honk their horns repeatedly until they sped past the Keenans' house and around the corner to the next street. The mysterious parade of cars that seemed to have come out of nowhere had strangely disappeared as quickly as it had appeared.

"What was that?" Harry felt he should ask even though he wasn't ready for the answer that he knew Cora was about to give him.

"Why, that's just one of the touring groups that will be touring around Sunlit Avenue lately to find out what the neighbourhood is like where The Sunlit Avenue Group lives."

"You mean one of many, don't you?"

"Yes, I do. And it was me that started it."

"You? How did that happen?"

"I asked them to tour around and see the houses on the Avenue. I put up a flyer on the wall at the nightclub where Cally Ryerson plays."

"Cora, you didn't."

"Yes, I did indeed."

"You're quite the gal. I have to ask though. What made you do it?"

"It's just that my old neighbours of Sunlit Avenue and I like it when it gets interesting. That's the reason why I did it. To make it interesting for them."

"Geez. Let's face it Cora, you like to be spontaneous."

"I guess I am a little bit spontaneous Harry."

"I really think you are. But it's good sometimes to be spontaneous from what I have heard before from people."

"It's funny you mention that." She was overcome by emotion. So much so she shed a tear. She wiped the tear with her hand and opened the passenger side window by pressing a button. She let the cool winter breeze of the morning that was blowing outside calm her down a little. "I'm so glad they like the robot that I brought to them. It's making for one exciting day."

"I'd say so. You're full of surprises today."

"Yeah. Anyway, my boyfriend Brooke is going to miss not seeing a Sizel Coolbeans robot standing beside the Catchy Petunia robot in my apartment like he pictured."

"Uh-huh. But it sure was fun delivering the robot to the Keenans' wasn't it? That's something a person doesn't do every day."

"Except for you." Cora reminded Harry.

"Yeah, except for me."

CHAPTER 26

Monday, May 28, 2012

More than three months had passed since The Keenans received the Catchy Petunia robot from Cora Pepper. It had been that long since the touring groups had first been seen visiting Sunlit Avenue to get a glimpse of what the neighbours had been keeping busy doing. During that time there were some nights of car tires screeching and horn blasting that kept the neighbours wondering who would go so far as to make the loud noises in the quiet of the night. Their curiosity kept building and building until they were left to wonder if somebody, anybody, might finally tell them who it was peeling their car down the street late at night. Then, on this particular day, the telephone rang at Hazel and Cally's house. Cally happened to already be awake at the time the telephone rang. He was having trouble sleeping.

He answered the telephone saying, "Hello?"

The voice that responded soon replied. "Tell Hazel that Hugh sped the car. My brother drives a NASCAR race car." After that there was a click and the call had ended.

Cally was quick to wake Hazel and tell her what the person on the telephone had said. After some puzzled looks of bewilderment, Hazel and Cally let out some sighs of relief after waiting so long for the unveiling of a great mystery that had occurred all within a moment's notice. Hazel and Cally were up for the rest of the day after the great mystery had finally been solved.

Later that day, Cally had spotted Damien weeding his front lawn as he looked through his bedroom window and he thought he would go over and talk to him.

"Damien…Damien…Damien…" Cally shook his head. He sounded as though he had some feelings to express.

"What?"

"What have you been doing with Rita lately? I get up early in the morning and I see you two going somewhere in her car."

"We have been going to the beach each day to see the sunrises. Except she keeps her camera in the car."

"Why?" She is a photographer after all. And she loves sunrises. Why would she leave her camera in the car?"

"Rita and I have been going to the beach secretly together to see the sunrises early in the morning whenever there is a clear sky. I have found a more spiritual meaning to life since my kidnapping ordeal occurred and I was released from the kidnappers."

"Go on."

"Because I'm seeing a change in how I think of my life. I explained to her in detail about remembering to be still sometimes and treasuring life and such. I value my life each day that goes by. After I was released from the kidnappers I have kept busy noticing in quiet reflection how important life is to me."

"Gee."

"I take time these days spending the hours in quiet thought. And that deeply touches and moves me. It soothes me for I know that God is always there in such moments and I listen to life differently than before."

"You have a way with words my friend."

"Yup. And I bet it's something you weren't expecting me to say."

"That's right."

"Say, why don't we invite all the neighbours to the beach tomorrow morning before sunrise and we can all watch the sun come up? We'll spend some time celebrating together because last May was the month exactly one year ago that we all decided to go for it and go for our goals. It's been one year now. Let's do that. Let's all celebrate the year we had by going to the beach."

"Before sunrise, eh?"

"Exactly. How about it?"

"Sure Damien. I'll go. What time?"

"Four forty-five a.m. That will give us only half an hour before sunrise."

"Cool. I'm with you. I'm all for it. Let me phone all the neighbours for you and then tomorrow we will go."

"Man, thanks a bunch." Damien patted Cally on the shoulder.

"I will see you tomorrow then. Early. Along with the rest of the group." Cally pinched Damien's cheek to be silly.

"I'm looking forward to it."

"Me too."

CHAPTER 27

Tuesday, May 29, 2012

All the neighbours, including Cora Pepper, gathered together one by one on a parking lot made of sand and stones and grass on a private beach nearby Shediac. It took about fifteen minutes for everyone to arrive but once they did the vehicles filled the parking lot with room to spare. There was already some faint light in the sky above and this helped them to see each other and notice what kind of vehicles they had pulled up in before the sun had come up.

Aleisha Forbes arrived in a white 2007 Honda Civic. Zoey and Ralph Holiday arrived in a mauve 2005 Hyundai Santa Fe. Brooke Akira arrived in a silver 2009 Ford Mustang. Sid Mathison and his dog Oazic arrived in a black 2005 Honda Accord. Mavis, Damien, Francis and Lulu Hemley arrived in a blue 2011 Lincoln MKZ. Doris, Mark and Edmond Keenan arrived in an orange 2005 Nissan Sentra. Rita Young arrived in a black 2011 Ford Fusion SE. Cora Pepper arrived in a white 2010 BMW 760 Li. Hazel Pepper and Cally Ryerson arrived in a black 2007 Toyota Tundra. Rain Woodrow and Cullen Dangsi arrived in a silver 2011 Lincoln MKZ. Sven and Vic Nicolos arrived in a 2008 white Nissan Pathfinder.

They did a head count of twenty people and one dog and walked to the shoreline. It was there at the water's edge where they huddled close to one another and continued on with their favourite pastime. Telling each other the latest on what has been happening in terms of their goals.

"Guys, you can buy copies of a children's book called Bubbles and Swirl now. Bubbles the whale and Swirl the dolphin. Last I heard was they are even going to make a frozen yogurt flavour called Bubbles and Swirl. Fantastic isn't it?" Aleisha said.

"Mmm. Frozen yogurt." Mavis replied.

Brooke cut in. "Let me tell you about the website I have on the sport of goal setting. People of all ages are writing emails to me telling me that they are finding it so much fun to write down a list of goals and going after their goals."

"That's cool enough." Cally said.

"Very much so." Damien said.

Cally remarked, "Guess what? It was Hugh that sped the car. Hazel's co-worker did it. I received a phone call from him recently. He hung up before I could say anything to him."

"Gee, that's a relief." Sven said.

"Oh my." Rita jumped in.

Cally went on to say, "By the way Cullen, my band and I finally finished writing the music for the food taster guy song you wrote for me. We have been practicing playing the song a few times and soon we hope to play it in front of large crowds at the Fen Fen Nightclub."

"That's nice." Cullen remarked.

Before Cally talked about in any further, he interrupted. "Wait a second. Hold it right there. Damien has something to say, haven't you Damien?"

"Why yes, I do. If you mean the spiritual view I have on life now, then yes I do."

"We're all ears." Cally said.

"I invited you all here to celebrate the year we have had together and to tell you that I came up with a timeless quote just the other day when I was sitting and relaxing. I will tell you what it is if you would like to hear it."

"Tell us Damien." Rain cheered him on.

"This one quote is so good to hear that you would pause to reflect on it and wonder how much money a person could earn if they sold copies of the quote on big posters for companies and businesses around the world to put up in their employee staff rooms and meeting rooms."

"This we have to hear." Aleisha said.

"Are you ready to hear it?" He asked.

"We sure are. Let's hear your quote Damien." Sven said.

"A bump in the road of life is only there to remind you to have more of a spring to your step."

"Yes. He said it." Sven certainly felt alive with passion for Damien's new quote. He could tell right away that there was great wisdom to it. And Sven really admired wisdom of any sort.

"Rita and I have been coming to the beach early in the mornings lately and talking about the quote while we watch the sun come up. Plus now I view life differently than before. It's in the quiet moments that I think of it more spiritually now."

"I already knew that. Damien told me about it. Didn't ya darling?" Mavis smiled.

"Yes dear." He nodded.

"Well that's new." Francis was caught off guard. Everyone could hear it in her voice.

"Yeah, sis. It is new." Lulu answered.

Everyone laughed a big, healthy sounding laugh once they heard the comments from Francis and Lulu.

"That's great. Let's do three cheers for Damien."

Everyone cheered for him. "Hip hip hooray! Hip hip hooray! Hip hip hooray!"

"Yay Damien. That quote is definitely one worth keeping." Rain said after the cheer. "By the way, did you hear what products Fine Point Rainforest Inc. has in its Great Emotion catalogue?"

"No, but I would like to hear about your products."

"Let me tell you then. One of them is a fine silver writing pen with the company name written on it. Another is a year's subscription to the Fine Point Rainforest Inc. magazine called "Let's Keep Goaling Strong" that talks about what goes on at the workshop at the Amazon rainforest. There are stuffed toys of Chuzzy the tiger mascot, hand sewn jackets with the company name on them, creative looking paintings of all sorts such as ones of super tall legged humans to mimic the tall trees of the rainforest. There are friendship necklaces of many different types and colors of plastic beads. It's going good. And soon there will be more. Lately we have been working on a few more products." She went on. "The workers at the Amazon rainforest shop are really finding it rewarding to be making the products for people and bringing in lots of money working for the company. And not as many trees will be cut down at the Amazon rainforest from what I hear."

"Nice." Damien took a big breath and exhaled. "That means more clean air."

"Yes it does, doesn't it?" Rain said.

"Hey Cally." Cullen began. "I recently read an article that talked about you thinking of an idea about having a whole street of rock bands making exceptional music the same way we the neighbours of Sunlit Avenue are entrepreneurs who have been working together. Have you heard if anyone has taken up your offer of having many rock bands working on making songs together?"

"No, I haven't Cullen. I'm still waiting to hear about it myself. Maybe it will happen sometime soon though. That's what I'm hoping. Wouldn't it be cool if they made lengthy songs that are like ten minutes each too? We should put something about it on The Sunlit Avenue Group's website so that maybe some rock bands will team up and make unusual and exceptional music like I've been hoping for."

"Sounds like a good idea to me. Yeah, we should definitely put something about it on the website. An idea is the first step to making something interesting happen."

"Yes, that's where it's at." Cally grinned with a sense of bewilderment in regards to Cullen's words.

From out of nowhere, the same man that Cullen kept seeing was now walking toward the group of neighbours from beside the water's edge and the waves were washing up close to where his bare feet were stepping. He looked for a few seconds for Cullen and found him. He gave Cullen a thumbs up as he passed by him and then he stopped to look for Rain. When he saw her, he approached her and started a conversation with her.

"Hi, you are Rain Woodrow right?"

"Indeed I am." She announced proudly.

"I'm Brooke's co-worker. Yeah, I'm the one who has been divulging information about all of you neighbours all along and I heard about you being in business with the Fine Point Rainforest company to reduce the emissions of pollution in the world by saving rainforest trees."

Cullen interrupted. "Hi, we meet again. Who are you anyway? I've been seeing you around so much. You just have to tell me!"

By this time the other neighbours had gathered around because Cullen's voice carried quite a bit and the other neighbours were all ears.

"I was threatened by Griffin and Lenny the kidnappers and they made sure that I spied on all of you here and there to see what you were up to."

"You spied on us?" Cally Ryerson scowled.

"Yep, I was a spy. I had to be a spy because Griffin and Lenny said they would be after me if I didn't tell them the details about you."

The neighbours talked among themselves for a very brief period of time. Then one of them, Rita, spoke out and said, "You mean to tell us that you acted as a spy for the kidnappers? Oh, that's too much. What did the kidnappers find out about us?"

"It's nothing at all."

Bad boy Cally led on the discussion. "Look, before we jump to conclusions why don't we listen to what he has to say? Go on. We're listening."

"They got to watch you progress along for one thing because I often checked up on you guys."

"How so?" Sven questioned.

"I have my ways. Right Cullen?"

"Well, I saw you walking around the Avenue a few times but it makes me wonder what else you may have been up to. Are you going to tell me or are some things better left unsaid?"

"Let's say that I combed the city and observed you while keeping a fair distance away from you so that you wouldn't notice me." He looked at Cullen. "Most of the time even you didn't notice me Dangsi."

"I wondered about you." Cullen went on. "You seemed to be a pretty spur-of-the-moment kind of guy by what I gathered.

"Hey, Cullen is this guy bothering you?" Cally gripped the man by his dark green shirt that had white sleeves. Cally looked him over and looked past his black shorts at his bare feet. "How about I lift you off the ground?"

"Easy there Cally." The man was quick to answer.

"Let go of him." Cullen saw Cally release his firm grip on the man's shirt. "I was going to say that I also found you to be natural and genuine in the way you were carrying about your business. I will go as far as to say that I admire you for your tendency to be so mysterious. Especially after the motorcycle incident."

"What motorcycle incident? Oh, do you mean that time when I heard a motorcycle accelerating outside when I was trying to get some shut eye?" Sid took a big breath. "I thought Sven and Vic had a visitor that day."

"A visitor?" Vic asked.

"He was parked in your driveway guys." Sid was nervous.

"That's nothing to worry about." Sven calmly assured him.

"I was going to say that since the kidnappers went to jail, I just feel like doing what I feel like doing now. I hope you guys can forgive me but I was forced to follow you around so that I could tell the kidnappers information about you."

"And?" Cally hoped to hear more.

"Oh, this is too much for me. How could you do something like just spy on us?" Rita folded her arms together and held her head high up in the air. She awaited an answer and the answer she was getting wasn't what she had hoped for."

"Cullen, we've met before. I have to warn you, Griffin has an evil streak. He sat up late at night wondering about how he was going to sell enough of those tribal art woodcarvings. He used to call me at odd hours of the night but I told him I was determined to let him figure things out for himself."

"Boy, this is news." Damien felt himself begin to sweat as he listened.

"Then he figured out that some investors could help fund the company he started. You see he was trying to sell as many of those doorknob tattoos as possible. So with the help of the investors he hired many workers to help carve the wooden carvings for him."

"Phew. This really is too much." Rita was hearing what he was saying.

Damien mentioned, "Yeah, I remember he told me about those over the phone once."

The man's attention was on Rain again. "Let me tell you where I'm going with all this. What I feel like doing now is being a spokesperson for your company to get the word across about the importance of Fine Point Rainforest Inc. so that people will hopefully continue to have clean, crisp air. I will talk in front of crowds of people doing seminars and charge a fee of fifteen dollars for those attending one of my seminars that I will be doing."

"That's just wonderful. What is your name by the way?" Rain asked.

"Marley Wilks."

"I'm so happy to hear it. So you were a spy? Even if that's the case I forgive you. I'm convinced that you will make a good spokesperson for the rainforest company that I started. What a way to advertise the business."

"Do you mean to say that you are going to do that for Miss Woodrow?" Ralph Holiday chuckled.

"Yes, I will be doing the seminars."

"I forgive you too mister." Cullen said, shaking his hand.

Rita blushed, "Oh gosh, I feel better about it now. You would understand me if I told you that all that has been going on these days has given me reason to be reluctant to hear what you had to say, as far as you talking to the kidnappers about us. Mr. Wilks, I forgive you too."

"Thanks. You must be...Rita. Yeah, that's it. You're Rita Young."

"Yes. That's me." She stared into his eyes.

"I like your spunk lady."

"You do? Hey, are you flirting with me? Because I can flirt back to you. Mr. Mysterious."

"What say we go on a date sometime Rita? I would really like to have a cup of coffee with you so we can get more acquainted."

"That sounds lovely. Why don't me and you go do that after we view the sunrise that's just about to come up?"

"It's a date then Rita."

"Oh Marley…there's something unusual about you that I'm attracted to. I can't quite place it."

"How 'bout the fact that he's good at getting your attention?" Sven theorized.

"I would say so. But for now he's Mr. Marley Mysterious to me."

Marley gave a little chuckle.

"Nice to meet you today Marley." Rain said warmly. "Keep in touch with me through the company website. Email me anytime."

"Yup. I will keep in touch Rain. It's been great meeting you all today."

"I think you're okay man." Cally Ryerson finally decided. "C'mon, the sunrise is almost here."

Brooke said, "Funny running into you like this Marley. I'm kidding."

"Isn't it though? Good thing I get up so early every day to keep an eye on you guys or I would have missed your fun meeting here at the beach."

"You always seem to find out the latest about us neighbours, don't you Marley?"

"Sure Brooke. You must remember how I observe people a lot from all the gossip stories I have told you over the years."

"That's where you get all the information. Marley, I have to hand it to you, when it comes to studying people you are some good at it."

"That's why I gossip so much."

"Now you're moving on. I'm going to miss not seeing you at work. Have fun doing those seminars."

"I will." Marley held up his knuckles and Brooke held up his. The two then pounded their knuckles into each other the same way that a high-five is done.

The minutes went by and soon it was time for the sunrise. Everyone watched as it unfolded and many of the neighbours mentioned that they had not seen a sunrise for quite a while. It was spectacular. It had vivid colors of yellow, orange and red. And its sunrays seemed to reach on to the heavens. And that is when they stood in a single line along the water's edge and lifted their hands up in the air in one big wave of joined hands. Sid's brown and white Chihuahua Oazic barked and jumped up in the air a few times.

Damien shouted happily to everyone in the group. "Okay, here's what we are going to shout. One word. Gloria. Okay, on the count of three. Here we go everyone. One, two, three…"

"Gloria!"